Tell Me It's Real

Also by Megan Byrd

Tell Me It's Real

Megan Byrd

ARDENVILLE PRESS

To Auntie Dee and Mrs. P

thanks for your love and support

CHAPTER ONE
Kat

Some people have the Northern Lights as a must-see event. Others cite a safari or swimming with dolphins as their lifelong dream. Me? On top of my list is Athens, Greece, the oldest city in Europe. Why Athens? Because I'm a bit of a history nerd. Old buildings and stories of the past enthrall me like nothing else.

While Charleston is an infant city compared to Athens, some of its buildings are designed in the Greek Revival style, which boasts majestic columns and symmetrical façades and draws my mind back to ancient Greece. I haven't had time to tour the city yet, but I read up on it before I arrived to film my movie and am looking forward to doing a little sightseeing while I'm here.

I study the mix of old and new buildings through the car window as we drive further into downtown. It's amazing some of these buildings are older than the founding of our country. While not as impressive as some places I've visited in Europe, the local historical buildings still have their own interesting stories and I'm eager to learn more about them.

The vehicle comes to a stop, and I peer up at the bright lights on the front of the building. Dozens of people stand behind velvet ropes framing a red carpet that leads from our vehicle to the door. Bliss, the name of the club, is written in fancy neon above the awning. I doubt bliss is what I'll find inside. A headache from the mix of sweat, perfume, and alcohol is more likely.

I spot a trio of young women huddled together behind the ropes. Two of them throw their heads back in laughter, while the third grins, clearly pleased by their reaction to whatever she said. My mind imagines them venturing to a different hot spot every weekend to have fun, catch up on their lives, and offer support to one another. I wonder what that'd be like. The closest person in my life is Lila, and she's my employee, so I don't know if that counts. Especially since we haven't done anything outside of work since…I can't even remember when, which is sad. My eyes dart away from the enviable friend group and I slump back against the cool leather seat, my hands smoothing the hem of my dress to distract me from my thoughts.

"You excited?" Rick asks with enough enthusiasm for the both of us.

Excited about what? Acting like I'm having a good time surrounded by a bunch of strangers while they stare and take pictures? I realized I'd be losing a lot of privacy when I became an actor, but I didn't think there'd be so many publicity events apart from hyping the movies I make. "What is it I'm doing here again?"

"We're taking photos of you having a blast in this new club and ordering your signature apple cider mimosa with Moët champagne. Make sure the labels are visible to the camera."

"Why not orange juice?"

My agent shrugs. "I found a cider company who wants to do an endorsement deal with you."

Of course he did. It's a good thing I like apple cider. "Where's Lila?"

"Already inside, waiting to film your grand entrance and earn you some more money."

I roll my eyes. "How long do I have to be here?"

He checks his phone. "At least an hour, but three would be great. I reserved a table in the VIP area if you need to rest your feet." He shoots a pointed look at my sparkly three-inch heels and shakes his head. "I still don't understand why you insist on towering over everyone else."

I lift a shoulder. "It's not my fault I was so genetically blessed." I honestly don't know where my height came from. If only it didn't come with equally gargantuan feet. I sigh. They're the real reason I wear heels. With my feet angled up, they don't look quite so large compared to everyone else's.

It's also the reason I don't have an amazing collection of designer shoes. Most fashionable styles only go up to size ten for women and I wear elevens. I buy a lot of my tennis shoes in the men's department, though I definitely don't advertise that.

I realize Rick didn't even hear my response because he hasn't looked up from his phone. I'd be surprised if his palm doesn't have a permanent indentation. He carries two portable chargers with him because he's on his phone so much. Being accessible twenty-four seven is probably what's made him so successful.

While he's focused on his screen, I take a moment to study him. His hair is still perfectly styled and his suit has nary a wrinkle despite it being ten o'clock at night. There are small bags under his eyes, the only sign he may not be getting enough rest. The lines at the corners of his eyes and around his mouth remind me he's aging, just like the rest of us. He must consume massive amounts of caffeine, considering how much energy he has most of the time.

As if to prove my point, he suddenly looks up, excitement dancing in his eyes. Or are those dollar signs? Sometimes I swear that's all he sees when he looks at me—a tall, blonde cash-making machine. "Alright, Kat, everything's ready inside. Let's do this!"

My door swings open. I lean out and grab the offered hand of my driver, who effortlessly lifts me to my feet. I thank him with a smile, then turn up the wattage as I step away from the car and wave to the crowd. There are squeals, cheers, and a few people calling my name. I pose for a few selfies with fans and sign some autographs before Rick ushers me inside with a hand on my lower back.

Once we've passed through the doors, he drops his hand and fades into the background. I see Lila, a phone raised in front of her. I walk straight toward her with a wide grin and wave before passing by and making my way to the bar. A handsome bartender is already there with a bottle of champagne and a glass container of apple cider. My life is so strange sometimes.

He opens the apple cider and pours some in a flute, then pops the cork on the champagne and fills the glass to the brim. I twist both bottles so the labels are prominent, then take the glass, cheers the camera, and tilt it up to my mouth, the bubbly beverage fizzing in my throat. I'm surprised at how I don't hate the apple cider and bubbles combination. It has a more pronounced flavor than apple juice.

"Okay," Lila says, approaching me. "Let's get a few photos for Instagram. Stand behind the bar with Will here."

There's no sense refusing, as Lila is a force. One who gets great results. I've learned it's quickest to just do whatever she says. My one hundred million followers love everything she posts.

Lila has Will make a second mimosa and then we clink glasses and sip. She instructs me to accept a glass from him while looking into his eyes like we have a connection. Then I'm told to kiss his cheek after a fresh application of Starstruck Red, my signature lipstick color. A few more with Will showing off the lipstick print on his face, and then she's satisfied.

I grab a cocktail napkin and kiss it to get rid of some of the excess still on my lips. Will hands me a pen with his eyebrows raised, so I write "To Will," sign it, and hand the napkin and pen to him.

"Thanks so much, Miss Sonnett. It's so cool you're shooting a movie here in my hometown. If they need someone to play a bartender, let me know." He hands me a napkin with his name and number on it.

"Sure thing. Thanks for your help tonight."

Amazingly, I think he's genuinely interested in a role and not trying to hook up with me. That's a rare thing these days. As evidenced by the dozen more napkins I acquire over the next hour while I alternate between dancing among a bunch of strangers and hiding out in the VIP section with Rick so I won't be groped or hit on. Lila joins me on the dance floor to shoot footage and also tries to act as a buffer, but is only moderately successful.

When the DJ puts on a slow song, couples flock to the floor, jostling me out of the way so they can squeeze up against each other like they're trying to meld into one being. I head over to the table in the VIP lounge. My eyes keep wandering back to all the people on the dance floor, my heart constricting with longing for my own dance partner. I'm usually too busy to think about how lonely my life is, but when I have it thrown in my face, the yearning roars inside like a starving lion. Of course, with so many work commitments, the only way I could feasibly have a relationship is if I scheduled it in or started dating someone I work with. Co-workers and employees are the only people I see on the regular these days.

I head to the bathroom for a break from the noise, grateful to find it empty. While I'm touching up my makeup, a woman comes in with tears streaming down her face. She grabs toilet paper from the stall, but she's crying so hard her whole body is shaking. My heart twists with sympathy.

"Oh, honey. Do you need a hug?"

She barely looks at me before walking into my open arms, gripping my shoulders tightly. I hug her loosely, one arm lightly circling her back, hoping the motion soothes her. This isn't the first time I've encountered a crying woman in a club bathroom, and it probably won't be the last.

After a few minutes, her shaking stops and she takes a few deep breaths. When her hold on my shoulders lessens, I let go. She takes a step back, wiping her eyes with the back of her hand. I grab some more toilet paper and hand it to her.

"Do you want to talk about it?" I ask.

She shakes her head. "Just my boyfriend being a jerk."

"He obviously doesn't appreciate you like he should."

"No, he doesn't." She smiles weakly, then freezes, her eyes widening. "Are you...?"

I shrug. "Yeah, I suppose I am."

"Oh my gosh. I'm so sorry. Did I get mascara on your dress?"

I wave her off. "Don't worry about it. We've all been there. What I'm concerned about is if you're okay."

"Yeah, it's stupid."

I touch her shoulder and wait until she meets my eyes. "No one should make you cry. Whatever he did or said is not a reflection of you. It's his issue and one you don't have to deal with if you don't want to. You have so much to offer and shouldn't waste your time with someone who doesn't see what a treasure you are."

She sniffs, dabbing her eyes, then straightens her shoulders. "You're right, Kat Sonnett. I *am* a catch."

I notice the mascara lines down her cheeks and dig into my clutch before handing her a makeup remover wipe. "This might help."

"Thanks." She leans toward the mirror and wipes away the remnants of her tears. "Do you mind if I get a photo?"

"Sure." Anything to help turn her night around.

She leans into me, and I wrap an arm around her shoulders. She takes a couple, then looks at her phone screen. "Wow, you look great in these. How are you still single?"

I chuckle. "Just haven't found the right guy, I guess."

"Me neither," she says, lips turned down.

She heads to the door, but pauses and looks back at me.

"Thanks again, Kat. I hope you find your Mr. Right soon."

I smile and nod, knowing that soon is impossible. Someday, though, I hope. I try to do something about the black smear on my dress, but realize it's futile. Reluctantly, I head back out to the dance floor.

When I slide into the VIP booth again after a few songs, Rick glances up from his phone. "We ready to go?"

He's not asking me. I'm just the talent.

"Yep," Lila says. "I got everything we need."

"The car's out back. We just have to slip through the kitchen."

I stand and smooth down the royal blue dress Lila had waiting in my hotel room this afternoon. It's not too short and, although tight, still comfortable to sit in. Plus, the color makes my blue eyes pop.

I follow Lila to the exit, Rick bringing up the rear to make sure no one tries to follow me out. He's talked about hiring bodyguards to be with me wherever I go, but I don't think that's necessary. I've never received a threat or felt unsafe anywhere I've been. Sure, I have to deal with handsy drunk guys at places like this, but having someone standing over me all the time feels like overkill.

Back in the car, I slump into the seat, feeling the weight of the day catching up to me. I spent the morning filming a scene for the movie we're shooting, then had an hour with my trainer before the afternoon was swallowed up with me memorizing the next part we'll be doing. Blocking is tomorrow with filming in the afternoon if the director feels confident we're ready.

I've had fun with this project. I'm one of the leads in a romantic comedy called Stuck With You. It's an enemies-to-lovers, second chance story about two people who went to high school together being paired up for an Amazing Race-type competition. My co-star for this project is Grady Hawkins. He's been fun to work with, a consummate professional. He's married, so I don't have to worry about any rumors of us dating, though

I'm sure at least one gossip magazine will make something up about an affair. It comes with the territory.

I wonder if I could find a guy who'd understand it's just part of the job and not believe everything that's posted or printed about me. I remind myself I'm too busy for a relationship. Plus, I'd have to actually put myself out there for that to happen and I've already been burned enough for one lifetime. These days it's impossible to know if a guy is actually into me or just infatuated with a character I've played, the potential to get into the spotlight themselves, or some other not-me-as-a-real-person reason. I'm exhausted just thinking about it.

"The car will be at the hotel at six-thirty," Lila says. "Breakfast will be on set. If the morning goes well, you'll be in hair and makeup after lunch."

I press a hand to my forehead, feeling the beginnings of a headache. Is it from the mimosa or just my schedule?

When we reach the hotel, Lila and I get out. I lean down to look at Rick. "See you tomorrow."

He doesn't look up from his phone, but waves a hand in acknowledgment. I close the door and it disappears down the block. I wonder where he's off to so late. We take the elevator up to the top floor. Lila opens the door to my suite, then hands me a leather tote bag containing my room key, wallet, phone, makeup, a brush, and the clothes I wore to the set this morning.

"Do you want a wake-up call?" she asks me.

"Yes, please. See you in the morning."

She nods, then heads down the hall to her room. I get ready for bed, then crawl under the soft sheets and fluffy down comforter with my phone. No new texts, which is unsurprising considering how infrequently I communicate with people who aren't part of my work world. My parents, whom I love dearly and have been nothing but supportive of me and my career, are used to short, sporadic phone calls with me, as my free time is usually late at night or early in the morning. You know, when most people are asleep. I keep telling myself to add a visit to Atlanta to my calendar and keep the commitment, but Rick doesn't seem to care whether I have a personal life. My older brother, Mason, has gotten so fed up with my inaccessibility that the only texts I receive from him are guilt trips about how I've neglected or forgotten my family. He's not totally wrong, but I definitely don't need him to pile it on.

My finger hovers over the little red notification bubble on my Instagram account. It's not the one Lila curates, but a private one. It has zero followers, zero posts, a generic handle, and follows one account. Which account, you ask? Why @katsonnettistrash of course. I know, I know. Why deliberately expose myself to an obvious hater? Lila's asked me that on more than one occasion. My response has been to keep me humble, but really, I'm morbidly curious why this user seems to dislike me so much. At first, the posts were just about how terrible I was at acting. And then I won a statue. So it moved on to talking about how I'm really not that pretty, posting very unflattering photos of me. But recently it's gotten a little more personal—claiming to be a close contact who knows how terrible I am as a person. I know this is a lie because I have no close friends, but I feel like I must have done something to this person at some point in my life because why else would they feel the need to bash me for the past several years? Whoever it is publishes a scathing post every week or two. Talk about dedication to a cause. I'd almost admire them if the words didn't hurt so much.

Giving in to the impulse, I open the app, which tells me @katsonnettistrash has a new post. They have several thousand followers, which means they aren't alone in their dislike of me. I know not everyone is a fan of teen dramas or rom-com movies, which is what I'm known for. However, there are many more people who enjoy my work, based on the box office numbers. The post is a cropped photo taken from my public account that shows just my shoes, a pair of white Adidas sneakers. The caption reads: *Take a look at these boats. Does she wear the same size as Shaq? #ifoundbigfoot*

Oof. Now that's just rude. I can't help the size of my feet. I wonder if they even know that, to me, this is the most hurtful post to date. Doubtful. They're probably grasping at straws because I've been avoiding public appearances lately. I have a few weeks until the run-up to my latest movie's release and wanted a breather. Which lasted for about two weeks until tonight's event.

I thoroughly regret opening the app now. I plug my phone into the charger, then grab my kindle. Perhaps some light reading will help me wind down. I downloaded the book my movie is based on after Grady complained that it's supposed to take place in Asheville, near where he lives, but the screenwriter adapted it to take place in Charleston. It got me curious to find out what all they changed. Many people insist the book is always better than the movie. I'm determined to make my own judgment in this particular case, but I'm so tired after my long day that I fall asleep after only a few paragraphs and wake up the next morning with the kindle pressing into my cheek.

CHAPTER TWO
Zach

I twist the knob and use my shoulder to push the door open. I breathe in and my stomach growls at the smell of tomatoes, sausage, peppers, and cornbread.

"Are we having what I think we're having?" I call, walking down the hall toward the kitchen.

"If you guessed jambalaya and cornbread, then yes," Mom responds.

I join her at the stove and kiss her cheek, then scan the kitchen to see how I can help. Grabbing a plate, I pop the muffins out of the tins and carry them into the dining room along with butter and honey. Next, I fill water glasses and take them into the dining room along with plates, silverware, and cloth napkins. When I return, I'm handed two bowls heaped with jambalaya, which I carry to the table. Mom follows me with two more bowls and I return for the final one. The dining room bell chimes, bringing the sound of several pairs of feet pounding down the stairs.

Mom sits in her chair at the head of the table. I chose a place next to her. Jonah, Will, and Nora—Mom's live-in tenants—enter the room. "Hey, man," Jonah says, "you're in my seat."

I shrug. "Maybe you should help set the table next time."

He squeezes his lips together and nods. "Fair point. This smells delicious, Mrs. Fontaine."

"Thanks, Jonah. Everybody have a seat. Nora, please say the blessing."

After the prayer and passing of the cornbread muffins, it's time for the good part—eating. The first bite of Mom's famous jambalaya practically has my eyes rolling back in my head from enjoyment. I don't think anyone makes it as good as she does. Of course, her recipe is from her great-grandmother, so you know it's out-of-this-world delicious.

"What's new with everyone?" Mom says. "Will, how's your job at Bliss going?"

Will straightens in his chair, his eyes sparkling. "We had a VIP show up last night and I got to be part of a promo she was shooting for her social media. In fact, I wonder if it's already online." He reaches into his pocket, but quickly pulls his hand back out after a pointed look from my mother. She has a very stringent rule about no devices at the dinner table. "Oh, sorry. I'll look later."

"Who was the VIP?" Jonah asks.

"Kat Sonnett."

Jonah whistles. "She is one fine woman. Did you get to talk to her?"

Will grins. "Better. She kissed me on the cheek."

Jonah's mouth drops open. "Whaaaat? You're so lucky. I never see anyone famous at work."

"Probably because you work with animals all day," Nora says. "I see celebrities all the time. In fact, one who shall not be named is staying at our hotel right now."

Jonah narrows his eyes. "It's Kat, isn't it?"

Nora pretends to lock her lips with a key and then shrugs, but her smile tells all.

"Man, why did I have to choose a nerdy profession?"

"I think it's pretty cool you're a marine biologist," Nora says. "Isn't that what most kids aspire to be?"

"Well, yeah. Whenever we host a school group, I get a lot of questions about my job. Nevertheless, a celebrity sighting would be pretty cool." He turns to Will. "Think Kat would want to come by and see the sea turtles we're rehabilitating?"

"I don't know, Jonah. I just met her. Though I gave her my number in case she needs a bartender for whatever she's filming. If she calls, I'll ask."

Nora chuckles. "Don't hold your breath. I doubt she'll call. She's a world-famous actor."

Jonah elbows me. "You've been pretty quiet, Zach. Have you ever seen any celebrities in your store?"

I grunt and take another mouthful of food. Apparently that's not enough to get me out of answering, because when I look up, everyone is staring at me. "What?"

Mom places a hand on my arm. "How are things going at the store, honey?"

"Uh, they're okay." I really don't want to lie to my mom, but I also don't want to tell her I haven't sold anything in several weeks. "No celebrities have come in."

"Wouldn't that be great?" Nora says. "If you could get someone famous to talk about your products, I bet your store would be overrun with customers."

"Or gawkers, hoping to see a celebrity," I say.

"Anything to get more people in the door, right?" Will says.

It certainly would be nice to have more foot traffic in Worthy Wood, my custom-made furniture store. I'm barely keeping the doors open right now. I have some commissions for side tables and dining room sets I'm working on, but they're from clients in other states which doesn't help with local business. It almost seems pointless for me to even have a storefront. If I could connect with a local interior designer, I'd probably be set, but I don't know how to make that happen.

Ideally, I'd hire someone to manage the store while I work on creating new pieces, but there's no way I can afford to have another person on my payroll right now. If I wasn't living at home for free, the store would have already closed. As it is, with the commissions and occasional walk-in sale, I'm just barely able to cover expenses. I don't enjoy trying to talk to people who come into the store into buying my products. I'd rather just have a website and let people come to me, but Mom leased the storefront as a thank you for taking care of her and her business while she was sick and I don't want her to feel like she made a poor investment. Thankfully, the lease ends in a few months and, if I'm still struggling, I can thank her for her support and tell her I've discovered I prefer having my business online. However, even the thought of that gives me hives. I don't want to disappoint her and it feels like being a failure at owning a storefront is a surefire way to do it.

"Yeah, sure. You're all welcome to send any famous person you meet over to Worthy Wood."

"Who's on the clean-up crew tonight?" Mom says when dinner is wrapping up.

"It's me and Nora," Jonah says. "Thanks again for a delicious dinner."

"Yes, thank you," Nora, Will, and I echo.

"Are we having game night tonight?" Will says.

"No, it's next Wednesday. Is everyone free?"

Nods from everyone except Mom. "I've got my book club," she says, which is code for wine and charcuterie with a group of longtime friends.

Mom never comes to game nights. It's for the "younger folks" as she likes to say. However, being a decade older than her tenants, I don't feel like I really fit in with them either. They just keep getting younger while I continue to age. Okay, I'm not *that* old. I'm thirty-six, but when I hang out with twenty-somethings, I feel every one of my years. They don't hold it against me, though. They're all pretty cool and accepted me with open arms when I came home two years ago to keep the house running and care for Mom after her cancer diagnosis. I threw myself into keeping up the weekly meals with her renters and fixing whatever was needed to be done with the house while also taking her to appointments, keeping her fed, and doing all I could to make her comfortable. She's in the clear now, but the twice-a-month game nights I started have continued.

"I'm going to head out."

I give Mom a hug, tell her I love her, then walk across the driveway to the front door of the carriage house where I live. Once inside, I plop down on the couch, pull out my phone, and do an internet search for 'Cat Sonnet.' Google asks me if I mean 'Kat Sonnett' and when I click, up pops a photo of a tall blonde with brilliant blue eyes and bright red lips. She's gorgeous, though I'm surprised by her youthfulness. I've never seen her before, so I peruse her Wikipedia page for more information. She's twenty-seven—I would have guessed twenty-two—and is known for some teen shows I've never heard of and a long list of movies I haven't seen. Which makes sense since I'm a documentary and action movie kind of guy. If there's a special on woodworking, I've seen it multiple times. Ron Swanson's hobby is the reason *Parks & Rec* is my favorite show.

I close the browser and check my email. No new furniture requests. Guess I'd better get back to work on the table in my shed. After changing into old clothes, I get lost in my work, only stopping when a glance at the clock tells me it's past eleven p.m. I smile, loving how immersive woodworking is for me. I could literally do this all day and never tire of it. It's so much more enjoyable than sitting at a desk, whittling scrap pieces of wood, while I wait for customers. Actually, the whittling part isn't so bad. It helps me with focus, precision, and detail. Plus, the tiny animals are actually kind of cute. Too bad they don't bring in the big bucks with how much time they take. At least most of my time is spent doing something I love. Not everyone can say that. I don't love *everything* about my job, but who does?

After a quick shower, I lay in bed, my mind turning to a subject I'd pushed to the side while taking care of Mom. Now that I'm refocused back on my job and future, I've definitely noticed the hole in my personal life. I'd been seeing a wonderful woman when I lived in Asheville, but ended things when I moved here. Part of me wants to see what she's up to, but I know I'm going to be staying in Charleston indefinitely in case something happens with Mom again, so it's not really fair to stir up those waters again. No, I need to look for someone to date here. But where would I find her? My last relationship came from a blind date set up. Maybe I should ask if anyone knows someone at our next game night? Nah, I'd just get made fun of. I'll figure something out. Too bad furniture stores are couples' meccas rather than a single person's paradise. I can't count on running into a pretty bachelorette in need of a dining room table.

CHAPTER THREE

Kat

After wrapping up another day of filming, I've decided to do a little retail therapy in the downtown area. One thing I love about shooting in new locations is the opportunity to explore the local culture and craft scene. I've already got my eye on a sweetgrass basket or two. My mom would love one. I know it won't make up for my absence, but it'll at least show that she's on my mind.

After a swing through the City Market, I've accumulated half a dozen baskets, a few pairs of earrings, a candle, and a hand-painted sand dollar depicting the city's famous pineapple fountain. Thoroughly shopped out, I look around, trying to figure out which way back to my hotel. I notice a small group of teenage girls casting curious looks my way. Normally, I'd interact with them but I'm too tired and just want to relax in my room.

I pull the baseball cap I'm wearing down further over my eyes and scan the area for an escape. I cross the street and look in shop windows, hoping for somewhere to duck into for a few minutes. A contemporary art gallery has a surprising number of patrons, so I keep going. The candy store next door is also crowded. The third store is a ghost town compared to the other two. It doesn't even look open, but when I tug on the door, it moves, so I slide inside. After the door shuts behind me, I turn to see if anyone followed me. I seem to have made a clean escape. Just to be sure, I'll browse for a few minutes.

Releasing a breath, I turn and realize I'm in a furniture store. There's definitely not anything I need here, but the clerk at the desk in the back probably saw me come in, so I'd feel rude if I didn't at least pretend to be interested. I start at the front, where there are a handful of wooden tables. Running my hand across the top of one, the smooth, lacquered wood calms me. I pause at the second one, entranced by the blue inlay that looks like a river running through the middle of pale wood. I've never seen anything like it before. The shimmery blue conjures images of a bubbling brook and makes me smile. I snap a photo of it.

Next are chairs that look well made. The seats look like they were custom made for comfort and, when I impulsively sit in one, I find I'm right. I can't help but try out all the different chairs and feel like Goldilocks looking for the perfect fit, which I find when I sit in a dark brown one with a curved back and thin wood slats inside a sturdier frame. It has thin arms set at the perfect height for me to rest comfortably in. I run my hands along the smooth arms, feeling like this seat was made just for me. A silly thought. Especially since there's nowhere for me to put a chair like this, especially when I'm living in a hotel.

Reluctantly, I stand up but take a picture of the chair. I don't see a price tag, which makes me wonder how expensive it is. It's definitely high quality. I turn toward the clerk, but his back is to me and he appears to be working on something. I'll ask him later.

There's another river table at the back of the store covered with flower pots, vases, and other bric-à-brac. A pair of bookends shaped like old books catch my attention. My brother is a big reader and I could see those on his bookshelf. I assume he has a bookshelf in his new place. I haven't been home in over a year and he bought a new house a few months ago. Guilt twists my stomach. I really need to make time to visit my family. Atlanta's not that far from Charleston. Maybe there'll be a gap in the schedule and I can dash over there. It would be great to catch up in person after so long. Assuming my family is available, of course. I don't expect them to drop everything just for me. I'm not that much of a diva. I'll have Lila check the schedule and see if there are any breaks coming up.

I pick up the bookends, then move toward what I assume is the checkout area. On the desk is a bowl of small wooden animals. Curious, I grab a handful. In my palm are several dogs, two hippos, a penguin, and an elephant. The swoop of the trunk makes me smile, so I set it down next to the bookends.

The clerk still has his back to me, so I clear my throat. When he doesn't move, my brow furrows, and I take a few steps to the side of the desk. "Excuse me." He still doesn't move, so I tap him on the shoulder.

"Aaaah!" He jumps out of the chair and spins around, his arms raised like he's going to karate chop me.

I can't help chuckling. "Hi." I give a little wave.

He pulls out an earbud, then quickly stabs at his phone to silence the loud, pulsing music coming from the tiny speaker.

"That sounds like some intense music. No wonder you didn't hear me."

He rubs the back of his neck. "Yeah, sorry. I wasn't expecting anyone."

I frown and look around. "You're open, right?"

"It's hard to tell some days."

I shake my head. "I can tell you love working here."

He shrugs. "How can I help you?"

"I'd like to get these, please." I point to my little pile.

"The wooden animals are buy one, get one free."

"Oh." I dig around in the bowl for a minute. "You don't have an otter in here, do you?"

He presses his lips together, his brows pushing together in thought. "Can't say I've ever made an otter before, sorry."

I can't hide the surprise on my face. "You made these?"

He holds up a small piece of wood which has the face of a cat sticking out. I take it from him, in awe of the intricate details.

"That's amazing. How do you see the animal in the wood?"

Another shrug. "I don't know. I've always been able to do it."

My eyes snag on another block of wood on the desk and point to it. "What is that going to be?"

He follows my finger, then picks up the wood, turning it as he studies it, his fingers sliding along the wood grain. "I could see a wolf or a snail."

I laugh. "Wow. Those two things are not alike at all."

He sets the wood down without a word, wrapping my purchases in brown craft paper. Did I insult him somehow? I certainly didn't mean to. I quickly grab an animal out of the bowl and hand it to him, not even noticing what I've selected.

The silence feels a little awkward, so I search for something to break the tension. "How much are the chairs?"

"Which ones?" he asks without looking up from his task.

"The dark brown ones with the arms and thin slats on the back."

"Shaker?"

I frown. "What?"

He finishes putting my items in a paper bag with a logo depicting two interlocking Ws. "Why don't you show me which ones you like?"

He walks with me over to the chair section and I slide my hand along the back of my favorite one, enjoying the smooth feel of the wood on my palm. "This one."

"It's made in the shaker style. Simple, unadorned, clean lines."

"Oh. Yes, I like that. This one is very comfortable. It almost feels made for me." I smile, but his serious expression doesn't change.

"Glad you like it. I have more in the back if you need a set for a table."

"No, I was just wondering how much such excellent craftsmanship was worth."

"This chair is fifteen hundred."

I whistle. "I have very good taste."

One corner of his mouth twitches. I am suddenly desperate to see what his smile looks like. He meets my eyes and freezes. My heart picks up as I wonder if I've finally been caught out. I've been enjoying pretending to be an anonymous customer and having a normal, non-work conversation with a stranger, but it looks like that's finished. He blinks and his mouth is once again a straight line.

"Does that mean you don't want the chair?"

I'm confused for a second. I was expecting him to say my name and announce that he knows me from such-and-such movie. That's what usually happens. "Uh, no. Well, yes."

It's his turn to look confused, and I laugh. "Sorry. What I meant to say was, I'd love the chair, but unfortunately I'm just visiting, so I don't have any place to keep it."

"We deliver within a three hundred-mile radius or we can ship it if necessary."

"That's good to know. Unfortunately, I'm going to have to pass today. Just the bookends and animals for me."

He nods, then heads back to the desk with me trailing him. I still can't tell if I'm relieved or disappointed he doesn't recognize me. I give him my credit card to pay for my purchases. When he hands it back, he says, "I hope you enjoy your stay in Charleston."

"Thanks."

He hands me the receipt to sign, and it feels like I've been shocked when our fingers touch. That's never happened to me before. "I'm sorry, this may be obvious, but I have to ask. Did you make all the furniture in this store?"

He looks up, a vulnerability to his expression, and I know the answer before he speaks. "I did."

My stomach squeezes with something like longing. I noticed he was handsome when I first saw his face—blue eyes as brilliant as the table in the front of the room, beard and mustache the same brown as his wavy hair. He looks like a cross between a lumberjack and a surfer with the muscular chest and arms I can't help but notice in his form-fitting black T-shirt. But add a dash of uncertainty and my heart gives a definite swoop.

I blink a few times to get my thoughts back in order. "I'm very impressed. You're a talented craftsman."

He looks away and shoves his hands into his pockets. "Thanks. Enjoy the bookends."

Have I embarrassed him? How cute. Plus the fact that he either doesn't know who I am or doesn't care? Well, that feels like icing on the cake. It's such a breath of fresh air to be seen as a regular person. Which I am, of course, but most people don't treat me like one and I miss it.

"I will. Keep up the good work."

Oh, Katie. That sounded stupid. Oh well. I grab the bag off the table and head back out front, smiling about this innocuous interaction. Which is why I fail to check my surroundings before leaving the store and am immediately mobbed by a large group of teenagers.

CHAPTER FOUR

Zach

Piercing screams make my head snap up from the desk. I turn toward the front of the store and see the woman who was just in here, surrounded by at least a dozen people all yelling and waving at her. *What is going on?* Concern for her safety wells up and I'm yanking the front door of the shop open before I've even had time to think.

The swarm of teenage girls, many of them waving notebooks and pens at her, is yelling things my brain can't comprehend as anything other than noise. I grab the woman's wrist and pull her back through the door, turning the lock and pressing my back against it. "Are you okay?"

Her eyes are wide with shock, locked on the glass door behind me. People are now banging on the front window and door. I press gently on her lower back, guiding her across the floor to the storage room in the back. When I shut the door, everything goes quiet. I grab a chair and motion for her to sit. She sinks down into it and puts a hand over her eyes, visibly shaken.

"Do I need to call the police?"

She releases a strangled laugh. "No, that's unnecessary."

"Did that group attack you?"

She drops her hands, an amused smile on her face. "Not exactly. They're fans."

"Fans of...?"

"Me."

This isn't computing. "And you are...?"

She removes her hat and gives me a bright smile. "Kat Sonnett."

I recognize the name from my recent google search. My eyes widen as I realize Jonah is going to have a fit when he learns I had a celebrity in my store. I noticed the woman was beautiful when I was talking to her about the chair, but hadn't connected her face with the name.

"So you *have* heard of me."

My face warms. "Actually, just recently."

She looks skeptical. "Are you just joshing me?"

I shake my head. "No, sorry."

She laughs at my contrite expression. "Don't be. It's actually kind of refreshing. It's not often I get to be anonymous."

My eyes stray to the door, thinking of the crowd out front. "I can't even imagine. Are you mobbed often?"

Her shrug says it all. "It's part of the job."

I wrinkle my nose. "Sounds terrible."

Her smile widens. "It's got some perks, too."

"If you say so."

"Is it cool if I stay here for a bit? Just until the crowd disperses."

She shouldn't have to hide out in my back room like this. "How about I sneak you out the back instead? It goes into an alley, but the end is far enough up the block that you won't be seen."

"That sounds good, except how do I get to the Marion Fox Hotel from here?"

She's staying where Nora works? It's not very close. I'd feel terrible if she was accosted by another mob of fans. "Why don't I walk you back? I know the best route to stay unnoticed."

She looks around. "What about work?"

"You're the first customer I've had all day. I think it'll be okay."

"Are you sure?"

I grin. "Walking through the city with a beautiful woman is a much more pleasant proposition than sitting alone in a quiet store."

Surprise flits across her face, and I immediately regret my words. Before I can backtrack, she responds.

"I'd be grateful for a guide through this lovely city."

She seems to have missed my comment about her looks. Not that she doesn't know she's gorgeous. She's a movie star, for Pete's sake. I'm sure she gets complimented all the time. Her fame doesn't matter to me. In fact, it's a bit of a turnoff. I have no desire to be in a spotlight of any kind. I'm happy with my quiet life where I can work on my furniture in peace. I don't need anything else. Okay, a person to share my quiet life with wouldn't be bad, but a starlet definitely doesn't fit into the picture.

"Great. Let me grab my keys out of the desk and we'll go."

I peek out the back door, just to be sure we're in the clear, then motion her out. She's got her hat back on and has added sunglasses. She's wearing jeans, tennis shoes, and an oversize sweatshirt so she doesn't look like anyone special, which is probably the point. Standing so close, I realize we're nearly the same height. I pause my perusal, inspecting her sneakers. They're white Adidas with black stripes.

"Nice shoes. I have the same pair."

Her cheeks tinge a light pink, which only enhances her beauty. "Thanks. I wear them all the time."

I take her shopping bags from her, pointing out the sights during the fifteen-minute walk to her hotel. There's not a lot to see because we're avoiding the major thoroughfares, but I show her the Center for the Arts and a local sandwich shop I like. When we reach the entrance to her hotel, I stop, not wanting to impose. She peeks inside, then turns to me. "Would you mind walking me to the elevators?"

Is she inviting me up to get to know me better? I noticed a bit of a vibe between us while we walked, but I'm not interested in her public lifestyle. She must notice my hesitation because she leans closer and whispers, "There are some reporters inside and if I look like I'm with someone, they probably won't notice it's me."

Ohhhhh. She needs my help. That makes sense. "Sure. Should we hold hands or something? Really sell it?"

Her eyes brighten and she nods. "Good thinking. They're so used to seeing me alone, I bet they won't even cast a second glance our way."

I want to spend some time ruminating on her words, but she takes her bags from me in one hand and slides her other one into mine. Her fingers fit smoothly into mine like our hands were made for each other. I pull the door open with my free hand and use my body to shield her from the people in the lobby until we get to the elevator. The door opens immediately, and I usher her on, stepping in behind her to continue to block her from view. She pushes a button, the doors close, and then she releases my hand and laughs out a breath. "I feel like a spy."

I grin, trying not to focus on the sense of loss I feel without her hand in mine. "Who knew famous life could be so dangerous?"

Her smile drops. "It's certainly not all roses and kittens."

My stomach twists with concern. "Is everything alright?"

She waves a hand and rolls her eyes. "Don't mind me. I have a flair for the dramatic. I'm an actor, after all."

Her attempt to lighten the mood isn't completely successful. I narrow my eyes, unconvinced until she playfully pats my shoulder. "I'm fine...uh..." Her mouth twists to the side, her eyebrows pinching together.

"What?"

"I'm sorry, but I just realized I don't know your name."

"Zach."

She smiles. "Thanks for saving me back there. The crowd was a bit much."

"Where were your bodyguards?"

"I don't have any." My thoughts about that must be written on my face because she shakes her head and glares. "Don't give me that look."

I spread my hands, trying to wrestle my face into neutral. "Don't you think it's a little reckless wandering around an unfamiliar town alone when you're so famous?"

"You sound just like my agent."

"I think your agent is trying to keep you safe."

She looks down at her shoes. "I know. It's why I don't go out by myself much."

I try to process this. "You'd rather be trapped inside alone than have freedom with one or two people to help protect you?"

She huffs out a breath. "The way you say it makes it sound like a no-brainer, but I don't know. I think it'd be weird having someone follow me around all the time."

It's really not my business. I just met her after all. "You know what you need. Ignore my opinion."

She places a hand on my arm, and I feel a jolt across my skin. "You're just trying to be helpful, which I appreciate."

The elevator dings and the doors open. "This is me," she says. "Thanks for everything, Zach."

I nod, press the lobby button, then wave as the doors close. Back in the lobby, I hear someone call my name and walk over to the front desk. Nora gives me a wide-eyed look. "Did I just see you walk through the lobby, hand in hand, with *the* Kat Sonnett?"

"Shhhhh, we were trying to avoid the reporters."

"We?! Since when are you and Kat a 'we'?"

I grin. "She came into my store earlier but was accosted by fans when she tried to leave, so I helped her get home unscathed."

Nora's eyes round even more. "She was in your store?! Oh man, Jonah is going to lose his ever-loving mind when he hears about this."

I press my lips together and wave my hands. "Quiet down. Don't draw any attention, please."

Nora narrows her eyes. "Are you trying to say you're going to be assisting Ms. Sonnett in the future?"

I shake my head. "No. But aren't you supposed to be discreet and professional when you're representing the Marion Fox Hotel?"

She waves her hand dismissively. "Right, right. But still. Please, can I tell Jonah?"

"Do it at game night. I want to see his face."

CHAPTER FIVE

Kat

"There's something I want to talk to you about," I say, entering Rick's makeshift office at the hotel where we're shooting today's scenes.

He holds up a finger. "Send it over to the Marion Fox and we'll make sure it gets seen and photographed in public later this week." He pivots toward the window, nods once. "Yes, no problem. Thanks."

He taps a button on his bluetooth earpiece, then swings back around to me. "Have a seat, Kat. What were you saying?"

I drop into one chair and Lila, who followed me in, sits next to me while Rick takes up half the couch across from us.

"I think now's the time to pursue a more serious role in a film. Maybe do a period piece."

Rick rolls his eyes. "Are we back on this? You're killing it in the rom-com arena. Why do you want to mess that up by switching to drama?"

I sigh. "I doubt it'd mess anything up. I just want to flex a different acting muscle. All these rom-com roles feel the same. I need something new, something that's exciting and challenging."

He scowls, but then a lazy smile unfurls, which reminds me of the Grinch when he gets his "brilliant idea" to steal Christmas from the Whos. I've seen this look before and I didn't care for what he had to say last time. Still, he is my agent, and he's good at his job of making me money, so I'll give him the benefit of the doubt.

"If you're looking to play a new role, how about an immersive role where you turn a bad boy into a model citizen?"

"Is this like a coach who motivates their players to become the best they can be? I haven't seen too many movies with female coaches, but this could have potential."

Rick shakes his head. "It's not a movie part."

I look over at Lila. She shares my confused look. "Then what are you talking about?"

"Talon Jacobs wants to make a fresh start. He's ready to drop the immature, slacker look and have a proper glow up to a respectable man. What do you say about dating him for a bit?"

My jaw drops. Rick wants me to associate with the creator of the gross and grossly popular YouTube channel *Drop Your Drawers*? Why would I want to date someone whose claim to fame is helping other guys hook up with women? That guy has sleazy written all over him. Literally, because *Sleazy* is the name of his skateboarder apparel line. "What?! You can't be serious."

He shrugs, not even a hint of embarrassment about what he's suggesting. "Talon's ready to turn his image around. He wants to get into movies and his agent thinks if he's seen with America's Sweetheart for a few months, it'll go a long way toward seeing him as reformed and reputable."

"But what about *my* reputation?" And what about the fact that I'd have to spend time with a guy who was recently in the news for cheating on his girlfriend with her best friend? It sure doesn't look like he's really interested in becoming someone who respects women.

"Right now, you're untouchable. Being associated with Talon would make you more desirable to men in the eighteen to twenty-nine-year-old demographic because you'd be seen as attainable. It's guaranteed to get them to your next movie."

I don't really care about being more appealing to men. That hasn't ever really been a problem. However, if my name is attached to someone like Talon Jacobs and then he continues to be a misogynistic jerk, there goes my chance of ever being taken seriously for a dramatic role. "I fail to see a real upside for me, Rick."

He sighs, like I'm being unreasonable. "You know it's only a persona for him, right? He's not really the jerk he portrays. It's all acting. And he's ready for a new role."

A few years ago, when I met him at an awards event, he certainly didn't seem to be acting when he catcalled me with a few phrases that don't bear repeating. Regardless, there's no way this will help me with any of my goals. "It's a hard pass."

I look at Lila for support, but she's busy typing away on her phone.

"Fine. I'll let his people know. By the way, a local designer is sending you a dress they want you to wear out this week. I'll set up a pop-in somewhere around town for Friday and send Lila the details."

I narrow my eyes, suspicious. Rick doesn't normally schedule my appearances. That's Lila's responsibility. Nor does he capitulate so easily when we disagree. Maybe he actually understands my perspective for once. I'm less enthused about going to another loud club surrounded by strangers. "Can't wait," I say, the flatness of my voice expressing my true feelings. Rick either doesn't notice or doesn't care.

"You're doing great on this shoot. Too bad Grady's married or we could sprinkle some hints that the two of you are falling in love for real. That always seems to help these kinds of movies."

I roll my eyes. He's always trying to force me into a fake relationship for publicity's sake. I really shouldn't have been surprised about the

Talon angle. It's just another way to get my name in the news, not that I'm too worried about that. If I had an actual boyfriend, I could easily avoid all these manipulations. Of course, when would I have time for that? It makes sense why so many celebrities couple up. They're busy, they understand what the other person is dealing with, and will ignore all the rumors about hooking up with coworkers.

My mind wanders to the furniture maker I met the other day. He'd make a great fake boyfriend. He's very nice to look at and doesn't seem to care about fame. Of course, I only spent like half an hour with him, but it rarely takes long to see someone's hunger for the spotlight. Not that I need a boyfriend. I put a stop to Rick's suggestion just fine on my own.

After our meeting wraps up, Lila rides with me back to the hotel so I can do my prep work for tomorrow.

"Can you believe Rick wanted me to date Talon Jacobs?"

Lila pauses her typing to meet my gaze. "He is kind of cute, even if he acts like a jerk sometimes."

I wrinkle my nose. "I think personality matters a lot in relationships. Besides, isn't he like 5'5"? I'd tower over him. We'd just look weird together."

She shrugs. "I agree that there's no benefit to you for helping him out, despite what Rick thinks. You've already got the male demographic locked. Especially once Maxim's Hot 100 list comes out this fall."

I roll my eyes. "Yes, because my greatest ambition is to be a sex symbol."

Lila chuckles, then her expression turns serious. "Look, I know you want to do something different, and I think you should pursue projects that interest you. This is your life and you should go after what you want, regardless of whether Rick thinks it's 'on brand' for you."

I give her an appreciative smile. "Thanks for your support, but if I can't get him on board to set me up with auditions for serious roles, there's no other way to get my foot in the door."

"Come on. You're Kat Sonnett. I'm sure if you made an announcement that you're interested in doing drama, scripts would be piled up at your door by the end of the night."

My eyebrows shoot up my forehead. "You really think so? I haven't been pigeonholed into light, romantic roles?"

She pats my arm. "Rick may not believe in you, but I do. I see how hard you work, doing promos you hate with a genuine-looking smile the whole time. If you can fake that, you can definitely make anyone believe you're mad or sad or whatever you're trying to do. Besides, you showed your serious side when you were making those teen dramas."

She's right. I got my start doing somewhat serious work. Teen drama is, of course, a little ridiculous at times, but it's in the same vein as what I'd like to do next. I give Lila's arm a squeeze. "Thanks, Lila. I needed to hear that. Have I told you how much I appreciate you?"

"Yes, but keep telling me because I like it."

Her words draw a genuine smile from me. She's worked with me for five years now and is hands down the most amazing assistant I've ever had. "You really are the best."

She gives me a wink. "I know."

"And because you're so incredible, I'm setting you up with a full day at the Four Seasons Spa when we get back to Los Angeles. Massage, facial, body scrub, manicure, pedicure, and whatever else you want. It's on me."

Her eyes light up, a smile spreading across her face. "Thanks, Kat!"

I grin, pleased I can do a little something to show my appreciation.

CHAPTER SIX

Zach

"Who's closest to winning?" Jonah asks, dealing cards around the table.

I consult the notebook. "Dane only has forty-eight, but Nora is at eighty-six, so depending on who goes out, it could be a nail biter."

Dane sighs. "I really hate the 'exactly one hundred back to fifty' rule. Can't I just be the assumed champion?"

I shake my head. "Sorry, bro. You know how we play Flipper. Besides, haven't you won a time or two by hitting one hundred?"

He grins sheepishly. "Yeah, but can't we make an exception tonight?"

"Yeah, no," Nora says. "I'm coming for you Dane-O."

He narrows his eyes, picking up the pile of cards in front of him. "Bring it, then."

The game ends after only a few turns around the table when Jonah lays down his cards. Dane ends up with three points and Nora slaps down a triumphant fourteen. "Read 'em and weep, sucker!"

"Man," Dane shakes his head, but his smile lets me know he isn't that bummed. "Guess that means I'll have to take you down in the next game. Whose turn to pick?"

It humors me how worked up everyone gets while playing a bunch of card games my family made up. I lift the bowl with the names inside, shuffle it around, then pass it over to Nora, the winner of this game. She pulls out a piece of paper and opens it up, her shoulders dropping.

"It's Greg. I know what game we're playing."

"Blackout!" shouts Greg, putting away the Flipper deck and pulling out a standard pack of cards.

Dane rubs his hands. "Alright, I've got a chance now."

I set up the scorecard while Greg shuffles. There's a knock at the door, but then I hear it open and shut.

"Sorry I'm late. What'd I miss?" Will says, coming into the kitchen.

He sets down a bag of chips and a pitcher of margaritas.

"Not much," I say, pulling out the empty seat next to me. "Just Nora cleaning our clocks at Flipper."

"Oh, man." He glances down at the notebook in front of me. "Ooh, Blackout. Just in time!"

Dane groans. "There goes my chance."

Will slaps Dane on the shoulder. "Buck up, dude. It's all in the deal."

While Greg deals the cards, I stand up to get some more snacks and a drink. Nora follows me over to the counter. "Now that Will's here, can I share the news?"

The twinkle in her eyes lets me know it doesn't matter what I say, she's doing it anyway. "How about after this first hand?"

"Sure, sure. Will you record Jonah's reaction?"

I give her a look. "Really?"

"Yes! It's going to be epic."

"Fine."

We play the round of eight and everyone makes their bid. It's Nora's turn to shuffle and deal. After the cards are out, she clears her throat.

"Hey gang. I saw a certain tall, statuesque blonde walking through my lobby the other day."

Jonah's head whips over to her and I subtly point my phone in his direction and start filming.

"Was it Kat? It's Kat. I know you can't officially say, so wink if it is."

Nora gives a slow wink and Jonah's eyes widen, his smile wide. "I knew it!"

"But that's not all I saw…"

Jonah's leaning forward, his arms on the table. He's all in.

"She was with someone. They strolled through the lobby hand-in-hand and took the elevator to her floor."

His mouth drops. "Kat's dating someone? Is he also famous? Describe him!"

She laughs, her eyes darting to me briefly before looking back at Jonah.

"Well, he was a little taller than her, with wavy brown hair, a beard and mustache, blue eyes…"

A couple of heads swing my direction and heat creeps up my neck. Jonah, however, is lost in thought. "Hmmm. Tall, famous person with blue eyes and wavy brown hair? Chris Pine could fit, but he's like forty. Too old for her. Zac Efron is too short and also a little old."

"Hey, he's my age," Dane says.

"Exactly."

Dane frowns, then looks at his cards. "Whipper snappers," he mutters, making everyone chuckle.

"Timothée Chalamet is kind of tall, but doesn't have a beard or blue eyes."

"How do you know all this?" Greg asks. "Are you that into celebrities?"

Jonah grins, a little shamefaced. "I try to keep up with pop culture for when I finally get on Jeopardy."

I smile, remembering that's his dream. He's applied half a dozen times, but never gotten a call. "And you think the questions will be about celebrity heights?"

He looks at me and shrugs. "Can't be too careful."

He picks up his cards, then does a double-take at me. "Wait a minute..." he says, looking over at Nora while pointing at me.

She gives him another wink and his jaw goes slack. He whips around to stare at me. "You?! No. No way. *Zach?* Nuh-uh."

I shrug, keeping my phone trained on his stunned face. Jonah blinks a few times, clearly stunned and trying to process this information, then gapes at me. He explodes out of his chair, slapping his cards down on the table. "You *held* her hand?! Are you dating? Tell me everything now!"

Nora cackles. "That was better than I imagined!"

Jonah swivels between her and me until I stop recording, pocket my phone, and motion for him to sit down.

"It's not a big deal. No, we're not dating. Yes, I held her hand."

"What? How? Why?" he splutters.

"She was in my shop earlier this week—"

"She came into your store?" Jonah interrupts. "And I'm just now hearing about it? How come everyone's seen her but me?" He slumps down in his chair, defeated.

"Anyway," I say, "when she left, some fans practically assaulted her, so I helped her escape out the back and returned her safely to her hotel. There were reporters in the lobby, so we pretended to be a couple to sneak by them, and it worked. That's all."

"Oh man," Jonah says, shaking his head. "Some people have all the luck."

"Speaking of luck," I say, ready to move on, "what is everyone bidding?"

After a few more card games, Jonah and Nora head to the main house for some sleep before another work day. Will heads out for his shift at the club, while Dane and Greg help me clean up.

"I can't believe you met Kat Sonnett," Greg says, rinsing off bowls and glasses and sticking them in the dishwasher. "Tara loves her movies. Which means I've seen most of them as well."

I shake my head. "I don't think I've seen any of them."

"They're better to watch with a significant other," Dane says. "Women usually feel pretty warm and romantic after watching one of her rom-coms, if you know what I mean."

"I sure do," says Greg with an exaggerated wink.

"I'll keep that in mind," I say, "if I ever find someone."

"Are you looking?" Dane asks.

I tilt my head back and forth. "I mean, I'm ready for a relationship, but I'm not sure how to find someone. I'm too old for clubs and too young for pickleball."

"You're never too young for pickleball. I can teach you if you'd like."

"Have you tried a dating app?" Greg asks.

I grimace. "I'm worried about what kinds of people are on there."

"It's how Tara and I reconnected."

"Yeah, but you two knew each other from high school."

They have a cute love story that I may be a little envious of. Dane and Sienna, too, but I'm happy for all of them. Maybe I should go to our next high school reunion and see who's still available. Okay, now *that* sounds a little desperate, which I'm not. At least not yet.

"Speaking of significant others, are your wives ever going to come to game night? They know they have an open invitation, right?"

"They decided they'd rather have ladies' night than compete against their husbands for bragging rights," Dane says, rolling his eyes. "Go figure."

Greg puts the last bowl in the dishwasher, then comes over and grasps my shoulder. "I'll keep an eye out for you. And maybe ask Tara if she knows anyone. We'll do whatever we can to help."

I smile, appreciative of my supportive network of friends. "Thanks, man."

CHAPTER SEVEN

Kat

I'm impressed by the cool, artsy atmosphere inside Twisted Ivy. Glancing around at the tables, my stomach grumbles at the delicious-looking food. Okay, an upscale restaurant sounds like a perfect evening. But then Lila heads through the restaurant and ascends a set of stairs. Looks like we're not having cocktails and apps. Bummer.

A door at the top of the stairs emerges onto a rooftop patio with seating, umbrellas, and plenty of neon lights. The music is thumping and there's quite a crowd dancing, all attired in collared shirts or cocktail dresses like mine. My red dress is a Sara Jane original, which I'm supposed to share with anyone who asks and have Lila tag in her social media posts. My head is already pounding from the music, but the open-air roof helps the sound escape rather than reverberate off the walls.

I bob my head to the catchy tune, beginning to warm up to the atmosphere until a familiar face heads my way. My brow creases as I try to place the man. Everything snaps together when he grabs my waist, pushes up onto his toes, and kisses me right on the lips. So much for avoiding unwanted touching tonight. I push him off me, sure the disgust is clear on my face, though Talon doesn't seem bothered.

"There you are, gorgeous. I've been waiting for you. Can I get you a drink?"

I look over at Lila, trying to make sense of what's happening. She has a deer-in-headlights look. This must be Rick's doing. No wonder he's conveniently absent. No, wait. There he is, with his phone up, motioning for me to put my arm around Talon. What. Is. Happening?

Talon slides a hand around my waist. He grabs my hand and brings it up to his lips, holding the pose for a few seconds before releasing me.

I stare daggers at Rick. He doesn't even have the decency to look ashamed, just shrugs, then examines the photos he just took. I march over to him. "I told you 'no,'" I hiss in his ear.

"What's the big deal? I thought you enjoyed helping other people."

I grind my teeth together, wanting to keep my head even if I am furious. "Not like this. My agent is supposed to look out for *my* best interests."

He rolls his eyes, not settling my ire one iota. "Guys want to see that you're approachable and attainable. Like I said, this will only boost your appeal. Lighten up a little." He gives me a once over that makes my skin crawl. "Go show off that dress."

Oh no, he didn't. My fists clench and I open my mouth to respond, unsure of what to say, when I get a sudden flash of inspiration. "I *have* a boyfriend, Rick."

His skeptical look doesn't do anything to diminish the anger pulsing through my veins. "Yeah, sure you do."

"I do. And I don't think he'd appreciate some other guy putting his hands on me."

He frowns, his face mirroring disbelief. "How come this is the first I'm hearing about it?"

"Maybe I'd like to maintain some privacy. Not everything has to be for public consumption."

He scoffs. "It does when you're famous." He turns away, like the conversation is over.

His blatant dismissal feels like the final straw for my restraint. I take a step toward him, gearing up for a heated confrontation, when Lila grabs my hand and tugs me across the room.

"What are you doing?" I say through gritted teeth.

"Preventing you from making a scene in front of all these people."

I turn around to find half the crowd with their phones pointed toward me. My outrage ratchets down to frustrated irritation. "Did you see what Rick did? I mean, Talon just *kissed* me!"

She wrinkles her nose. "Yeah. That wasn't cool. But look, nothing good can come of you yelling at either of them. Let me get some video of you dancing in that beautiful dress and then we can go."

I sigh. Lila's right. What's done is done, though I am definitely starting to rethink my relationship with Rick. While he's helped push me into the upper echelon of actors, his recent actions are making me wonder if our ideas about my future are no longer compatible. Of course, I'm grateful for all he's done, but his recent comments about my image and career aren't vibing with my desires. Maybe it's time to look for new representation. I'm not looking forward to that conversation. I perk up when the DJ plays a song that never fails to get my booty shaking. Determined to salvage the night like the professional I am, I turn my mind away from the last five minutes.

I nod at Lila, then shimmy my way into a small circle of women who are dancing together. I smile, a thrill pulsing through me as I see their eyes light in recognition. There's definitely a bit of an ego boost to this fame thing sometimes. We dance to a few songs; me pretending like I'm actually hanging with a group of friends until there's a tap on my shoulder and a thumbs up from Lila. Looks like she's gotten what she needs. I wave to the women, and one of them motions taking a picture. I nod, then turn to Lila, who already has her phone up. The five of us squeeze together and smile. Lila has one woman share her email address and then promises to send her the photo after some edits. It'll be the same one she posts on my social media later tagging Sara Jane and Ivy Rooftop and Lounge.

Relieved that my duty is done, I take one last look around, noting Talon over by the bar, surrounded by a cluster of people. He's got an arm around a young woman, looking at her in a way that makes my lip curl in disgust. It just confirms my belief that he's not really looking to change. I don't know what Rick was thinking. Not bothering to find him, I link my arm with Lila's and we head back down the stairs and out to the street.

"The hotel's just a few blocks that way." Lila points down the street. "Unless there's somewhere else you want to go."

"No, a quiet hotel room sounds nice. I'm game to walk if you are."

We get a lot of looks from people and I realize we're a bit dressy for a casual Wednesday night walk through downtown Charleston. Oh well. I'm used to people looking at me.

"I still can't believe Rick blindsided me like that. And that Talon just kissed me right on the lips like he knew me? The nerve!"

Lila purses her lips. "Rick didn't tell me Talon would be there or I would have warned you. You were pretty clear you were against his dating idea."

"Thank you. I bet none of this would have happened if I were in a serious relationship. Men don't seem to care about what women want, but they sure work hard not to offend other dudes."

She nods her head. "Too true."

We lapse into silence until we reach the hotel where a few photographers are waiting outside. I sigh, but paste on a sparkling smile while I pose for a few seconds before heading into the lobby to the elevator. At least Sara Jane is getting some publicity from all this. The dress really is gorgeous and feels silky and smooth against my skin. And the sweetheart neckline is quite flattering. I may actually wear this one again.

Lila deposits me in my room with the promise of a wake-up call and room service in the morning before another day of filming. I get to make an ice cream sundae, according to the script. Actually, I'm "accidentally" spilling one and yelling at my co-star while he flirts with a camera woman. Maybe I can funnel my real rage about tonight's events into the scene tomorrow.

After a shower and my nightly skin care routine, I get into bed, still stewing over the evening's debacle. If I was really dating someone, surely Rick would show me some respect then. Not that he shouldn't have honored my wishes, regardless. I suddenly go cold at the realization that I told Rick I'm dating someone. Obviously, that wasn't true, but I couldn't stand seeing him look so smug. Does this mean I'm now on the hook to produce a boyfriend? But who could I get to play the role? The only single guy I know is my brother, and we barely speak to each other. Plus, gross. That would cause all kinds of headlines I don't want to be part of.

The furniture store guy pops into my mind and I get a tingly feeling in my chest. He's ruggedly handsome with his mountain man vibe. And a smidge taller than me, which I don't hate. Of course, he's not an actor, so could he pretend to be into me? Would he even be willing? I mean, what would it entail? Being seen around town a few times cozied up together? He willingly held my hand to avoid reporters the other day, so the idea doesn't seem completely far-fetched. And once filming wraps, we could conveniently break up. No harm, no foul. I'll even pay him. I mean, I'm pretty desperate to avoid a repeat of tonight, so whatever it takes. Who would say no to getting paid handsomely to fake date a celebrity?

CHAPTER EIGHT

Kat

"No."

"What do you mean 'no'?" I'm gobsmacked. Have I found the only guy on the planet who's immune to the Kat Sonnett charm? Okay, Rick isn't a pushover either, so maybe there are two.

"I mean just what I said. I don't want to pretend to be your boyfriend for a few weeks."

"Months," I correct. "Filming is scheduled to last through the summer."

"Months?!"

It's obvious Zach doesn't know the intricacies of the movie business. It's almost refreshing. I've been surrounded by people in the industry for so long I've nearly forgotten what non-acting life is like.

"Then it's a definite no."

I sigh. "What's the big deal? Am I that hideous to look at?"

His brow furrows as he studies my face. He shakes his head. "You know you're beautiful."

Why do his words cause a hitch in my breath? It's not like I haven't been on half a dozen magazine hot lists. Could it have something to do with the frisson of attraction I feel when I look at him? Not important right now. I'm supposed to be getting him to agree to this harebrained scheme. "Do I have a terrible personality?"

"I don't know you well enough to comment, but probably not if you're 'America's Sweetheart.'"

I'm not a fan of his air quotes, but at least he knows a little about me. Which means I'm still perplexed by his objection. Unless... "Oh, you already have a significant other. I understand."

He frowns and rubs the back of his neck, giving me a feeling of déjà vu. Is that a habit of his? "Uh, no. I'm not seeing anyone."

I release a breath. Thank goodness. That would have been an obvious deal breaker. "Then what?"

He looks at me in disbelief. "Did you not hear yourself when you said you want me to lie to my family and friends for weeks—"

"Months," I correct.

He scowls. "It means allowing strangers to dissect my life, seeing unauthorized photos and videos of me splashed all over the internet, and then breaking up with you and becoming the most despised man on earth."

When he puts it like that, it doesn't sound so good. I'm used to pretending, but I forget that's not everyone's life. "If you want, I could dump you in the end."

He throws up his hands. "Great. Then I'll just be pitied. Poor guy couldn't please a gorgeous, successful, talented woman."

"You think I'm talented?"

I realize that's not what I was meant to take from his words, but I just can't help it. Sometimes I need my ego stroked. All the better if the compliment comes from a good-looking guy.

He shakes his head. "I mean, you won an award, right? Honestly, I haven't seen any of your movies."

And just like that, my ego is back on the floor. "What? None of them? Not even *For Love or Money*?"

"I don't watch romance movies."

Huh. I suppose that's not surprising. He is a man, after all. Still, a lot of guys see them because they think I'm hot. Or they're on a date. Zach has admitted I'm beautiful, but maybe he's saying it objectively, like a piece of art is beautiful. Everyone agrees, but it's personally not his thing. Am I not his type? This doesn't matter. If he's not into me, then it will make things easier for this scheme. We can date and then break up with no hard feelings.

"What if we say we parted by mutual agreement?"

He's still frowning, which is definitely not in line with how I saw this interaction going. Who knew it would be so much work to arrange a fake boyfriend?

"I suppose that would be okay. I just don't like the idea of pretending in front of my friends. This is my community. You'll leave and I'll still be here."

Oh yeah. I hadn't really thought about that. How can I appease his conscience? I immediately feel guilty for trying to con him into something he obviously doesn't want to do, but I'm desperate. I can't have another Talon incident. And desperate times call for desperate measures. "Well, it wouldn't actually be lying. We would go on real dates, so we would technically be dating. There just wouldn't be any feelings attached."

His scowl hasn't budged, and I really need him to see things my way. "The thing is, my agent is trying to force me to date a sleazeball, and the only way he'll stop is if he thinks I'm already dating someone." I know I'm playing dirty by appealing to his protective side, but I'm willing to do whatever it takes.

Internally, I wince at the half-truth. Outwardly, I'm practically staring a hole through Zach, willing him to come to the dark side with me.

"How can your agent make you date someone? That doesn't seem possible."

His skeptical expression forces me to bring out my ace. "I didn't think so either until said sleazeball stuck his tongue down my throat."

"What?! That's assault. You should report it."

Now he's just angry. Oops. I guess I told a little too much truth. Technically, he's right, but I just want to get rid of Talon and put the whole thing behind me.

"I'm fine, but I want to ensure it won't happen again. Which is where you come in."

He looks conflicted, which is infinitesimally better than being obviously opposed. Is there anything I can say to push him all the way over the line to my side? "And to keep things on the up and up, we can set up some rules."

"Rules?"

The wrinkles in his forehead are a little less pronounced. Maybe he's softening. "Yeah, like guidelines. Things that are and aren't okay while we're 'dating.'" I use quotes to show him how cool and breezy this can be. Maybe even fun.

He crosses his arms, frown fully intact. "Like what?"

He's putting me on the spot. Maybe I should have spent a little more time thinking this idea through. "Um, like only touching in public when people might see us."

His eyes widen a little, but then narrow. "What kind of touching?"

Wow, he's being thorough. "You know, holding hands, hugs, a guiding hand on the back, helping me out of a car. Standard relationship stuff."

He nods slowly. "Okay. That sounds reasonable. What else?"

"No dating other people while we're together."

He rolls his eyes. "Obviously."

I guess he's a one-woman guy. As it should be, though, I've definitely dated guys with a different mindset. Not that I knew this until I caught them cheating. I'd certainly rather not deal with that again, even in a fake relationship.

"Okay, I think there's just one more rule to discuss. Kissing."

His Adam's apple bobs up and down. "What?" His voice sounds a little hoarse.

"If we're really going to sell this thing, we're going to have to show some affection." He's got a startled look on his face, so I rush on. "Obviously, no super long make-out sessions or anything. Just, like, an occasional cheek kiss and maybe a few pecks on the lips. When it's called for."

"And when exactly would it be called for?"

Good question, Zach. When indeed? All this talk of locking lips has me studying his. I've never kissed a guy with a beard before. All my rom-com co-stars have been clean-shaven, as have the handful of guys I've dated. I wonder what that would feel like? Perhaps I'll soon find out. Why does that cause a shiver to race down my spine?

"I don't know. Maybe at the end of a date if there are photographers around to make it look more authentic? We can play that by ear."

He presses his lips together, still not convinced.

Maybe a financial incentive will seal the deal. "I can pay you."

He shakes his head. "That's a hard no. I'm not your call boy. This isn't *Pretty Woman*."

Yikes. Is he saying he feels like Julia Roberts? That would make me Richard Gere in this scenario, and the thought makes me feel a little icky. I am seeking his companionship, but it's not seedy. Just one person helping out another.

"No, you're right. Regardless, I want to help." I glance around the room, the absence of potential customers glaringly obvious. "Maybe I can help drum up business for your store?"

He follows my gaze. "Uh, no, that's okay. I'm doing alright."

It doesn't look or sound like he's raking in the dough, but what do I know? I guess he's happy with the way things are. Who am I to rock the boat? Though I will have to find some way to compensate him for this huge favor. The main thing is, it sounds like he's coming around to this little plot of mine.

"So you know the approximate timeline of this situation, plus we've laid out some ground rules, which we can modify at any time, of course. Any other questions?"

He's quiet for a minute. "Yeah." I hold my breath, wondering what he's going to say. "Why me?"

I blink, surprised. That's a great question, actually. While I'm thinking this through, he continues talking.

"I mean, it doesn't seem like it'd be a hardship for you to find someone to date. You could probably open a dating app and have a thousand willing guys in two seconds. Heck, you could walk outside, flag down a guy, and, if he's single, he'd agree in a heartbeat." He pauses. "Maybe even if he's not single, actually."

I don't think he's trying to be funny, so I hold in a chuckle. He's right. It really wouldn't be too hard to get a date. Why is he the one I'm asking? "Well...I wouldn't use a dating app because I'd worry the guy might think we're really dating and then be hurt when I end things. Or he'd just want to hook up and I'm not into those kinds of connections. And I'd feel kind of weird asking a stranger to be my fake boyfriend."

His eyebrows knit together. "Isn't that exactly what you're doing with me?"

I guess he's right, but he doesn't feel like a stranger to me. There's just something comforting about him. "I suppose, but we've met before and it's obvious you're not star-struck or even into me. Dating someone who doesn't have feelings for me seems perfect because we know it's fake going in and no one will have their heart broken when things end."

He nods, and there's a little twist of disappointment in my gut that he agreed with my assessment so easily. Maybe I have drunk a little of the celebrity Kool-aid and kind of like having people attracted to me. But I know I'm right. Just being work colleagues, so to speak, is best.

Though maybe a promotion to friendship is an attainable future goal? It'd actually be really nice to have a genuine friend. Does that sound pathetic?

He gives a decisive nod and looks me in the eye. "Okay, I'll do it."

"You will?" The surprise in my voice is almost laughable. I guess I really didn't think he'd agree. "That's great."

"Do I need to sign a contract or something?"

Why does creating a legally binding document sound so unappealing to me? Maybe because it would underline the fact that this is strictly a professional thing. Which is what I want, I remind myself.

"I don't think that's necessary. I don't know you very well, but I trust you. You rescued me from a crowd the other day, after all."

"When do you want to have our first 'date?'"

His use of air quotes makes me frown briefly. "We should probably work up a schedule. Maybe do something together in public once a week?" That should convince Rick this is real.

"Weekly seems reasonable. Forgive me, but this public relationship thing is a new concept for me. Could we sort of ease into it? Maybe do something low-key to start?"

Oh, he's nervous about all the attention. It's been so long since I thought about people looking at me. I just assume I'm being watched at all times and act accordingly. It's easy to forget not everyone lives like me.

"Sure." I don't know where to even start. "Do you know someplace we could go that doesn't have a lot of crowds or that people wouldn't expect to see a celebrity, but would still give us an opportunity for a social media post?"

For the first time since I walked into his store, a smile ghosts across his face. "I actually think I have the perfect spot, but we'd have to visit sometime between nine a.m. and three p.m. When are you available?"

I'm definitely intrigued. It's not a bar or a club based on the hours. Maybe we're doing something fun like mini golf. I want to know, but the idea of a surprise is more enticing. "Let me check with my assistant and I'll get back to you. Are you sure you can leave your store in the middle of the day?"

He looks around. "Like I said last time, I think it'll be fine." He scribbles something on a scrap of paper and hands it to me. "Here. You may need this."

It's his name and phone number. Zach Worthy. That sounds nice together. "Is your middle name Trust?"

His lips turn down briefly, but then he seems to realize I'm messing with him and he shakes his head, the corner of his mouth quirking up. "No, but that's actually the first time I've heard that one."

His almost smile just makes me want to try harder to see the full thing. "Guess I'll have to keep thinking. Is it Michael?"

"Nope, but your middle name is Rae."

My mouth falls open in shock. "How did you know that?"

He shrugs. "It was on your credit card. Katherine Rae Bissonnette."

Oh yeah. Duh. "Please call me Katie."

"Katie it is." He tips his head to the side, studying me. "It suits you."

I don't know why his words thrill me. Or why I told him to call me Katie rather than Kat. Everyone in my professional life knows me by my stage name. I guess dating someone, even if it's not real, feels more personal. My phone buzzes in the pocket of my leggings and I pull it out.

> **Lila:** You're wanted at the set in an hour for blocking.

"I have to get to work, but I'll call you later and let you know what day I'm free."

He shrugs. "You can just text."

Why does that feel like rejection? Everyone communicates over text these days. "Yeah, sure. And Zach?" When he meets my gaze, I give him a grateful smile. "Thank you so much for helping me out. You don't know how much I appreciate it."

CHAPTER NINE

Zach

I can't believe I agreed to be Kat Sonnett's boyfriend. *Pretend* boyfriend, if I'm being accurate. What was I thinking? I'll tell you what. I saw a beautiful, vulnerable woman seeking my help and I just couldn't say no. I'm still not sure why she needs this ruse, but from her earnestness, there seems to be something amiss. What is wrong with this world that a famous movie star needs to hire someone who will pretend to adore her? Creepy guys who don't take no for an answer—that's what's wrong. Of course, she didn't *actually* hire me. I'm working out of the goodness of my heart. But oh, will it be a struggle to lie straight to my mother's face. I've never been a good liar and I don't really want to gain a lot of practice. I think honesty is generally the best policy. However, something in my gut told me to play along with this scheme of Katie's. I'm not exactly sure what my body is trying to tell me, but it's normally good at steering me in the right direction.

Jonah is going to blow a gasket when he sees us together, which is why the aquarium was the first place that popped into my head when Katie asked about date locations. He said he never sees a celebrity at work. Well, buddy, that changes today. As soon as I heard from her, I arranged a behind-the-scenes tour with him so he can see us up close and personal.

And maybe it might even impress Katie a little. Not that I'm trying to knock her socks off or anything. This is all just for show, but it might be good practice for when I actually get back into the dating scene. In fact, that's exactly how I should view this arrangement. An opportunity to reacclimatize myself to putting myself out there and discover all the cool places Charleston has to offer couples. I guess this arrangement will benefit me after all.

When Katie texted me with her free day, I told her I'd pick her up. Now I'm standing outside her room, gathering myself before knocking on the door. I've spent the last couple of days trying to prepare myself for being seen in public with a movie star. Truth be told, there's probably no way to really be ready for something like this. I raise my hand to knock, but then the door swings open and I'm staring into the confused face of a petite woman with stick straight shoulder length black hair.

"Hi, I'm here for Katie."

She scowls briefly before schooling her face into one of indifference. "You must have the wrong room number. There's no Katie here."

"What about Kat? This is the room number she gave me."

Her eyes narrow. "Who are you?"

Oh boy. Guess we're jumping right into this fake dating adventure. "I'm Zach. I have a date with Kat."

This causes her eyebrows to shoot up to her bangs. "Just a minute," she says and shuts the door in my face.

Does this mean Katie hasn't told anyone she's seeing someone? Maybe she's not all that keen on lying to others, either. After another minute, the door opens again and Katie scoots out.

"Sorry about that. I forgot to tell my assistant about my plans."

"She seems...nice?"

Katie chuckles. "She isn't a fan of surprises. So, where are we going?"

I take a moment to peruse her attire. Jeans, sneakers, sweatshirt, and a baseball cap with the Charleston RiverDogs logo. I nod. "You look like you belong here in that getup. The hat's a nice touch."

She smiles and touches the brim. "Thanks. Every place I shoot, I try to find something from the city. A memento of sorts."

"Is it always a hat?"

"No. Sometimes, I get a shirt or a piece of jewelry. Whatever strikes my fancy."

My lips quirk up. "And a dog biting a bat is what you've decided best memorializes your time here. Nice."

She laughs. "Hey, I didn't choose the mascot."

"Fair enough. Anyway, you'll blend right in where we're going."

Her smile dims slightly. "It's not a baseball game, is it? I didn't pack any sunscreen."

"Nope. Our adventure is indoors."

We take the elevator down to the lobby and out front, where my truck is parked. I open the passenger door for her, then walk around to the driver's side, wiping my damp hands on my jeans. Even though my brain knows this isn't a real date, I'm feeling nervous like it is.

A handful of minutes later, we're pulling into the parking lot. Katie's eyes light up when she sees the sign. "An aquarium?"

She lets out a little squeal of delight, which is so cute it makes me grin. "You like animals?"

"I love them!"

My shoulders relax a little. This might actually be fun. Especially once she sees what I have in store. I show an employee our tickets who lets us in without seeming to recognize Katie. I text Jonah that we're here, but he doesn't respond. There's nothing to be done except wander around until I hear from him. We take the escalator upstairs to the first exhibit, which contains river otters.

"What?!" Katie shrieks, before quickly covering her mouth. "I love otters! How did you know?"

I actually didn't, but my brain recalls her request for one when she was searching through my bowl of wooden animals. I shrug. "I thought you'd be excited about the sea turtles."

She turns to me, wide-eyed. "There are sea turtles?"

I laugh at the expression of pure delight on her face. I know she's trained to show emotion, but she's definitely not pretending right now. Why am I so charmed by her child-like enthusiasm?

"Yes, but they're downstairs." I motion toward the glass. "One adorable creature at a time."

She nods solemnly. "You're right. Carpe diem, as they say."

"Or carp diem, as the fish might say?"

She chuckles and rolls her eyes. "That is a terrible pun."

I lift a shoulder. "You still laughed."

"Touché."

She turns her attention back to the otters, watching them swim gracefully through the water. A staff member comes out and tosses them some food. Katie's face is practically smashed up against the glass. I watch her quietly, amazed at how unassuming she is at this moment. It actually feels like I'm on a date with a regular person.

I shake my head, reminding myself this is not a real date, only for show. While I can practice my skills, I shouldn't let my heart get any ideas that this might have actual potential. There's a fine line between enjoying an experience and getting immersed. I will have to remember which side I need to stay on.

Eventually, Katie turns to me, a wide smile on her face. "That was amazing! What's next?"

We continue along the corridor, checking out river life. Katie skirts around the trading post, which focuses on reptiles and amphibians.

"Not a fan of frogs?" I say, a teasing lilt to my voice.

"Those are fine. It's the snakes I don't care for."

"Why snakes?"

She gives me a sheepish look. "You're going to laugh."

Now I have to know the answer. I make my face serious. "Try me."

She sighs. "I saw *Anaconda* at a birthday party sleepover in fifth grade. I didn't sleep for a week."

I curl my lips in to keep from smiling, imagining a room of ten-year-olds screaming their heads off when the giant snake took its first victim. "I'm sorry. If it helps, seeing a movie too soon is why I'm not a fan of toddlers."

Her face scrunches in confusion. "Toddlers? Like small children?"

I nod solemnly. "Yes. Did you ever see *Pet Sematary*?"

Understanding dawns and she pinches her lips together, but not before I see the edges tip up. Mission accomplished. She definitely doesn't feel silly about her snake fear now.

"Yeah, a two foot tall person with glinting eyes and a scalpel can make for some bad dreams."

I shiver, just thinking about it. "You're telling me."

"Does this mean you don't want kids? Mitigate the risk of suffering Jud's fate?"

"I hadn't thought about that until right now, so thanks for that."

She giggles. "Sorry."

I give her a wink to let her know I'm not really bothered. "I have a confession to make. I'm not really afraid of small children. Truthfully, I don't know if I want kids. I think I would be happy either way. What about you?"

She looks to the side, considering the question. "You know, I haven't given it much thought either. Ideally, I'd like to have a long film career, so I don't know how well a family fits in. Especially since having a baby would mean taking time off for the pregnancy and recovery."

I nod. "Yeah, that's a valid concern. I bet some actors adopt or use a surrogate."

"They do. I appreciate you bringing this up, Zach. I haven't had a relationship serious enough to think about this, but I probably should figure out what I want for my future."

"Do you want a serious romantic relationship?"

She turns away from me slightly toward the tank in front of us, but I can see her downcast expression in the reflection of the glass. "Maybe? I just don't see how that would happen with who I am."

"What do you mean?"

She keeps her eyes glued to the tank, but I don't think she's really seeing anything. "I haven't had the best luck at finding guys who like me for me, you know? They see the fame and the money, but not the woman. It makes it really hard for me to trust that people are genuine around me."

Ouch, that sounds rough. I'd hate to only be a status symbol for someone else. No wonder she objected to finding a date online. It solidifies my conviction to treat her well during our time together. She obviously needs people who like her for who she is rather than her fame. However, we've crossed into deep territory for what's supposed to be our first date. Time to lighten things up.

"I bet those fish in there don't see your fame and money. They're probably terrified of the giant monsters leering at them through the glass."

My inane comment seems to do the trick, because she turns to me, gives me a huge eye roll, and lightly shoves my shoulder. "You're so dumb, Zachary Ryan."

I shake my head at her attempt to discover my middle name and smile wide, glad that she's perked up slightly, but then she freezes. Uh, oh. What did I do now? "Are you okay?"

She blinks, then shakes her head, pressing her lips together. "Yeah, fine." Her eyes look over my shoulder and she brightens significantly. "Ooh, a touch tank!"

She grabs my hand and pulls me along until we're staring down into an open tank with stingrays, sea urchins, and anemones. I'm oddly disappointed when she lets go of my hand, but hide my true feelings with a chuckle. "No snakes, but stingrays are just fine. Gotcha."

"Come on, Zach. If it wasn't safe, they wouldn't let us do it."

She's got me there. When we're finished at the tank, we wash our hands before continuing our exploration of the aquarium. My phone buzzes while we're walking down a long ramp to the first floor. Perfect timing.

"The next part of our experience is ready. Let's head over to the sea turtle recovery area."

Katie gives me a curious look, but says nothing. What could she be thinking? More importantly, is she enjoying this as much as I am?

CHAPTER TEN

Kat

W hen I woke up this morning, I definitely didn't think I'd find myself strolling through an aquarium having a deep conversation with a practical stranger. And, really, that's what Zach is. These get-to-know-you questions are quite informative because, before today, all I knew about him is where he works and that he's objectively handsome. I could definitely see him on a movie screen or in a magazine modeling for a clothing campaign. Not that he's interested in either of those. At least, I doubt it. I haven't actually asked. Oh, I know his last name too! So, not that much. I've also learned that I experience a strange tingling sensation whenever I touch him, as evidenced by the surprising jolt I felt when I nudged his shoulder upstairs. However, questions will have to wait because, when we reach the sea turtle area, a man in khakis and a blue polo waves us over.

"Hey, Jonah," Zach says.

"I'm shocked you're finally dating again."

My brow furrows. Zach doesn't date? I wonder why not. There's no way women don't find him attractive. And from what I've seen so far, he's not a jerk. I mean, he opened my car door for me. Who does that anymore? Uncertainty creeps in. Does he have a hidden flaw? I'm sure to discover something I don't like the more time we spend together. At least, part of me hopes that's the case, so I don't get too attached to this possibly perfect man. I paste on a smile when Zach turns toward me.

"Katie, this is my friend, Jonah. Jonah, this is—"

"Kat Sonnett!" Jonah finishes for Zach, eyes wide.

This is what I'm used to. I make sure my eyes are warm as I extend a hand. "Nice to meet you, Jonah."

He blinks a few times, then slowly places his hand in mine, wrapping his other one over the top, and pumping our hands up and down. "The mine is all pleasure."

"What?"

He shakes his head. "I mean, uh, nice to meet you, too."

He's still shaking my hand, so I soften my grip. He gets the message, releases my hand, and quickly pulls back. "Sorry about that. I wasn't expecting you."

He turns to glare at Zach, who is far enough ahead of me I can't see his face. They have a silent conversation, during which Jonah makes some strange faces. Finally, Zach turns to me and I see a mischievous sparkle in his eyes. What's that about? Whatever it is, I like how it makes his lips quirk up in a pleased smile. I've seen him smile twice today and both times it's made my heart rate kick up. I definitely could get addicted to it.

"I asked Jonah to give us a behind-the-scenes tour of the aquarium. He's one of the marine biologists here. He mainly works with the sea turtles."

"Wow, that's so great. Thanks, Jonah."

He looks pleased. "You're welcome. If you two want to follow me, we'll head back to where we keep and care for the rescued turtles."

He scans his badge at a door, and we follow him down a short hallway. It's loud with the tank pumps and other machinery. He stops in front of a tank with two turtles inside. One has some barnacles attached to its shell, but otherwise looks fine. The other is missing part of its left flipper.

"In this tank are Marmalade and Croissant. They're green turtles. Over here," he says, walking to the next tank, "we have Beignet who is a Kemp's ridley. All three were rescued from the beach only a few miles from here."

"Why do they all have food names?"

"Good catch. The first turtle rescued years ago had a quirky personality, so the staff named him Ham. Things just kind of escalated from there."

That story sounds made up. I narrow my gaze at him. "Are you pulling my leg?"

Jonah raises his hands in front of him, his face serious. "No, I swear it's true. I'd never lie to you, Kat Sonnett."

I manage to stop an eye roll. It always bothers me when people call me by my full name. And it's not even my real name. At least it's a litmus test for who sees a real person versus who only sees a celebrity. It makes me even more grateful that Zach doesn't seem to be like that.

"Just Kat, thanks. Do you ever work with the river otters?"

Jonah deflates a little. "Unfortunately, I don't. I take it you're infatuated with Charlie and Beau?"

I straighten up, clasping my hands together. "What adorable names! Are they brothers?"

He smiles. "They are, actually. They came to us from Potter Park Zoo in Lansing, Michigan. Their parents' names are Nkeke and Miles."

"Oh, that's so amazing. But so are these turtles," I motion to the tanks. "I'm sure it takes a lot of hard work to care for injured animals."

He nods his head, looking more somber. "It's rewarding work, but sometimes we lose a patient. That's always tough."

I nod. "I'm sure." I reach out and grasp his shoulder. "What you do matters, even if you can't save all of them. Remember that."

His shoulders roll back and he stands taller, a smile curling his lips. "Thanks, Kat. That means a lot coming from you."

He takes us to the infirmary, which houses a variety of fish and sea creatures, including an octopus. The octopus has one red arm suctioned up the side of the glass, and I place my hand over it. I don't know what's wrong with it, but hope it recovers. It's a beautiful animal. A flash reflects in the glass and I turn to see Jonah with his phone out in front of him.

"Did you just take my picture?"

"Put that away," Zach says, reaching for it.

"No, it's okay. Actually, we're supposed to get a few shots while we're here." I turn to Jonah. "Would you be willing to help?"

He nods. "Anything for you, Kat."

I shut my eyes. Oh, boy. He's like an eager puppy. I definitely prefer Zach's cool demeanor, even if it makes him hard to read.

"Great. I was thinking of maybe a silhouette shot against a cool background. Any ideas?"

"What about in front of the ocean tank? We might be able to get a shark or large fish in the shot."

I smile. "Sounds perfect." I pause, turning to Zach. "I mean, if the tour is over. If not, let's keep going."

Zach looks at Jonah, who says, "This is pretty much all I can officially show you."

"Alright," says Zach, sighing. "Let's take some pictures."

He doesn't seem thrilled, but what I have in mind should ease any concern he's feeling. I figured we'd start with an amorphous shot, let people speculate about his identity before a big reveal. When we get to the tank, there are a few other people, but that will just aid to the natural look of the shot. I give Jonah my phone and explain what I'm looking for, then take Zach's hand and walk over to the glass.

"What are we supposed to be doing?" Zach asks out of the side of his mouth.

"Just watching the fish."

We stand, hand in hand, and stare into the blue. A small school of yellow fish swim by. Something about this shot doesn't feel right, but I can't quite figure it out. I look down in thought and realize our fingers aren't entwined. Isn't that how a genuine couple would hold hands? I loosen my grip and slide my fingers between his. Yep, much more intimate for sure. I look over at him, but he's staring straight ahead.

He must sense my gaze because he turns slightly and then his breath catches. He points off to the right and I turn. There's a shark swimming toward us and behind it is a giant sea turtle. Its lazy path through the water is mesmerizing.

"What kind of sea turtle is that?" I whisper.

"It's a loggerhead," he rasps back.

"I see you've found Caretta."

Jonah's voice right next to my ear makes me jump, releasing Zach's hand.

The turtle turns toward the glass and seems to stare into my soul. *Are you trying to tell me something, Caretta?*

"She likes you," Jonah says.

Now that the moment is officially broken, I hold out my hand to see the photos Jonah took. The first few look awkward and stiff, and I delete them. We both look more relaxed in the pictures with the sea turtle. Even I could almost be convinced we're an actual couple. In the last photo, you can see Zach's profile. He appears to be watching me watch the turtle. It almost looks like he's smiling. I look up at him, but he's whispering with Jonah a few feet away. Whatever they're talking about, it looks heated.

"Hey Jonah," I say, interrupting their discussion. "These look great."

He puffs up. "Thanks. I'm glad you're pleased." He glances at Zach, who gives him a warning look. He steps forward. "Um, would it be okay to take a picture with you?"

"Oh, sure." I'm surprised it took him this long to ask.

He hands his phone to Zach, then rushes over to me. "Is it okay if I put an arm around you? No, wait. Can we do clasped hands like in *For Love or Money*?"

This is not the first time I've had this request, and honestly, it's less awkward than hugging someone I don't know. "Of course."

We face each other and grasp hands. I notice his hands are smaller than Zach's. Who knew I had a thing for large hands? We smile for the camera. Zach hands the phone to me for inspection. How thoughtful. He must know this will be on social media before the end of the day. I heart my favorite then delete the others, including the one he took of me with the octopus, before handing back his phone.

"You can post it if you'd like, but please don't tag Zach. We're still keeping things on the down low because it's so new."

Jonah's eyes widen, and he turns to Zach. "Does that mean you haven't told anyone yet? Not even Nora knows?"

He sighs. "No. We're keeping our relationship quiet for now, so we'd appreciate it if you'd keep this news to yourself until I say otherwise. From *everyone* in the house."

His emphasis on the word everyone piques my curiosity. Is there someone he's trying to hide our relationship from? Maybe it's someone he's actually interested in. I hadn't thought about how our arrangement might complicate his life. It's fine if he likes someone else. Hopefully, whoever she is will still be single when our charade is through. The thought doesn't console me like it should.

"Can I at least tell them I met Kat Sonnett?"

Zach motions to his phone. "If you have permission to post that photo, I think that's a yes."

"Will's going to be so jealous. This is even better than a kiss on the cheek!"

What in the world is he talking about?

"Thanks for the tour," Zach says, shaking Jonah's hand. "We're going to get out of here."

He looks at me for confirmation, and I nod. We walk back toward the exit.

"Do you want to visit the gift shop?" Zach asks.

I see an adorable stuffed otter just inside the shop, but there are too many people for my comfort. "No, I'm good."

He opens the passenger door for me once again, and I smile my appreciation. When we arrive in front of my hotel, he puts the truck in park.

"Can I walk you to your room?"

His words make my mind spin. Normally, if I heard that type of question, I'd assume he was hoping to kiss me. But this isn't a real date, so that can't be it.

"Why?"

He gives me a strange look. "In case there are reporters."

My heart drops. It should be a relief he's being so considerate of me, but I'm oddly disappointed.

"No, I think I'm good, but thanks. This was fun, Zach."

He nods, adjusting his grip on the steering wheel. "I'm sorry about Jonah. I knew he was a fan, but I didn't think he'd be so weird."

"He was fine." There's a long beat of silence. I should get out of the car, but part of me wants to stay and talk a little longer. "How do you two know each other?"

"My mom rents rooms to young people, and he's one of her current tenants."

That's interesting. "Does that mean you're from this area?"

"Born and raised. Though I lived in Asheville, North Carolina for a little while. What about you?"

I like that he's curious about me. Or maybe he's just being polite. "I grew up in Atlanta, but have lived in Los Angeles for about a decade now. When I'm not traveling for work, that is."

"Do you get back home often?"

His words hit a tender, guilt-filled spot in my gut. "No. I keep meaning to take time between projects, but then Rick seems to fill all my free time with photo shoots or sponsorship activities."

"Is Rick your agent?"

I nod.

"Is he good?"

"I mean, he's done an excellent job of getting me parts and making me money."

He shakes his head slightly. "Yeah, but does he look out for your best interests? I'd think spending time with your family would be important." He pauses, something darkening his expression. "Unless, of course, you don't have a good relationship with your parents. I don't want to assume."

I shake my head. "My parents are great. I'd love to visit them. I just haven't been all that great about voicing what I want, I guess. I'm sure Rick would help if I told him."

How do all our conversations seem to hit topics I didn't even know I should think about? I look at Zach. There's definitely more to him than I first thought. What has made him so perceptive?

"What do you want to do next week?"

Zach's words snap me out of my thoughts.

"Um, maybe dinner? Are you ready to show your face to the world?"

His mouth twists up to the side while he thinks. "It has to happen sometime. Do you mind if I pick the restaurant?"

"Sure. Can it be someplace with seafood? I've been dying to try some authentic shrimp and grits."

He nods. "Not a problem. Text me an evening and I'll get us a reservation."

I say goodbye and head up to my room without incident. Except for Lila giving me the third degree about my date, asking where I met him and why I was being so secretive. After I agree to keep her in the loop for scheduling purposes and she teases me about how lucky I am to have found such a hot guy to date, I text Zach a day for our dinner date, then pick up the script to prepare for work. My mind keeps drifting back to my time at the aquarium and the interesting guy I've paired myself up with. The knowledge that I'll see him again soon makes my heart beat faster.

CHAPTER ELEVEN

Zach

Jonah has been grinning at me like the Joker since I walked into the house. He obviously wants to spill the beans about me and Katie. I probably should do it tonight since we're having dinner tomorrow evening and, after that, our faces will most likely be plastered all over the internet. I'm feeling really uncomfortable about putting on this front with my mom. I know relationships end, but I just hope she doesn't get her hopes up too much with this one. Deep down, I know her primary concern is my happiness, so I suppose as long as I act thrilled about this, no harm, no foul.

I stand up from the table with my empty plate. "I'm going to grab a little more chicken. Would anyone else like anything?"

I stare meaningfully at Jonah. He leans back and rubs his belly. "I'm near about stuffed. That was so good, Mrs. Fontaine."

I roll my eyes at his obliviousness.

"I wouldn't mind some more asparagus," Nora says, raising her plate to me.

"Excellent. Jonah, would you like some more water?"

He considers my question for a moment. "Yes, that would be great, thanks."

He lifts his glass, but both my hands are full of plates.

"Why don't you come into the kitchen with me?"

I raise my eyebrows and jerk my head toward the doorway. He frowns, but then seems to catch my drift.

"Oh! Yes, of course. Does anyone else need a refill?"

"Why I'd love some more iced tea, if you please, Jonah," Mom says.

"Anything for you, Mrs. F. We'll be back in two shakes of a lamb's tail."

Once we're hidden behind the swinging kitchen door, I set down the plates and turn. Jonah's at the fridge, pulling out the pitcher of tea.

"I'm impressed you've kept things quiet this long. It's time."

He spins around, nearly spilling the full glass in his hand. "Yesssss!"

I hold up a hand to calm him. "Just tell them you saw her with me at the aquarium."

He grins. "Oh, I'll tell them. But I'm going to put a little flair on the story."

"Whatever, but only the truth. Don't make things up."

He sighs. "*Fine.* So what's it like dating a famous actor?"

"So far it's the same as dating anyone, but it's only a matter of time before someone discovers who I am. Then, who knows what will happen?"

He nods. "There's been a lot of speculation about the mysterious man at the aquarium. People are guessing Austin Butler or Chance Campbell."

I shake my head, assuming the people he's named are actors. "Boy, are they going to be disappointed."

"Nah. I think fans will love that she's dating a normal person. It makes her more relatable, I think."

He's really into celebrity culture. Or maybe it's just Katie he likes. It might actually be nice to hear his perspective as someone who pays attention to this stuff. "What is it you like about Kat so much?" It feels weird to call Katie by her stage name, but it's what Jonah calls her and I don't know if she'd want me to divulge something so personal.

He leans against the counter. "Well, first off, she's gorgeous." I nod in agreement. "But she also seems very down to earth and approachable. That's the characters she plays in her movies, but I think it mirrors real life. Plus, she works with animal charities, which is always going to be a hit with me."

She does charity work? I'd like to hear more about this side of her. I've always had the impression that actors are self-absorbed and focused only on becoming more rich and famous. Of course, that's probably just me making rash assumptions. "Do you know which charities?"

"She starred in a commercial for Los Angeles's no-kill shelter. She makes pet adoption look very sexy."

I frown, not thrilled at Jonah's giddy look. I shouldn't care, obviously, because Katie isn't anything to me, but I can't stop myself from saying, "She's more than just her looks, Jonah. She's a genuine person."

He holds up his hands. "Sorry, Zach. Didn't mean to sound like I'm drooling over your girl. It's gonna take me a bit to wrap my head around this situation. My friend and my Hollywood crush—I would never have guessed something like this could happen."

"You and me both," I mutter.

"Well, I'm happy for you. I just hope she doesn't break your heart."

Fat chance of that happening. Still, I'm a little insulted by the insinuation. "Are you saying she's going to tire of me or something?"

His eyes widen. "No. Not at all." He pauses. "I really hope it works out, but I just don't see her hanging around here after her movie wraps. No offense, but you don't really fit into her world."

He's not wrong. That's exactly what's going to happen after she's done shooting her movie, but he doesn't know that.

"I appreciate your honesty. You make a good point."

He frowns slightly. "I hope for your sake I'm wrong, but I would hate to see things end poorly between you two."

I force a smile. "Tomorrow is only our second date. Even if we keep seeing each other while she's here, I doubt we'll spend enough time together for me to fall head over heels. Besides, whatever happens, it's probably good for me to get back into the dating world."

Jonah nods toward the door to the dining room. "You ready to share the news?"

I swallow, suddenly second guessing everything. No, this is fine. I'll be fine. One day it'll be a great story I can tell at parties. "Yeah, let me get Nora's plate and I'll be there. Don't start without me."

He tops off his water glass, then heads back to the table. I put a few stalks of asparagus on Nora's plate, before joining everyone else in the dining room. Nora frowns.

"Where's your chicken?"

I'd completely forgotten about my ruse. "Oh, uh. I decided I'm full."

"Why'd you two take so long in there? Were you sharing secrets?"

Uh oh. We've been caught. I guess that works for a segue into the news. I nod at Jonah. "It sounds like you're up."

He puffs out his chest and clears his throat. "I've got some exciting news. As you know, Kat Sonnett visited the aquarium last week."

Nora rolls her eyes. "Yes, Jonah. You showed us the picture a hundred times already. We've all met Kat Sonnett."

"Well, not everyone," Mom says, "but I don't mind being left out of celebrity dealings."

My heart beats harder. I hadn't even thought about how this might affect her. Though surely no one's going to mess with her. It's just my life everyone will dissect. Which includes my mother... I really wish I had thoroughly considered the repercussions of dating someone famous. Too late to back out now, though.

"Anyway," Jonah says, a little of his bluster diminished at the inter-ruptions. "If you've seen the online photos, you know she wasn't alone."

Nora's eyes shine. "Ooh, are you going to tell us which famous person she was with? I thought you said you signed a non-disclosure." Her eyes narrow. "Breaking something like that is a big no-no."

Jonah sighs. "I may have lied about having to sign something, and yes, I'm going to tell you who she's just started dating." He looks around the table to confirm everyone is alert for his next words. "It's...our very own Zach Worthy!"

Heads swing my way, but my eyes are focused on my mom's face. Her forehead crinkles, but then she tips her head back and laughs.

"Oh, that's a good one, Jonah!"

He frowns. "I'm serious."

She shakes her head. "When would he have met an actress? He hardly even goes to the movies."

"Actually..." Nora says, her phone in her hand, her gaze moving from it to my face and back a few times. "This guy has your build. And it did kind of seem like you had a little pep in your step when I saw you at the hotel."

Oh great. Now Nora's reading into things.

"No phones at the table, dear," my mom chides. "Hand it over."

"Sure. You probably want to see this picture, anyway."

My mom takes the phone and I lean over to get a peek at the screen. It's the one Jonah took at the aquarium with the fish tank in the background. I haven't actually seen it yet. Our backs are to the camera, our fingers intertwined. Definitely nothing to give me away unless you recognize the shirt I'm wearing.

"Is that the sweater Josie made you one Christmas?"

Josie is a local artist who works with wool and rented a room at our house a few years ago.

"Yes, Mom."

Her eyes meet mine, her mouth slack with surprise. "Are you really seeing this woman?"

Here we go. Stay calm. Stick to the facts. "It's really new. Our second date is tomorrow."

"He's taking her to Bishop 28," Jonah says, not wanting to be left out of the conversation.

"That's Cecily's restaurant, right?" Mom says, referring to another former tenant of the house.

"You're pulling out all the stops, huh?" Will says. "That place has a months-long waiting list."

"Cecily hooked me up."

"Smart," Jonah says. "Having Kat there is only going to increase the restaurant's hot factor."

I hadn't considered that part of it, but I'm glad to give Cecily's place even more exposure. Perhaps I should use this opportunity to help other local businesses.

"There's a good chance we'll be photographed together tomorrow, and I wanted to make sure you all were aware of the situation ahead of time."

I look over at Mom, trying to figure out what she thinks of all this.

She smiles and pats my arm. "If you're happy, I'm happy. It's nice to see you getting back out there."

"Even if it's with a celebrity?"

She shrugs. "You can't help who you're attracted to. As long as she's a nice person and treats you well, that's all that matters."

Those are definitely good qualities. Unfortunately, I barely know her. Hopefully Jonah's right and she is a good person. I suppose ultimately it doesn't matter since our relationship is only temporary.

CHAPTER TWELVE

Kat

"I can't believe Kat Sonnett has a boyfriend."

I roll my eyes at Lila. She's been razzing me ever since I told her my plans for this evening, but is also using this opportunity to have me show off another dress from a different up-and-coming designer. It's strapless, which is not my favorite, and tight but stretchy, which means it shows off all my curves. I usually prefer to leave some things to the imagination, but it'll certainly make sure I'm noticed tonight, which is the point.

"What's hard to believe? That someone is interested in me?"

She shakes her head. "Of course not. The surprise is that you've found time to connect with someone outside the industry and are making them a priority. How long have you been sneaking around behind my back, anyway?"

Tell the truth, but not the whole truth. "It's fairly new. And do you really think a weekly date night shows he's a priority?"

"With your schedule? Definitely. He's pretty much taking up all your free time."

She's not wrong. The work schedule I've got is pretty all-consuming. Not that I mind. It means the director's efficient and not wanting to waste anyone's time.

"So, what's the plan tonight?" she asks. "Am I sitting at a nearby table and sneaking photos of the two of you?"

I wrinkle my nose. If Zach knows he's being watched the whole time, I bet he'll be stiff and stilted. Things should look natural. Plus, a small part of me wants to pretend this is a real date. It's been a long time since I went on one of those. Like Lila mentioned, I've been busy.

"Zach isn't used to the limelight, and I'm trying to ease him in, so I don't scare him off. How about you take some shots either going into the restaurant or coming out?"

"Sure. Where are you going, anyway?"

I pause and think. "He hasn't told me, actually. I guess I'll text you the name of the restaurant after we arrive and you can come by an hour later."

"Works for me. You look gorgeous, by the way. The coral color really brings out your eyes."

I smooth my hands down the sides of the dress, tugging it a little lower on my thighs.

"Thanks. Though, please let designers know I'm not a fan of strapless."

Lila types into her phone for a second. "Noted. Though you have great shoulders, so why not show them off?"

"I'm honestly afraid of a wardrobe malfunction."

She chuckles. "Honey, that dress isn't going anywhere. You look like you were poured into it."

There's a knock at the door, and Lila's eyes widen. "Is that him?" She grimaces. "Do you think he remembers how rude I was to him last time?"

I shrug. "I doubt he'll hold it against you." Zach doesn't seem like the type.

Lila steps toward the door, but I rush over to cut her off, wanting Zach to see a friendly face, and open the door without looking through the peephole. Probably not the smartest move, but luckily it's not a reporter. Standing at my door is a very handsome man in khaki pants, a white dress shirt, a navy sport coat, and tie. I swallow, shocked at how my body zings at the sight of Zach in business casual. I've only seen him in jeans and T-shirts, but he cleans up very well.

"Wow," Zach says, handing me a small bouquet. "You look amazing, Katie."

The sound of my name in his voice does something strange to my insides. I blink a few times, trying to get myself under control, then drop my nose to the flowers for a distraction. Something in this bouquet smells good and I take another appreciative sniff. Finally getting my wits about me, I smile at him and give him another once over.

"You look really nice, Zach. Come in."

He steps inside and looks around the room. I scan the area, wondering if I've accidentally left some dirty clothes lying around. Thankfully, there's only my script, a water glass, a rumpled blanket, and my purse.

"Are you ready to go, or do you need a few minutes?"

"Let me put these in water, grab my shoes, and I'm all set."

Lila takes the flowers from me. "I'll do this. You finish getting ready."

I hustle through my bedroom door, not wanting to leave Zach alone with Lila for too long. I'm sure she's dying to hound him with questions. I grab the first pair of sandals I see and carry them out to the living room. Sitting down on the sofa, I slide my foot into the first one and buckle the strap, then the other one. When I'm finished, I realize it's oddly quiet and look around. Zach's standing stock still, his eyes glued to my legs. Has he been watching me the whole time? He swallows, then his eyes dart up to meet mine before he turns and walks over to a window.

I turn toward Lila, who has the flowers in a glass of water and is grinning at me like she knows a secret. Her head tilts toward Zach and she mouths "wow," her eyes sparkling. Guess she agrees with my assessment of Zach's wardrobe choices.

Grabbing my purse off the table in front of me, I stand. "I'm all set."

Zach walks to the door, then holds it open for me.

"You two kids have fun," Lila says with a wink.

I manage to stop my eye roll, though there's definitely a buzz of energy coursing through my body. It feels like I'm headed to prom. I'm just missing the corsage. "Don't wait up, Mom."

I walk past Zach into the hall, my nose picking up a pleasant scent as I pass. Something woodsy. Maybe that's how he smells working with wood all day? Whatever it is, I definitely like it.

He escorts me through the lobby to his truck. Surprisingly, I don't see any cameras. Maybe everyone's gotten used to me hiding in my hotel room. This is definitely in my favor because it means I have some control over the narrative.

We drive south for a few minutes before Zach pulls into a parking garage. He opens my door and extends a hand, helping me down out of the truck. He offers his arm, and I slide mine through, appreciating the feel of the fabric. It's soft, which makes me think this is a quality jacket. I look at him out of the corner of my eye, my gaze catching on his tie. It's navy to match his jacket, but has small red and white parallelograms all over it. I'm itching to run my fingers along it and my mind conjures a scene of me grabbing the tie and pulling Zach toward me, drawing our mouths together.

I stumble on the sidewalk and Zach's arm comes around to steady me. "You okay?"

"Yeah." Just daydreaming about kissing you. No biggie.

"There are some loose stones around here. Be careful."

We stop at a cream-colored building with a black awning. The wrought-iron gate is open, and he guides me inside.

"Worthy, party of two," he says to the host. The gentleman leads us out to a back patio and stops at a table situated under a gazebo strung with white tea lights. There are large plants on three sides of us, giving our table a secluded, intimate feel. Zach pulls out my chair for me, making sure I'm situated before sitting on the opposite side of the small rectangular table.

A server in all black appears almost immediately, sets down two waters, and hands us each a menu. "Welcome to Bishop 28. Would you like anything else to drink?"

We decline and the server leaves us alone to study the menu. All the food descriptions make my mouth water. "What sounds good to you?" Zach asks.

My stomach rumbles in response. "Everything, obviously. I said I wanted to try the shrimp and grits, but the crab cakes sound great too."

"Just about every good restaurant has both, so get whatever sounds most appealing to you. I was considering getting an appetizer or two to share. What do you think?"

I look over my menu at him. "I'm pretty hungry. Get whatever you know is good."

He gives me an embarrassed smile. "I haven't been here before, but I know the sous chef, so I can promise whatever we get will be fantastic."

He's got connections. I guess that's what happens when you live somewhere for most of your life. The server returns with two glasses of champagne. "From the chef," he says with a wink. "Have you decided what you'd like to order?"

Zach looks at me, and I make a quick decision. "I'd like the barbecued shrimp and grits, please."

"Excellent choice. And you, sir?"

"I'll have the crab cakes. And we'd also like to start with the fried green tomatoes and southern pickins."

"Very good." He takes our menus and disappears.

"So...Zachary *James* Worthy?"

"Wrong," he says, "but good try, Tiger."

I pull my lips down in a frown, but I'm not really upset. I'm going to figure it out, eventually. My mind snags on something he just said. "Tiger?"

He shrugs. "You seem feisty and cunning. Though, I doubt you'll figure out my middle name."

Is that a challenge? My eyes narrow, not liking the idea of losing this game we're playing. Maybe I am a little feisty. "I know you lived in Asheville for a while. What took you there and brought you home?"

He grabs his champagne flute. "First, I think we should toast."

"Okay." I hold mine in the air and look at him expectantly.

"To new friends and good food."

I smile. "Amen to that." We clink glasses and take a sip. The fizz tickles my throat pleasantly.

Zach sets down his glass, then meets my gaze. "I heard Asheville was a good place for artists and thought I'd spread my wings a little. I enjoyed being in the mountains and also found a solid customer base. I'm working on some chairs right now for someone in North Carolina." He pauses. "I came back to take care of my mom after her cancer diagnosis."

My arm reaches across the table and gently squeezes his forearm. "Oh, I'm so sorry. How is she doing?"

"She's in remission. Her last several scans have been clear, so she's good for now."

I can tell he's worried about his mom and the potential of her cancer returning. That's a lot of responsibility for one person to handle. The way he's talking makes me think his father isn't in the picture, but I've already bumped into one sore subject for the evening. Time for something more light-hearted.

"That's good to hear. Is Asheville where this mountain man look came from?"

I motion toward his face, and he runs a hand down his beard. I wonder if his hair is scratchy to the touch. It doesn't look long enough to be soft.

Finally, he shrugs. "To be honest, my focus was completely on my mom until recently and I guess I let a few nonessential things slide. Are you saying it's time for a haircut?"

His teasing smile lets me know he's not offended by my comment. However, I want to make sure he doesn't think I was insulting him. "It looks really good on you. If you like it, keep it."

His cheeks hitch higher. "It sounds like you like it. Maybe I'll keep the beard a while longer. At least while we're dating."

Several things happen rapidly in my body. My heart rises when I realize he's saying he wants to please me, and I wonder if that means I'll actually get to experience a kiss with a bearded guy. But the reminder that all this is temporary makes my stomach dip like it's just crested a hill and is now careening down toward a valley.

His smile turns down, making me realize I've been quiet too long. I sit up in my chair and force my face into a pleasant expression.

"Either way. I'm sure you'd look just as hot without facial hair."

My eyes widen and I wish our appetizers were on the table so I could stuff something in my mouth to stop words from coming out of it. Two comments on his appearance in a row has to be a dead giveaway that I'm attracted to him. Out of desperation, I grab the flute and chug the rest of the champagne, spluttering as the bubbles dance down my throat.

"Whoa there," Zach says, half-standing from his seat. "You okay?"

I cough twice, then dab my lips with my napkin. "Yeah, fine," I rasp. A gulp of water calms my throat, though my cheeks are warm from embarrassment.

Our server appears with two plates and sets them down between us. "Here are the fried tomatoes and southern pickins. Enjoy." Another server places small white plates in front of each of us.

"Please, do the honors," Zach says.

I transfer a few things to my plate, then Zach does the same. My first bite is a piece of tomato dipped in the tomato-bacon jam and a dollop of grits. I close my eyes and drop my head back, enjoying the combination of flavors in my mouth.

"That good, huh?"

I frown at Zach's amused face. "What?"

He chuckles. "You might have made a little noise and danced in your seat."

I shut my eyes, feeling my cheeks rise another couple of degrees in temperature. "Sorry."

"Don't be. It's cute."

My eyes fly open and over to his face, but he ducks his head and cuts his own piece of tomato. He is appropriately silent while he chews. No unfiltered moans from him. After swallowing, he smiles at me. "What do you like to do for fun?"

That's a random question, but perfectly in line with something we'd talk about on a date. What do I like to do for fun?

"I like history." At his puzzled frown, I continue. "Sometimes on shoots, when I have time, I'll visit local museums or read books about interesting things that happened in the area."

"You've come to a great place for history. Did you know Charleston had the first public museum in the United States?"

I lean forward, amazed that he knows such a random fact. Of course, this is his hometown. "No, I didn't know that. Tell me more."

"The Arthur Ravenel Jr. Bridge is the longest cable-stayed bridge in the country."

I deflate a little. "I already knew that."

He twists his lips to the side and looks away. It gives me another opportunity to study him. His blue eyes look darker this evening, probably because of the navy blazer.

"Charleston was the state capital until 1790 when they moved it to Columbia. The British held control of the city for two years during the American Revolution. It exported cotton and rice to the Caribbean for many years, and is about three and a half miles from Fort Sumter, which was captured by confederates and precipitated the Civil War."

My interest is fully captured now. "Okay, Mr. Encyclopedia. Did you learn all this in school?"

He shakes his head. "Nope. My summer job in high school was giving city tours."

Okay, that's pretty hot. Not that any normal person would be turned on by someone knowing so much history. He must see something in my face because he adds, "I can take you around town to some sights if you're interested."

I lean in. "Oh, I'm interested." And maybe I'm talking about more than just seeing Charleston's history.

He grins and gives me a wink.

What. Is. Happening? My whole body flushes at that dangerously addictive wink. I clear my throat and lean back, stabbing something on my plate and sticking it in my mouth. I don't trust my voice to not sound strangled if I speak.

Zach seems nonplussed and takes a few bites of his food. We eat without speaking until our server appears with our main courses. The grits look like creamy gold and the shrimp form a ring around the bowl with crumbled bacon and scallions scattered on top. This looks incredible.

I glance over at Zach's plate. The crab cakes over succotash also look equally appetizing. Did I choose the right option? Guess I'll never know. I take a bite of shrimp and grits. Okay, I do not regret my choice one iota.

Zach cuts a piece off of one of his cakes, then adds it to his forkful of vegetables. He holds his hand under his fork as he moves it across the table.

"Do you want to try it?" He looks at me earnestly. "It's a clean fork."

Oh, my goodness. Did he order the crab cakes so I could try them? From the little I know of him, he seems like that kind of guy. One who's willing to help others out from the goodness of his heart. I lean forward and open my mouth, closing it around the tines. He holds it steady, allowing me to use my lips to slide the food off the fork, then leans back, watching me. I chew, then swallow.

"Those are very good, but I think I like mine better."

He nods. "I prefer shrimp over crab too."

He *did* order the crab cakes for me. I don't know how to feel about that. I motion toward my plate. "Do you want to share some of mine?"

He waves me away. "No, you enjoy. I can eat here whenever I want."

My brow furrows. He just said he's never been here. Probably because it's kind of pricey. Though I suppose if he sells one chair, he can afford several meals here. And he lives here, so he could conceivably come again whenever he wants.

I motion to our gazebo seating. "Did you and the chef go to school together?"

He takes a bite of his food with the same fork he used to feed me. Guess he's not worried about my germs. That'll be good when we kiss. Assuming that's necessary. Why is my brain trying to come up with scenarios where kissing the man across from me is essential?

"No," he says, startling me out of my daydream. Is he reading my thoughts or did I say something out loud? "Cecily used to be one of my mom's tenants."

"Tell me about how your mom decided to rent rooms to others."

He smiles, obviously at ease with this turn in conversation. "When my grandparents owned the house, they set it up as a bed-and-breakfast. When Mom took over, she decided she wanted more long-term residents. Charleston isn't the most affordable place to live, so she charges well below the going rate to give her tenants a chance to go after their dream careers. The process includes an interview and references to ensure they have a plan for achieving their goal."

I nod, thinking Zach's mom must be cool and laid back like he is. It's hard for me to imagine allowing other people free range of my house. "I take it being a chef was Cecily's dream."

He nods. "She's incredible too. One day she'll have her own restaurant, but she's already made a name for herself working here."

I like this talk about dreams. My goal of being a working actor came true. I assume Zach's dream is making furniture for a living or he wouldn't have moved to Asheville for it. This thought makes me feel a kinship with him. He seems like someone who would be super supportive of whatever I wanted to do. I can imagine him cheering me on, clapping from the crowd whenever I win an award. My heart twists with longing. When I won my statue a few years ago, Lila was my date. How much better would it be to share that experience with someone I love? Too bad my time with Zach is only temporary.

CHAPTER THIRTEEN
Zach

After I pay for dinner—which was a whole thing in itself, what with Katie trying to pay for the meal and me gently rebuffing her—we head out front where we run into Katie's assistant.

"I forgot to tell you," Katie says. "Lila's going to take a few photos and post them to my socials."

I wonder if this is one of those times when kissing might be necessary. I've been staring at Katie's mouth all evening while she ate and talked and I definitely don't think it'll be a hardship, but I don't want to seem too eager. This is a business arrangement. If she had any idea I've had a few more-than-friendly thoughts about her, I bet she'd call things off. It's not every day a beautiful woman asks you to be her fake boyfriend. I'd like to ride this train as far as it'll go.

"Do we need to pose or something?"

Lila waves at us. "I want it to look natural. Maybe wrap your arm around her and look into each other's eyes. You know, like you like each other."

I furrow my brow briefly. Does Lila know this isn't real? I'll have to ask Katie later, just in case. Of course, I don't have to pretend to like her. This gives me an excellent opportunity to look at her like I've been wanting to. I slide my hand around her waist and turn into her slightly. With her heels, she's slightly taller than I am, but I'm not bothered. I take a moment to study her ocean blue eyes. It's a little awkward being this close to someone without kissing them, and my eyes dip down to her lips at the thought. I quickly pull my eyes back up to hers, but she's looking down as well. Is she thinking about kissing me, too?

Her left hand grasps my shoulder and her right one comes up and gently tugs on my tie. She gives me a mischievous grin that makes me wonder what's going through her mind.

"What are you thinking?" I whisper.

Her eyes widen and she splutters, her voice an octave higher than usual. "What? Oh, uh...nothing! I, uh, thought maybe you had something on your tie but I was wrong."

She rubs the fabric of my tie, then flips it over.

"This is an Armani tie."

"Yeah...is that okay?"

She readjusts my tie against my shirt, then smooths it down, her hand caressing my chest. It's all I can do not to flex against her touch.

"I like your outfit. This jacket is so soft. As is this shirt. Are they also Armani?"

This is a weird conversation. I guess Katie likes designer clothing. It probably comes with the job. "The blazer is, but the shirt is probably Tom Ford."

She takes a step back and peers closely at my feet. When she looks back up at me, her eyes are huge. "Don't tell me those are Berlutis."

I shrug. "Okay, I won't."

She gently slaps my chest. "Zach! No wonder you look so good. Your clothes were tailored to you."

Okay, I don't hate that she likes how I look. "Why is that so surprising?"

She looks away. "I mean, I don't know you that well. You could be a secret billionaire or something."

I scoff. "I don't think that's a thing."

She raises an eyebrow. "You'd be surprised."

"Well, I don't know any billionaires."

She challenges me with a look. "How would you know? They're *secretly* rich after all."

I shake my head, amused. "I guess you've got me there. But I'm not one. My mom paid for these clothes."

"Is *she* a secret billionaire?"

I purse my lips together to keep from laughing. I don't want her to think I'm making fun of her. "Not to my knowledge, though she certainly isn't struggling."

She narrows her eyes at me. "Are you part of the money-so-old-your-family-founded-Charleston crowd?"

I don't answer, but my face must give me away because she pushes my shoulder away. "Zach!"

"What? It's not *my* money. My mom inherited it from her parents and grandparents. I'm really a paycheck to paycheck woodworker."

"Then why did you pay for dinner?"

Someone clears their throat and we both turn to see Lila staring at us. "As much fun as it is to listen you two bicker, it's not helping me get a good shot. Why don't you two take a walk or something?"

I'd forgotten she was even there. Right, we're supposed to be photogenic right now. Which makes me think of the perfect spot for some candid photos. "I know a magnificent spot, but it's a bit of a walk." I look down at Katie's shoes. "Can your feet handle it?"

She rolls her eyes. "Are you kidding? I can jog in these things. They're surprisingly comfortable."

I'm not that knowledgeable about women's footwear, so I'll take her word for it. Since we're supposed to be playing up our relationship for the camera, I offer her my arm, which she takes, and lead her down the street toward Waterfront Park. We walk along the edge of the park; the wind rustles our hair. Katie's hair is in some sort of updo, with a couple of strands hanging down around her face, showing off her long, elegant neck. I have an urge to lean over and kiss the spot where her neck and shoulder meet, but keep my desire in check.

Katie shivers next to me. I release her arm, shrug out of my jacket, and hold it open for her. She smiles at me and slides her arms into the sleeves. I offer her my arm again. She slides her arm over my forearm, then laces her fingers through mine. Oh, so we're going for more intimacy. I can play along. I bring our hands up, hers on top, then lean down and place a soft kiss on the back of her hand, my eyes never leaving her face. Her breath catches. She reaches her free hand up to brush my cheek. I close my eyes at the touch, concentrating on not leaning into it so I don't give too much away. She drops her hand. I open my eyes and give her a small smile.

"Ooh, that was great!" Lila says, breaking the spell. I'd completely forgotten we weren't alone.

"Hey, there's that pineapple fountain!" she adds, pointing. "Would you mind standing in front of it for a bit? It looks so cool lit up like that."

My gaze returns to Katie, who shrugs. "Let's do what the woman says."

I'm unsure if we're supposed to stand a certain way. Katie must be equally confused because she asks her assistant what to do.

Lila studies the area, then turns to us with a smile. She points to me. "You sit on that ledge. Kat, sit on his lap, angled toward him so you can see each other."

We do as she says. She frowns slightly, then adjusts the sides of the jacket so more of Katie's dress is showing. "Zach, put your arms around her waist."

I do as she says, a more than willing participant.

"I'm not hurting you, am I?" Katie says.

She's only hurting my chances of not falling for her now that I know what it feels like to hold her against me. "No, you're fine."

Her head is higher than mine, so she's looking down at me. I lean toward her and whisper, "Now, what are we supposed to be doing?"

She leans closer, a warm smile on her face. "I have no idea. This feels like a prom pose or something equally cheesy."

"You know what would make this more cheesy?"

She shakes her head, but her open expression lets me know she's curious.

"If we touched foreheads and stared soulfully into each other's eyes."

Her smile flashes, but then she quells it into something serious. "Sounds perfect. No smiling, either."

She drops her forehead toward mine until we're touching. Our noses are mere millimeters apart. Her eyes are bright and I can tell she's working hard not to smile. Her breath puffs against my lips and all of a sudden there's nothing funny about this situation at all. One of her hands is on my arm and the other is wrapped around my shoulders. We're too close for me to see her lips, but I can sense them a hair's breadth from mine. I bet if I tipped my chin up just a bit, I'd find them. The sparkle in her eye has disappeared, replaced with something more heated. Is she feeling this same tension between us? I want to ask, but at the same time I don't want to do anything to break our current state. Unfortunately, it doesn't end up being my decision.

"That's great. I can feel the attraction pulsing between you. Thanks for humoring me. I think you'll like the final product."

Katie quickly releases her hold on me and stands up, my arms falling to my sides. I immediately miss her warmth. The reminder that this is for show douses the feelings threatening to break through my reserve. This is an arrangement. She's an actor, paid to pretend all sorts of things. Faking feelings for a random guy should be no problem. I stand up and brush off the seat of my pants, unsure of what to do next.

"I'll leave you two alone to finish your date in private," Lila says with a suggestive wiggle of her eyebrows. "Have fun!"

With a wave, she disappears, and it's just the two of us and a big blob of awkwardness.

"I suppose we should head back to the car?"

Katie nods. "Lead the way."

She makes no move to grab my arm or my hand, so I stick my hands into my pockets and turn back the way we came. I motion in the direction Lila disappeared. "Does she know the truth about us?"

Katie shakes her head. "I'm not telling anyone. I think it's easier if everyone thinks this is real."

Makes sense. My heart feels a sharp stab at the reminder that I'm just playing a part for her. Obviously, she could be with anyone she wants. I was just in the right place at the right time for the right reason. Oh well.

"Do you have any siblings?"

I guess we're doing some more "get to know you" questions. "I'm an only child. How about you?"

"I have an older brother, but we've grown apart over the years."

The sadness in her voice makes my heart squeeze. "I'm sorry to hear that. What are your parents like?"

She smiles at that. "They're great. They've always been very supportive of Mason and me. When he was interested in baseball, they signed him up for every league, including special clinics. Even a summer camp with the Braves."

They sound like very involved and caring parents. "And, I assume, they did the same for you with acting?"

She nods. "I did community theater and summer intensives. They found out about a casting call for one of the Marvel movies and took me out of school to audition."

"Which one?"

She wrinkles her nose. "Doesn't matter. I didn't get the part. But the next call I went to turned into a non-speaking role." Her expression opens into one of wonder. "The entire process was so cool. I loved being behind the scenes and seeing how everything worked. After that, I was hooked. I begged my parents to take me to any casting call they heard about until I booked a small speaking role. That was even better."

"Was that the one that really started your career?"

"No, I was only thirteen. But the director said I had promise and asked me to audition for her next movie. I got a supporting role in it which caught the eye of my agent. He used that to get me an audition for a teen drama TV pilot and the rest is history."

"Pretty impressive. I guess you must not have gone through that awkward teen phase most of us have to deal with. Lucky you."

She laughs. "No, I just had movie-grade makeup to cover up my acne. What about you?"

"No makeup for me, unfortunately."

She shakes her head, the grin still wide on her face. "I find it hard to believe you ever went through an awkward-looking phase."

I appreciate her vote of confidence. We're nearing the parking garage when I remember what's right around the corner. I bet Miss History Buff would enjoy a quick peek at one of our notable buildings. I steer her around the block, stopping in front of a wrought-iron fence.

"Have you seen Hibernian Hall yet?"

When I wave my hand toward the building, she turns, her head angling up as she slowly takes in the two-story brick structure. Her mouth opens in surprise and she covers it with her hand. Since she seems to be speechless at the moment, I take the opportunity to dust off my tour guide hat.

"A historic meeting hall and social venue built in 1840, Hibernian Hall is a fine example of Greek Revival architecture with its six

Ionic columns supporting an entablature and pediment. The architect, Thomas Ustick Walter, modeled the columns from a small temple on the Ilissos River in Athens. The arched Italianate window was added after an earthquake in 1886 damaged the building."

She looks at me and shakes her head, but her eyes are shining. When she drops her hand from her mouth, she reveals a wide smile. "I can't believe you remember all that."

I chuckle. "Me neither."

We walk back up the street and around the corner to my truck. After helping her into the passenger seat, I drive to the hotel.

"I'm happy to walk you up," I say after parking at the curb.

"No, but thanks." She gets out, then turns back. "Oh, your coat."

"Keep it for now. I'll get it next time I see you."

"Speaking of which, check your schedule and get back to me about when we should get together next week." Look at how easy breezy I can be, even though my heart has picked up at the thought of seeing her again. "I had fun tonight, Katie."

She smiles. "Me too."

After a little wave, she turns and heads inside. She certainly looks good in my jacket. I bet she'd look even better in one of my sweatshirts. *Get yourself together, Zach. This isn't real.* I sigh and drive home.

CHAPTER FOURTEEN
Kat

"What is this?"

Rick spins his laptop around and slaps the top of his desk, making me jump. On the screen is a photo from my date with Zach on the TMZ website with the headline, *Kat Sonnett's New Beau?* Lila must have sent a photo to the gossip site. I wonder why she didn't post it on my socials like she did with the aquarium one. A glance to my right finds Lila focused on her phone.

"It looks like a picture of me and my boyfriend."

I can practically see steam rising off of Rick's red face. "Boyfriend?! This sure doesn't look like Talon Jacobs to me."

I scowl. "Because Talon *isn't* my boyfriend."

He leans way back in his chair, rubbing his temples. "We talked about this."

I lean forward, eyes narrowed. "Yes, we did. And if you recall, I told you I didn't want to do it because I was seeing someone."

He sighs like the world is ending. "I thought you were just joking. We've already released photos of you and Talon together."

It's my turn to look affronted. I point a finger at him. "From the rooftop bar? You blindsided me. I had nothing to do with that."

Rick breaks eye contact with me. He hates admitting mistakes, but I'm sure he'll find some way to spin this.

"Well, you said you were interested in a dramatic role. Looks like you've found one as a heartbreaker."

And there it is. I can't stop the scoff that comes out of my mouth. "What in the world are you talking about? Photos with two different guys weeks apart is not exactly a breaking story. Besides, you didn't say anything about the aquarium picture."

"That one didn't show any faces. It could plausibly have been Talon with you."

There's no way anyone would believe that. Talon's a head shorter than me, whereas Zach and I see almost eye to eye. "Shouldn't it have been a big clue I was telling the truth when I said I was seeing someone?"

Hopefully, my slight fib won't come back to bite me. Technically, I had seen Zach, but I wasn't actually *seeing* him. I guess I'm still not.

The look on Rick's face lets me know there's something he hasn't told me and I'm not going to like it. He types on his laptop for a few seconds, then spins it back around. The browser is open on *People* magazine's website. There's the photo of Talon kissing me, my eyes wide open in surprise. Below is the headline: *Talon Jacobs Reveals How Love Made Him Change His Bad Boy Ways.*

Lila groans next to me. I look over, but she quickly ducks her head and focuses back on her phone.

"What did you do?" I say between clenched teeth.

"I didn't see a reason not to run with this angle. If you'd told me you were seeing someone—"

"I did."

"—we wouldn't be in this mess. I suppose Talon will get sympathy after being dumped."

"We. Were. Never. Dating. This is your mess, not mine."

Rick shrugs, which only increases my anger.

"Who cares about Talon? What is this going to do for *my* reputation? You're *my* agent, after all."

Something like guilt flits across his face, but it's so brief I might have imagined it. "Eh, we can just let it blow over. I'm sure a few people will call you out, but all attention is good attention, right?"

I frown, not agreeing with his assessment. It sounds like he's not too worried about it. I'm not sure if that's because he's confident of my overall good standing or just isn't that concerned about how the public perceives me. I bet he thinks giving me a little "bad girl" energy will only increase the offers coming in. Either way, this doesn't sit well with me. I'm so worked up inside, I'm ready to get this meeting over with.

"Was there anything else you needed to talk about?"

Rick turns his computer around and clicks the screen a few times. "Nope. That was it. I'm hearing good things from the set. Grady Hawkins's agent told me you're one of the best actors he's worked with."

That unruffles my feathers a smidge. I feel the same way about Grady. Regardless, I need to vent some of this frustration. I stand up and Lila rises beside me. When I reach the door, I turn back and fix Rick with a glare.

"No more interactions with Talon. Promise me."

He holds up his hands like I'm attacking him without cause. "You're the boss."

I should be, but it really hasn't felt like I've been steering my career for a while, possibly ever. I suppose because I started so young, I looked to adults to guide me along the right path. However, now that I've been an adult for a number of years, I know many people are just winging it, so it really is on me to figure out what I want and go for it.

"Hey, Kat?"

I turn back around, dread pooling in my gut as I prepare for Rick to drop a bomb on me.

"Who is this guy you're seeing? He looks like a model. Have I seen him in any ads or commercials? I can see him working with Patagonia or one of those outdoorsy companies."

More confirmation I'm not the only one who recognizes how hot Zach is. I shake my head. "Nope, he's just a local businessman."

On the ride back to my hotel room, I can't keep my thoughts in anymore.

"Something about this whole scenario seems fishy."

Lila looks up from her phone. "What do you mean?"

"Why was Rick pushing this Talon angle so hard?"

She shrugs. "He can't do much now that your real boyfriend has been unmasked."

I'm slightly worried Rick's going to try to poach him as a client. He's always looking at people like they have dollar signs over their heads. Hopefully, he has enough integrity to leave him alone. Regardless, I'm wondering if our business relationship has reached its terminus.

"Hey, Li? Why didn't you post the pic of me and Zach on my social media?"

"I thought it'd get more buzz if the reveal was done on a national platform. No one told me about Talon's interview with *People*. I'm so sorry, Kat."

I grab her hand and squeeze. "None of this is your fault. In fact, your pictures will help put a stop to Talon's lies. It may be a little iffy for a few days, but surely people will be able to distinguish fact from fiction."

Lila's wrinkled brow tells me she doubt's the public's discernment abilities. Oh well, nothing to be done now except wait and see what people say.

"Hey, would you mind posting a photo of me and Zach on my socials with a caption that says something about it being new but real? Whatever wording that steers the narrative toward this being the truth rather than the Talon stuff?"

She nods. "Sure thing. By the way, your boyfriend's not only hot, but seems genuinely kind and gentlemanly. A stark contrast to Talon Jacobs."

I smile. "I know, right? Zach is sweet and very down to earth. He runs a business near the city market."

She shakes her head, but her smile lets me know she's teasing me. "You sure live a charmed life."

Not sure how charmed it really is since I'm not in a real relationship, but I should at least enjoy the perks of this ruse while I can. "Could you do one more thing for me? I'm questioning my current agent-client relationship. Any chance you could put together options for other representation? Maybe see if Jennifer Lawrence's agent is taking on new clients?"

She chuckles. "I'm pretty sure any agent would take you on in a heartbeat, Kat. But sure, I'll see who's representing other big name women and get back to you. Maybe also a few newer, hungry agents with connections, but not a star-studded roster as well." At my questioning look, she adds, "They're more likely to spend all their time working for you. You'd have their undivided attention."

She's got a point. "Okay, thanks. But please keep it quiet. Who knows what Rick would do if he found out I'm shopping around."

Lila zips her lips and returns to her phone. I open mine up and notice a little red circle on my social media app. Looks like @katsonnettistrash has been posting. Wonder what it could be? Maybe that I have legs like a giraffe? They really like to harp on my appearance when there isn't anything new about me in the news.

My mouth drops open when I see the new post.

Looks like Kat has sunk to a new low, cheating on Talon while he's trying to get his act together. Real classy, Kat.

There's the photo of me and Zach along with a link to the *People* article. There are already thousands of likes and dozens of reposts.

"What's going on?"

Lila's question startles me out of my stupor. I hand the phone over. She scoffs and hands it back. "You know it's bad to read your own hype. Especially someone with a user name like that."

She's right, but I just can't help myself. I shove my phone into my pocket, hurt that people are believing the fake news but also angry at Rick for creating this drama. Of course, if I had played along with his plan and not gotten myself a boyfriend, there wouldn't be an issue right now. Why am I even accepting a portion of the blame? This is not my fault. I should be in charge of my life and who's part of my circle. I slump back against the seat and stare out the window, not really seeing the buildings we pass.

When we get up to the hotel room, I drop onto the bed, arms and legs spread like a starfish, and groan into the comforter. My phone buzzes next to me, but I ignore it until it buzzes again. I grab it and roll onto my back.

Zach: What's the plan for this week? Have anything in particular you want to do or is it my choice?

The melancholy I was feeling moments earlier practically disappears, the smile returning to my face. I think for a moment.

Kat: The director is giving us Friday and Saturday off. I'm open to whatever.

There are a few dots while he's typing, but then they stop. They start again and stop. Then there's nothing for a bit until my phone rings and Zach's name pops up.

"Is everything okay?"

Zach chuckles. "Yeah, fine. I just thought it might be easier to talk than type."

Most people hate talking on the phone. I don't mind it. And I really don't mind hearing his deep vibrato in my ear. He's no James Earl Jones, but his voice relaxes me instantly. I get an image of him behind me, arms around my waist, his mouth near my ear. I shiver with delight and possibly also delusion. "Yeah, sure. What do you think about this weekend?"

"Unfortunately, I'm scheduled to deliver a table to a customer in Atlanta on Friday. I could do something Saturday afternoon or evening if that works for you."

Atlanta? I haven't been there in ages. A thought swirls around in my head. I'm not sure if it's a good idea, but it would knock a bunch of stuff off my to do list at once. Otherwise, I don't know how else I'm going to pass the time here if Zach's gone. I haven't exactly made any other connections in Charleston.

"I could go with you." The line is silent for a beat too long. I pull the phone away from my ear to make sure the call's still connected. "Zach?"

"Uh, yeah. Sorry. I mean, you could, but it won't be very exciting. Five hours one way, which means ten hours of driving in one day and not at all scenic."

Is this his way of saying he doesn't want me to ride along? I'll at least tell him my reasoning before I give up. The more I think about this, the better the idea sounds to me. A chance to see my parents, hours to get to know this interesting guy better, and time away from my agent and work. What's not to like about this plan?

"I appreciate the heads up, but I was thinking I could stop by my parents' house and see them for a bit. If it's not too far out of your way, that is. If I'm horning in on your trip, tell me, and I'll let it go. We can also do something on Saturday after you get back. Your choice."

"Of course I can take you to see your parents. Family relationships are very important. I think it's great you want to spend your time off with them. I must warn you I'm planning to leave early, like five a.m. I hope that's not a deal breaker."

I grin, getting more excited about this adventure now that it looks like it's happening. "I think I can manage. Do you want to give me your address and I'll meet you at your place?" I would like to see where he lives.

"Nah, I'll pick you up. You're in charge of coffee."

"Sure thing. Thanks, Zach."

We hang up and I lie back, a genuine smile filling my face. I don't know what it is about Zach, but he makes me feel all kinds of things—supported, cared for, excited, and safe. We're going to have a lot of hours to fill while we're confined in his truck. I'd better come up with a few activities to keep us entertained.

CHAPTER FIFTEEN

Zach

"Did you steal Kat from Talon Jacobs?"

It's the first thing Nora says when I walk into the house for the weekly dinner.

"Who's Talon Jacobs?"

Her mouth drops open. "You don't know who he is?" She dismisses me with her hand. "Of course you wouldn't. He's kind of a jerk. One of those shock jock YouTubers, though if you believe the interwebs, he was turning things around after meeting your girl."

I'm about to correct her, but manage to keep my lips clamped together. For all intents and purposes, Katie is my girl. Instead, I shrug. "I doubt you can believe everything the gossip rags print."

"This was in *People*, Zach."

"Okaaaayyy, well, I don't know what to tell you. She hasn't mentioned him to me."

Nora narrows her eyes. "She better not be cheating on you with him."

I doubt that's what's happening. She's so slammed with work, we don't see each other or communicate outside of our scheduled meetings. Well, except for our phone call last night.

"What are you smiling about?"

I look up, startled. "What? Oh, nothing."

She marches closer to me and sticks a finger in my chest. "That look isn't about nothing. You were thinking about Kat, weren't you?"

I lean away from her, feeling like I'm being interrogated by the police. I'm about to make something up when I realize I probably should be thinking about the woman I'm dating. *Duh, Zach.* I spread out my hands, conceding. "You caught me."

"I knew it! What's happening? I need details."

I shake my head, but a smile spreads across my face. "I have to deliver a table to Atlanta, and she agreed to go with me."

"Ooh, a road trip! Are you going to spend the night in a cute little motel?" She pumps her eyebrows suggestively.

"Come on, Nora." I look around to see if anyone else is listening in on our conversation. Mom's back is to us while she stirs something on the stove, but I don't trust her not to be utilizing her bat-like hearing. "I'm a perfect gentleman. Besides, it's just a down-and-back trip. No motels."

She deflates. "Aw, man. You're no fun."

"Dinner's ready," Mom says, turning and holding her arms out for a hug.

I walk over and embrace her while Nora rings the dinner bell. "Hey, Mom," I say, kissing her cheek. "I love chili night."

She pats my face and winks. "I know you do."

After everyone's seated at the table, and grace is said, Nora breaks the news.

"Our boy, Zach, is going on a road trip with Kat this weekend."

Jonah's head swivels to me. "Where are you taking her? Down the coast? There's a cute little bed-and-breakfast at Edisto Beach. And you can visit the serpentarium!"

I chuckle. "Yeah, she's afraid of snakes, so we definitely won't be doing that ever. I have a delivery in Atlanta, so we're driving over for the day."

"Don't her parents live in Atlanta?"

I'm surprised Jonah knows that, though I shouldn't be since he's a fan. I bet he's seen everything she's been in. "They do," I say slowly. "We're planning to stop in while we're there."

Will whistles. "Meeting the parents already? This is getting serious."

I glance at Mom, who's watching our exchange intently. "It's not like that. Katie doesn't get to see her family very often because she's so busy with work. We all know how important family is, so I don't see why I wouldn't make sure she gets quality time with the people she loves."

She smiles at me and pats my arm. "You're a good man, Zach Worthy."

My neck heats at her compliment. "Only because I was raised by an incredible woman."

She smiles, love shining in her face. I look away so I don't get choked up.

"Speaking of incredible," Nora says, "did anyone else see that photo of Kat and Zach at the pineapple? Whew! I could feel the heat radiating off of them."

"Oh yeah," Will says, grinning over at me. "My screen nearly caught fire."

"There's a photo?" Mom says.

Jonah pulls out his phone. "There is a *photo*," he says and starts typing before realizing what he's doing and freezing. He looks up, sheepishly. "My bad. I'll show you after dinner, Mrs. F."

She shakes her head. "Please show me now. You've got me very curious."

Jonah hands his phone over and I decide now is a good time to focus on nourishing my body.

"Mom, this chili is delicious, as always."

There's no response. The back of my neck breaks out in a sweat as I feel Mom's eyes on me. I may have looked at the photo in question a time or two or twenty over the past few days. It definitely looks like we're into each other. Just a glance and I'm transported back to that moment.

Feeling her weight on my legs, her arm around my neck, her forehead against mine, her sweet scent in my nostrils. I can't quite put a finger on the fragrance, but it's light and airy and I really like it.

I know there's no avoiding my mother, so after another bite of chili, I set down my spoon and meet her gaze. She's trying hard to suppress a smile, but there's no denying the twinkle in her eye. Guilt twists my gut. She doesn't deserve to be deceived, but I gave Katie my word and I will honor it. At least when this thing ends, I won't be the only one disappointed. I'll have friends to commiserate with me, which I'll probably need, because I'm enjoying spending time with Katie and getting to know her more than I should for a fake relationship. I wanted to keep her on the phone last night after we made our plans just to hear her voice, but couldn't come up with an excuse.

Which means I'm looking forward to our road trip on Friday. A lot. It'll either cement my belief that she is a genuinely nice person who I truly connect with or show that we're not as compatible as it has seemed thus far. I'm not sure which revelation I'm hoping for.

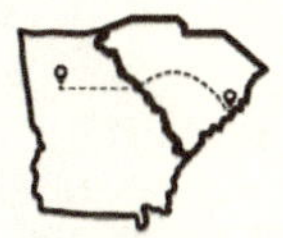

CHAPTER SIXTEEN
Zach

I'm surprisingly alert for being up and about while it's still pitch black outside. It could have something to do with a certain person I'm meeting momentarily, but I'll never admit it. The dining table I finished this week is padded, tarped, and secured in the back of my truck. The forecast doesn't call for rain, but I'd rather be safe than sorry.

When I pull up to the hotel, I debate whether to go up to her room or text her. Before I can decide, she pushes through the front door with a to-go cup in each hand. I get out of the truck to help her in.

"Good morning, Katie."

"Morning, Zachary Joseph."

I shake my head. She shrugs and hands me both coffees before getting into the truck. She sets the large tote bag that was on her shoulder between her feet, then motions for me to step closer. When I do, she takes the cup from my left hand and blows me a kiss.

I shut the door, perplexed by her playful behavior. Maybe she's a morning person. Or perhaps this isn't her first cup of coffee. I get back into the driver's side and set the cup in a holder while I buckle my seat belt. I type the address into the maps app on my phone, then put the vehicle in gear.

"Are you a morning person or just already full of caffeine?"

She smiles at me, and it warms me to my toes.

"It's the caffeine. If I had my way, I'd stay under the covers until eight. I prefer to wake up slowly."

Noted. "I'm the same."

I'm rewarded with another smile, and cover my own with a gulp of coffee. It burns my tongue, but I take another swig, not wanting to look stupid in front of her.

"Do you want to get breakfast now or drive for a while and then find a place to eat? I know at least one restaurant open this early."

She pats the bag between her legs. "I brought bagels and cream cheese for whenever we get hungry. Does that work?"

I nod, touched by her consideration. "That's perfect. I'll wait until we're on the highway for mine, but feel free to eat when you're hungry."

"I'll wait for you," she says, sipping her own coffee.

We ride in silence except for the music playing on the radio until we're about an hour outside of Charleston. I chalk the quiet up to the fact that we're still waking up, despite the buzzing in my body from being near Katie.

"I'll take a bagel now, please."

"Sure thing, Zachary Ryder Worthy."

"Not it," I say, grinning at her.

"Darn," she says, smiling back at me. "I've got plain, everything, cinnamon, and wheat bagels."

Options? That's impressive. Normally I'd go for an everything bagel, but I want my breath to be pleasant if I'm sharing cab space with a beautiful woman. With that in mind... "Cinnamon, please."

"Great. I'll take the everything one, then."

I guess she's not worried about it. Makes sense. I doubt we'll be taking pictures or kissing or anything today. She pulls a container of cream cheese out of a small cooler. After smearing it on our bagels, she puts the two halves of mine together and wraps half of it in a napkin. "Here you go."

"Thanks." I bite into it, surprised by how soft the bread is. "This is delicious. Where did you get them?"

"Holy City Bagels. I googled bagels near me and it's what came up."

"I love that place." I motion toward her lap. "You're going to love the everything. It's my favorite."

Her brow furrows. "Why didn't you choose it?"

I can't tell her the truth. What would she think if she knew I was worried about my breath? Plus, she's now eating it and I don't want her to feel self-conscious. What's another plausible reason?

"I thought the cinnamon would pair well with the coffee. A little sweet to offset the strong coffee."

This seems to satisfy her because she picks up a bagel half and takes a bite. When breakfast is finished, Katie pulls a small trash bag out of her tote for our napkins and the empty cream cheese containers. I lean over to sneak a peek in her bag, but her leg blocks my view.

"What else do you have in that magic bag of yours?"

She chuckles. "I brought a few things to keep us entertained."

I'm intrigued. "Such as?"

"Well, honestly, it's mostly snacks, but I also brought a mad libs book, a blanket, and a list of questions to ask one another if we run out of things to talk about."

I'm surprised at how prepared she is for this trip, but I don't know her that well. Maybe she's a super organized person. I'm sure she has to juggle a lot of different things in her line of work. Making lists and planning ahead are probably par for the course. I decide to tease her a little.

"Is the blanket for when you get bored with me and want to pretend to nap?"

She shoots me an insulted look. "What? Never. I tend to run cold, so it's better to be prepared."

"Fair enough. Why don't we start with some questions? I'm curious to hear what you want to know."

She ducks her head to root around in her bag. When she straightens back up, her face is flushed. I look down at the paper and my eyes catch the word "dates" before she turns it away from me.

"Can I see that paper real quick?"

"You're driving. You can't be distracted."

"I just want to see the title at the top of the page."

She presses her lips together, then sighs. "It says, 'Thirty-five questions that'll take your dates to the next level.'"

Whoa. Is she thinking she might like to change this arrangement? I'm definitely open to a discussion.

"But don't read anything into that," she says. "I just typed in 'get to know you questions' and printed off the first thing that came up."

Well, so much for that. She's made her desires, or lack thereof, quite clear. *Lock it down, Zach. You're just friends.*

"No worries. What's one that sounds interesting?"

She scans the list quietly for a few seconds. "What's the longest relationship you've been in?"

"Jeez. Diving right into the deep end, huh?"

"Sorry. I don't really like small talk. Would you rather discuss your favorite bands?"

I shake my head, interested that I'm learning more about her already. She likes to go deep. Does that mean she's interested in moving to the next level with me? I stop my thoughts with an eye roll. She just wants to know me more as a friend.

"It's fine. I dated a woman for about a year, but that was a while ago. My last relationship was only a few weeks. It probably would have lasted longer, but I moved and didn't want to juggle a long distance relationship while caring for my mother. What about you?"

She rubs her hands together before clasping them and dropping them in her lap. "Eight months, but I didn't know until afterward that he was cheating on me for half of them."

"Ouch. I'm sorry."

She shrugs. "It was his issue, nothing to do with me."

I'm glad she doesn't blame herself. We can't control other people's behavior, no matter how much we might want to.

"What about favorite music groups?"

"Mmm. I've got eclectic tastes. Obviously, I have a soft spot for Atlanta locals like Ludacris and OutKast, but I had a blast at a Taylor Swift show and Bruno Mars is a good time. If there's a show where the crowd is going to be dancing, I'm there."

I smile. "Sounds like you're in it for the experience more than anything."

She nods. "Do you enjoy live music?"

"Sometimes. My favorite bands are Two Left Feet and Imagine Dragons, but if I had a choice between going to a concert and doing something like hiking or kayaking, I'd choose to be outdoors every time."

"Fair enough. Can we stop for a bathroom?"

"Sure. I need to stretch my legs a little. Do you want to play a rest stop game?"

She turns to face me. "Sure. As long as you don't dare me to eat one of their hot dogs. I just don't trust that rolly machine."

I make a disgusted face. "Ew, no. Never eat hot stuff from a gas station. Only prepackaged snacks. That's road trip rule number one."

She smiles. "There are road trip rules? Tell me more, Oh Wise One."

I laugh at her ribbing. "Well, obviously, everyone uses the bathroom before you start and at every stop."

"Of course."

"If you fall asleep, you have to drive after the next stop."

She holds up three fingers, counting along. "I like that one."

"The driver chooses the music unless they give the power to someone else, rescindable at any time. No smelly foods. If you stop for a meal, eat somewhere local. No chains."

"That's six," she says, waving her fingers. "Any more?"

I run through the list to see if I've forgotten anything. "Navigator helps with directions, finding rest stops, and entertaining the driver."

Katie purses her lips into a pout and turns to look out the back window. "Guess that means no sleeping for me, since I have to keep you entertained."

I shrug. "Sorry. I don't make the rules."

She tilts her head, her forehead crinkling with her frown. "Um, I'm pretty sure you just did."

I laugh and her forehead smooths out as she chuckles along with me.

"You have a really expressive face," I say. "Has it always been that way, or have you honed your skills through work?"

"Probably both. I was a terrible liar as a kid because my face always told the truth. I've managed to learn how to manipulate it some over the years, but I still have a few tells."

"Oh yeah, like what?"

"Yeah, right. I'm not going to divulge *all* my secrets to you." She pushes my shoulder lightly and my body responds to the brief contact by sending heat coursing through my veins. "Tell me about the game."

I look at a blue sign on the side of the highway as we pass it. We're in luck that the next exit has multiple gas stations. There should be a clean one among the bunch.

"Okay, so after we fill the tank and use the bathroom, we'll have five minutes to buy each other a gift in the store. It can be only one item and you have to have a reason it makes a suitable present for that specific person."

She claps her hands together. "Ooh, I like it. I'm good at giving gifts."

We take the off-ramp, then turn left toward four gas stations.

"Which one should we visit?"

She points to the left. "That one. Any place with eighteen wheelers has to have kitschy stuff inside."

I stop next to a pump and get the gas flowing. My next plan of action is to clean the windshield, but Katie's already at work on that task. I'm surprised she's doing that, but then, there's been a lot about her that has amazed me. I should just expect it. She's put on her RiverDogs cap, her ponytail poking through the hole in the back. She's wearing yoga pants and a baggy sweater with her Adidas shoes. I doubt anyone will recognize her at a random truck stop, but she's had much more experience being her than I have, so I trust her judgment.

After we've visited the facilities, we both hit start on our phone timers and split up to peruse the store. I find a rack of baseball hats, but nothing is interesting enough for me to choose. There are lots of South Carolina keychains, but nothing that screams Katie. Ooh, maybe something cat themed? No, too obvious. Time is nearly up when I find the perfect item.

I look around for Katie, but don't see her in the store. After paying for the item, I put it in the pocket of my hoodie and head out to the truck. Katie's already seated in the passenger side, a wobbly smile on her face. I'm more excited than I should be to find out what she found for me. I slide into the driver's seat.

"Okay, whatcha got?"

She fidgets with her shirt. "I'm suddenly second guessing myself."

I make a "give it to me" motion with my hand. "It's your first time playing this game, so I'll cut you some slack."

Her eyes are almost apologetic as she reaches behind her, then hands over a black piece of fabric. I unfold it and laugh. In white letters, it says, *This is my road trip shirt.*

Katie still looks a little unsure. "It's not as personal as I would have liked. I mean, they didn't have anything about furniture or woodworking, and I don't see you as someone who'd appreciate a dolphin key-chain."

I give her a reassuring smile. "It's great. It's something to remember this trip by. Plus, it's super soft and I never turn down a comfy shirt. Thanks."

Her posture relaxes, and this time her smile is real. "You're welcome."

"Okay, it's your turn. Hold your hand out flat."

She puts both of her hands together to make a table and I set my gift on top. It's a plastic pineapple with arms and legs standing on top of a black square. She peers at it for a bit, then looks over at me.

"Push the button," I say.

Tinny music emanates from the box and the pineapple's legs and arms bend and twist in a bizarre-looking dance.

"Is that the Macarena?" she asks.

"Yep. You said you like music you can dance to, and I thought the pineapple would remind you of Charleston's famous fountain."

The one where we were so close we could have kissed, I think, but definitely don't say.

She chuckles. "Aww, that's cute. Okay, now I get the gist of the game. I'll be ready next time." Her eyes sparkle and I feel a rush of excitement that I'm responsible for the giddy look on her face.

Realizing I've been staring too long, I clear my throat, start the truck, and pull back onto the highway.

"What should we do now?" Katie asks. "More questions or mad libs?"

"I'm game for more intrusive questions." I give her a wink.

"Great. Let me know if you need a snack. I've got waters, trail mix, cut veggies, and a couple of apples."

"Good to know, but I picked something up at the gas station." I reach into my hoodie and pull out a bag of Nerds Gummy Clusters.

Katie looks at me with wide eyes.

"I know. Not as healthy as your options, but sometimes you just gotta have sugar." She's still staring at me. "You okay?"

"I love Gummy Clusters."

"Me too." I hold the bag out toward her. "Do you want some?"

"I thought you'd never ask."

She snatches the bag from me, tears it open, and dumps some into her hand. She pops a few into her mouth before holding one in my direction. I hold out my hand, but she shakes her head and moves it toward my mouth. Is she going to feed it to me? Why does that make my pulse jump? When her fingers are almost to my lips, I open my mouth and she drops it inside, her finger grazing my bottom lip. I shudder at her touch. Oh, man. I'm in trouble.

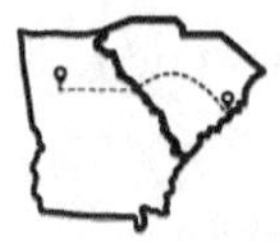

CHAPTER SEVENTEEN
Kat

Our drive from Charleston flew by with all the games Zach and I played on the way over. I've learned a decent amount about him from the questions game. He doesn't mind road trip detours, whereas, if I'm in charge, my aim is to get there as fast as possible. He thinks it's important not to let work take over his life and makes time for important relationships and having fun, as supported by his weekly dinners at his mom's house and regular game nights with friends. I can't imagine what it'd be like to have that kind of social calendar. I see plenty of people during the workday, but no one I'd feel comfortable asking to hang out. Perhaps my yearning for a life more like Zach's means I should do some rearranging of my own. I've also learned his middle name isn't Tyler, Woodruff, or Christopher and am no closer to figuring it out.

"Thanks for helping me carry the table," Zach says as he helps me back into the truck. "You didn't have to do that."

I shrug. "I didn't mind."

He shuts the door and walks around to his side. He buckles his seat belt and my stomach rumbles.

"Guess it's time for lunch," I say.

"You know this area better than me," he says. "Where should we go?"

I suddenly have a hankering for a burger from my favorite diner. I wonder if it's as good as I remember. Only one way to find out.

"There's a cute little diner in downtown East Point, if you don't mind driving twenty minutes."

He starts the truck. "Whatever you want. Just tell me how to get there."

I navigate us to the downtown area of my youth. Zach slides into an open spot out front of the brick façade block with green awnings.

"This is like something out of an old movie."

I chuckle. "Actually, this block has been in a couple of television series."

He looks over at me with wide eyes. "Really?"

"Yeah. A lot of Atlanta is recognizable in movies shot over the past twenty years. If you look closely, you can see my parents' house in an episode of *Stranger Things*."

"No way! You'll have to show me."

I unbuckle my seat belt and get out of the truck, Zach following me. "My parents framed a still shot, so you'll see it when we get there."

We order at the counter, then choose a booth near the back. At first, I'm sitting with a view of the front door, but then realize people might recognize me, so I slide out and scoot in next to Zach. He gives me a curious look.

"I'm trying to stay incognito," I say. "There's a good chance someone will recognize me since I lived here for several years."

His eyebrows knit together in confusion. "Several years? I thought you grew up in Atlanta?"

I've become so comfortable with Zach this morning, I sort of forgot we're new friends. "I did. We lived in Marietta, which is north of downtown, until I was in seventh grade, and then moved down here to East Point once I started getting movie roles. It was a beast of a drive from that far north. It normally took an hour to get to the studio, but we sometimes spent two hours battling traffic, depending on the time of day. Once I had steady work, my parents figured it'd be worth it to move us and cut down on the commute."

"Wow. Your parents are amazing. Not everyone has such a supportive family."

They really are. I probably haven't told them enough how much I appreciate them. "Yeah, Mason didn't love the move, though. He was in high school and had a solid group of friends in Marietta."

"I bet that was tough. I imagine it was hard for him not to feel some resentment toward you."

I lean back, absorbing Zach's words. I'd never really thought much about my brother's experience. He was definitely sulky for a good while, but seemed to find his niche at the new school. Maybe I should ask him about his view of our cross-city move sometime.

A server arrives and sets down our baskets of burgers and fries.

"Katie Bissonnette, is that you?"

I look up into the smiling face of Mrs. Lottie, the owner of South City Burgers, who served me my first hamburger here years ago.

I stand up and give her a hug. "It's me, Mrs. Lottie. So wonderful to see you!"

"What are you doing back in these parts?" She glances past me into the booth. "And you brought your sweetheart with you, I see."

No need to correct her, especially since that's the exact impression I was hoping to make.

"Just in town for the day. Thought I'd show Zach some of my old haunts before we visit my parents."

"Ooh, you're introducing the boyfriend to your folks. Big step." She gives me a wink.

Her words fluster me. I suppose under different circumstances it might be monumental introducing my parents to someone I'm seeing. Especially since it hasn't happened in almost a decade. Okay, now I'm getting overwhelmed. I really hadn't thought about the implications of seeing my family with Zach in tow. Now I get why Zach was concerned about lying to his friends. It really isn't fun knowing you're purposely deceiving someone you care about. I give her a smile and drop back into the booth.

"You two enjoy your meal," Mrs. Lottie says before heading back to the kitchen.

Zach takes my hand and gives it a squeeze, drawing my eyes to his face. "I take it you were in here a lot if she still recognizes you?"

I chuckle. "About as often as I could manage until I got my big break. After that, the studio hired a tutor so I could do school work while on set, which meant the end of my traditional schooling days. I never even got to go to prom."

"Bummer."

I shrug. "Eh, I experienced several fake ones on various sets. I don't think I missed much."

He shakes his head. "No, probably not. Besides, you seem to find occasions to dress up fairly regularly."

I give him a wry look. "That's the work of my agent and assistant. They hook me up with local designers and I try to give them a boost by wearing their products. Honestly, I'm more comfortable in stretchy pants and T-shirts."

"It's admirable you want to help local businesses. And for the record, I think you look just as good now as you did at dinner the other night. Maybe even better."

I can't help the smile that pushes up my cheeks. He's sweet and I think he even means what he says. I give him a once over in his faded jeans and gray hoodie. "I think the same thing about you."

He grins, but his smile fades as he glances over my shoulder. "Keep looking at me. I think there's someone filming you from the counter."

I really want to turn and look, but that would probably make things worse. It would be pretty easy to just ignore them, but a thought curls into my brain that makes me reconsider. There have been a few online threads about how I broke Talon's heart. A few commenters have defended me, talking about how you can't help who you love. Perhaps if I played up the head-over-heels aspect with Zach, people would drop the "poor Talon" angle.

"Well, then, why don't we give them a show?"

"What do you mean?"

"Put your arm around me and lean closer."

He pauses only for a moment before following my instructions. I grab one of my fries and lift it to his mouth. He takes a bite and then I pop the rest in my mouth, grinning at him like I can't get enough. Of course, being this close means I can smell his cologne, and it definitely beckons me closer. His gaze drops to my lips and my heart kicks in my chest. Yes, we should definitely kiss. Only because we have an audience. No other reason.

I lean toward Zach. "I'm going to kiss you now, unless you object," I whisper.

A slight shake of his head. "No objections, your honor."

I grin and then close the distance between us, my hand finding his bearded jaw. His lips are full and soft. I inhale his woodsy scent and sigh. His hands find my face, cradling my jaw like I'm precious and fragile. He tilts his head slightly, which only ratchets up the sparks I'm feeling from the kiss. His facial hair is a little ticklish but not rough, like I'd expected. And his lips...well, divine is the only word that comes to mind. They fit perfectly with mine. So perfectly, I don't want this kiss to end. After a few more seconds, the pressure of his mouth on mine lessens until there's air between us again. My breath is coming in ragged bursts. That sure didn't feel like a fake kiss.

Zach releases my face, his hand touching my shoulder and sliding down my arm. "Wow."

He looks a little dazed. My insides are wobbly. "Yeah. That was perfect." I take a deep breath, trying to regain my senses. "Is the person still filming us?"

The sparkle in Zach's eyes dims. He glances over my shoulder again. "They are. What do you want to do now?"

"Let's eat and then get out of here."

He nods, releases my arm, picks up his burger, and takes a huge bite.

I take a smaller bite, but sigh at the familiar flavors. "This is just how I remember it. What do you think?"

"It's good." His voice is flat.

I place a hand on his arm. "Is everything okay?"

He shrugs. "Yeah, why wouldn't it be?"

There's no hint of a smile on his face now. Maybe he's annoyed by the invasion of our privacy. I'm a bit perturbed myself. I wish that kiss hadn't been for a camera. I felt so cherished and desired, something I haven't felt in a long time. But it was all for show. Even if it felt real.

When we're finished eating and head to the front to pay, there aren't any patrons at the counter. I guess our paparazzo has left. Although the food was good, something isn't sitting right in my gut.

I sneak glances at Zach all the way to my parents' house. Something is definitely off with him. When we park out front, Zach turns to me with a smile that doesn't reach his eyes.

"Anything I should know before I meet your folks?"

My stomach twists a little at the reminder that we're playing parts for my family.

"They're probably going to hug you right away. They're very affectionate people."

"Fair enough."

I swallow down my nerves. "And, uh, they'll expect us to be joined at the hip. I, um, have a tendency to be a little clingy with people I care a lot about."

He raises his eyebrows but says nothing.

"Is it going to be too much for me to be hanging all over you? We can just stick to hand holding if that's more comfortable."

He shakes his head. "Do whatever you need to do. I'll follow your lead."

I give him an appreciative smile and open the truck door. We meet on the sidewalk and I lace my fingers through his. We're only halfway to the front door when it swings wide open and both of my parents step out onto the porch.

"Mom! Dad!"

I tug Zach along, then drop his hand to hug first my mom, then my dad.

"Great to see you, Katie Bug," Dad says after letting me go. "And who do we have here?"

I twine our fingers together again and snuggle up against his side. "This is my boyfriend, Zach. Zach, these are my parents, Judith and Lawrence."

"Please," Dad says, "call me Larry."

He pulls Zach forward, and I release him so they can hug. Mom is next, adding a cheek kiss.

"And I prefer Judith, but Mom is fine, too."

Inwardly, I cringe. My parents are just being themselves, but I'm sure it's overwhelming for Zach. Though he doesn't seem phased.

"Larry, Judith, so wonderful to meet you. You've raised an amazing woman here."

He wraps his arm around my waist and tugs me to his side. My heart skips with happiness. This may be fake, but perhaps I could pretend it's real just for today. See what it'd be like to really bring home a guy I liked. Because I do like Zach. Maybe not that way, but definitely as a friend.

Mom grins. "And she obviously has great taste in men like I do." She winks at Dad before turning back to Zach. "You're very handsome. Are you an actor as well?"

He chuckles. "No, I make furniture."

"You do?" Dad asks with a little too much enthusiasm. "Judith wants me to put some bookshelves in our den, but I'm not sure how to make that work. Would you mind looking and giving me your professional opinion?"

I groan, realizing where Dad's going with this. If I'm not careful, he'll have Zach working all afternoon. "Dad, he's not a carpenter. He makes tables and chairs."

"Actually," Zach says. "I appreticed with a carpenter for a couple years. I'd be happy to check out your project."

"Wonderful," Dad says. "Come in and I'll show you what we're working with."

The men disappear into the house, leaving me and Mom still on the front porch. So much for cutting Dad off at the pass. I sigh and Mom pats my arm.

"Don't worry, dear. I won't let him monopolize all of Zach's time, but he really has been puzzled about how to transform the room. Why don't we make some appetizers to entice them to join us in the kitchen?"

I'm still stuffed from lunch, but have nothing better to do. "Sure."

Mom grills me on Zach while we put together a small tray of cheese, crackers, and fruit. Thankfully, our Q and A at dinner last week plus our road trip questions this morning prepared me to answer just about everything she asks. I'm pulling plates out of the cabinet when the guys walk into the kitchen.

"I really think built-ins would look great in there," Zach says. "If we were here another day, I bet we could get it framed out. Then you'd just have to stain or paint."

Dad turns to me. "What do you think? Could you spare some more time with us?"

Oof, the guilt is pressing down hard on my heart. I know my parents miss me as much as I miss them, but I don't want to waste more of Zach's time. I'm already inconveniencing him by stopping here before we head back.

"I'd love to, but I think Zach has a schedule to keep. I don't even know if we can stay for dinner."

Zach raises his shoulder and gives me a look I can't quite interpret.

"If Katie has the time, I don't mind staying to help. I know she needs to be back in Charleston tomorrow night, so we'd need to leave by mid-afternoon."

My parents beam at him before turning their smiling faces on me and sandwiching me in a hug. "Excellent!" Mom says. "This will give me and Katie some much needed girl time. How about we go get our nails done before dinner?"

My mind is swirling with all that's just happened in a matter of seconds. We're spending the rest of the day with my parents, which is exciting, but also means extra pretending. It also means more time with Zach, though it sounds like he'll be hanging out mainly with my dad.

"Sounds delightful, Mom."

Dad grabs a handful of grapes. "I guess Zach and I will do some measuring and then head to the lumber store. You girls have fun with your spa day."

Zach comes over and gives me a peck on the cheek. "Don't worry," he whispers, his thumb smoothing across my wrinkled forehead. "Have fun with your mom. I'm looking forward to doing a little construction work."

"Are you sure?" I say. "You don't have to do this."

He gives me a smile that crinkles the corners of his eyes and makes my breath hitch. "I want to."

He presses a lingering kiss to my temple, squeezes my hand, then grabs a couple of apple slices and follows my dad back to the den. My skin is tingling from all of Zach's touches. My heart wants to believe they mean something, but my head is more sensible.

CHAPTER EIGHTEEN

Kat

Zach and my dad spent most of the afternoon together working on the den project. I'm impressed at the amount of work accomplished in such a short span of time. After pedicures, I helped Mom shop and prepare dinner. Just as we're setting plates on the table, the front door opens and shuts. A few seconds later, my brother, Mason, appears in the dining room.

"Just in time," he says, giving Mom a kiss on the cheek. He juts his chin up in a nod. "'Sup, Sasquatch."

I ignore the jab and walk over to give him a hug. He stays pretty stiff, his only response two quick taps on my shoulder with his hand. I know we haven't seen each other in a while, but he doesn't have to be so standoffish.

Dad comes in from the den covered in sawdust. Zach follows, his hair hidden by a RiverDogs cap, which is also sporting a layer of dust. I squint. Is that my hat? Zach touches the brim and dips his head, trying to contain a smile, which only makes me more suspicious. He comes up to my side, wraps an arm around my shoulder, and kisses my cheek. He smells more like fresh lumber than the woods right now, but it's equally appealing to me. I relax, appreciating how natural he seems at projecting a lovey-dovey front. I wrap my arms around his waist and squeeze.

"I see you've brought one of your boyfriends with you. Do you have just the two, or are there more?"

I glare at Mason. "Don't believe everything you read online. Zach is the only person I'm dating, despite what rumors you may have heard."

He scoffs. "I didn't know *People* magazine was known for making up stories."

Mom turns to me. "You're in *People*? We'll have to find a copy."

"I'm not. There was a small misunderstanding, but I'm trying to let it blow over."

Mason snickers. "Small misunderstanding. Never heard that phrase used to defend breaking someone's heart."

I huff out a breath of annoyance. "I didn't break anyone's heart. I've never even had a conversation with Talon."

"So now you're just going around kissing strangers? Sounds like something an entitled celebrity would do. No regard for anyone else."

I clench my hands into fists. Even though I know he's riling me up on purpose, I hate how he's painting me in front of Zach and my parents. The need to defend myself overpowers any thoughts of letting this go.

"He kissed me. I didn't lead him on or even know he was there. It was an ambush."

"Riiiight. You're so beautiful, people just throw themselves at you. I'm surprised your ego was able to fit through the front door."

I'm seeing red. I open my mouth to refute his statement, but Zach's hands are on my hips and he pushes me through the kitchen into the laundry room, where he shuts us in. Then he pulls me to him, wrapping one arm around my waist while the other cradles my head. I sag against him, my arms dangling. He rubs soothing circles on my back, hugging me until I pull away.

"You okay?" he asks, his voice mirroring the look of concern on his face.

I blow out a breath. "Yeah. He's so good at winding me up. I know I don't visit much, but I don't get why he always has to be so combative with me."

He shrugs. "Maybe he's got something going on in his life that you don't know about. It might not have anything to do with you, Katie."

Mason's comments seem way too sharp and personal not to be about me, but I don't want to sit under a cloud all night. "Okay, I'll let it go. But if he starts up again…"

"I'll be right next to you. Feel free to grab my hand and squeeze it to a pulp if that'll help."

I give him a grateful smile and lean in for a hug. "Thanks, Zach. I'm glad you're here. Sorry about being roped into spending the night. I'm also sorry you're meeting this version of Mason."

He hugs me back and I feel him shrug. "All families have their issues. Besides, it's been fun working on a project with your dad. I think it's going to look really good when we're finished."

I'm not quite ready to end this hug, so instead I burrow a little deeper, my forehead brushing against his neck.

"Can I ask you something?"

I'm nervous about what it might be, but nod.

"Is Talon the sleazeball you told me about when you were in my store?"

I nod again, touched that he remembered. Of course, I did use the story as emotional blackmail, which might be a little hard for anyone to forget. My stomach twists at the reminder that I'm using this sweet man for selfish purposes. And now I'm cuddling him against his will. *You're so selfish, Katie.* Startled by the thought, I quickly release him, shamed by my behavior. Maybe Mason isn't so far off the mark about my ego. I should take more care in my interactions with Zach. Treat him with the same respect and kindness he's shown me.

When we return to the dining room, everyone else is seated at the table, leaving two seats open across from Mason. Conversation starts out pleasant enough. My brother talks about his work as a portfolio analyst at a financial firm. He must have come straight from work because he's wearing a navy suit. My brain turns to the memory of Zach in a tie on our last date. He definitely wore it better. I smirk at the thought, but quickly school my face into one of interest and tune back into Mason's monologue.

After dinner, we all move to the den. Dad pulls the sheets off of the furniture so we can sit down. Sawdust coats the floor from the day's work.

"So Zach," Mom says. "Tell us what attracted you to our wonderful Katie Bug."

I choke on the sip of water I was taking, but thankfully, keep it all in my mouth. "Moooom," I say, my face heating.

Zach takes my hand and gives it a reassuring press. "Great question, Mrs. Bissonnette."

"I told you to call me Judith."

"Sorry, Judith." He meets my gaze and smiles. "I'd have to say it was her smile."

"She had braces for three years," Mason says.

I scowl over at him, but he looks nonplussed.

"That and her good taste in chairs," Zach says, redirecting the conversation.

I laugh, warmed by the teasing sparkle in his eyes.

"We met in his furniture store," I say, talking to my parents, but still caught in Zach's gaze.

"So you're a salesman," Mason says. "Do you work on commission?"

"He makes the furniture," Dad says before I can jump in. He waves his hand toward the partially built shelves. "He's been helping me with this project today. What do you think?"

Mason peers over at the wooden frame. "Uh, I'm not really sure. It just looks like you're framing out a wall."

"Well, sure. But imagine it stained a warm honey color and filled with books. It's going to be great."

He shrugs, looking less than impressed. "Whatever you say."

I hop up quickly. "Mason, I brought you something. Will you come with me to the kitchen?"

He reluctantly follows me. By the time he makes it through the door, I've already pulled his gift from my tote bag.

"I haven't had time to wrap it, but here is a housewarming gift."

He takes the bookends from me. While he doesn't smile, I notice the small lift of his brows revealing his surprise.

"I thought you could use it to showcase your vintage books."

"Did your *boyfriend* make them?"

I don't like his dismissive tone, but I'm really trying to get us back onto more friendly ground. "He did. I'm glad work is going well for you."

He just nods. My mind pings on my conversation with Zach earlier today.

"I also wanted to say I'm sorry my career taking off took you away from your high school friends. I know that must have been hard starting over as a sophomore. I never wanted my dreams to disrupt yours. If I could go back, I'd look for some way to keep us at our old house."

His eyes widen a degree, but then a door seems to slam shut on his emotions.

"Are you also sorry for blowing up my baseball career?"

My forehead crinkles. "What baseball career?"

He sneers. "Exactly. Thanks to you, I never got a chance to see how far I could go."

"I don't understand. You played baseball at your new school."

He rolls his eyes. "Yeah, but we had a terrible team. My old school won the state championship all four years I was supposed to be there. Many players received college scholarships, and a few went to the minor leagues. There weren't any scouts visiting teams with losing records, so I got forgotten at the new school."

The hurt on his face makes my heart ache. "I *am* sorry, Mason. I didn't know. That must have been devastating for you."

He shrugs, his face sliding into a mask of indifference. "Whatever. You got what *you* wanted."

It sounds like his life hasn't turned out as he hoped it would. While there's nothing I can do about his potential baseball career, I do have connections. "I thought you liked being in the financial industry. If you're looking for a new profession, I could see if I know anyone."

He rolls his eyes. "I don't need your help. I'm fine." He waves at his suit. "I can afford nice things. In fact, I'm thinking about getting a Rolex."

I glance down at his feet, careful to keep my face neutral when I notice his brown leather Berluti shoes.

"Yes, these are the shoes you gave me. They're excellent quality and very comfortable." He pauses. "I guess you're not completely self-absorbed."

Is that supposed to be a compliment? His words are followed by the smile Mason uses when he's trying to play nice. I guess it'll have to be enough for now.

"Do you always come for dinner on Fridays?"

His smirk is back. "No. I thought I'd come meet your new man."

I frown. "Did Mom text you?"

"Someone from high school posted a video of you at the diner earlier today. Way to announce your arrival, by the way."

He pulls out his phone, messes with it for a bit, then turns it to face me. It's surprisingly good quality for a phone video. You can clearly see Zach, but only the back of my head while we're kissing. The steaminess of that interaction is lost through the screen. I'm getting warm just thinking about it. After the kiss, I turn my head to take a bite of my burger, and you can see enough of my face to figure out who I am. Well, I suppose that was the point of the kiss. To get people's attention.

"I was just having lunch with my boyfriend. How was I to know someone would film us?"

He shakes his head. "You've got to be more aware of your surroundings. In this town, everyone knows you, so you should just assume you're being watched."

I shrug. "Well, it's really nothing new for me. I just try to ignore other people or else I'd be paranoid all the time."

"You sure are good at ignoring people," Mason mumbles, but loud enough for me to hear.

"I'm sorry if I haven't been in contact enough. But you know, phones and airplanes work both ways."

"Yeah, whatever." He glances toward the den. "I'm gonna go. I've got plans. Tell Mom and Dad I said bye. Guess I'll see you when I see you."

He's out the door before I can respond. My only consolation is that he took the bookends with him.

After Mason's dramatic exit, the evening winds down with a marathon game of Phase 10. Mom and Dad say goodnight and head down the hall to their room. I didn't realize Zach and I would be sharing a room until

Mom told me they turned Mason's old bedroom into a combination crafting and fly-tying room to house my parents' hobbies. That means the only guest bedroom in the house is my old room. We stand just inside the doorway, staring at the full-size mattress we're both supposed to sleep on tonight. I'm so freaked about the idea of sharing a tiny bed with my fake boyfriend that the rest of the room doesn't even register until Zach speaks.

"This is quite a collection of shirtless guys," he says, drawing my eyes up from the bed to the posters above the headboard. "You really had a thing for guys with swoopy hair."

I chuckle. "Did you just say swoopy?"

"Yeah. What else would you call that look?"

I study the photos. I suppose hair brushed across the forehead does fit his description. "I guess I'd call it swoopy."

"I'm not sure what I expected your childhood bedroom to look like, but it certainly wasn't this," he says, motioning to the wall of framed programs of shows I'd been in before I started getting movie parts.

"And your room looked so much better?"

He grins. "No, not really. I had posters from *Fight Club* and *The Matrix* even though I wasn't allowed to watch them until a few years after they came out. But the posters were pretty phat."

I shake my head. "Phat?! What are you, like forty?"

He clears his throat. "Thirty-six, actually."

"Oh." I guess I assumed he was closer to my age, though the beard kind of hides his face. Still, nine years isn't that big of a deal. No wonder he's so good at his craft. He's been at it for close to twenty years, I bet. "I'm twenty-seven."

"I know." He must notice my surprised look. "I googled you once."

I'm not sure whether I should be pleased or annoyed he researched me. Eh, who am I kidding? I did the same thing to him, just couldn't find anything.

"And it doesn't bother you?"

He shrugs. "I don't see how it affects me one way or the other. Besides, we're both adults."

That's right. This isn't real. Why do I keep forgetting that? *Because you want it to be real.* Do I? Maybe I'm just trying to fully immerse myself in the role like I do for movies. It makes my performance more believable to the audience. Yep, just being professional here. That's all. *You keep telling yourself that.*

"Should I sleep on the couch downstairs?" Zach says. "I'm not sure if this bed can hold us both."

While that would be the more comfortable option, something keeps me from agreeing to his suggestion. Better to just continue to pretend we're smitten with each other for the rest of our time here.

"It'll be fine. My dad is a very early riser and I doubt you'd want him accidentally sitting on you when he has a full mug of hot coffee."

He grimaces. "Probably not. I didn't bring an overnight bag. Do your parents have an extra toothbrush, maybe a spare pair of gym shorts I can sleep in?"

Oh, yeah. Neither of us were prepared to spend the night. Of course, we need pajamas. Thankfully, there are still a few of my things in the dresser. I find an oversized T-shirt and a pair of baggy sweatpants. I hold the bottoms out to Zach.

"Will these work?"

He grimaces. "I tend to sleep hot. But I suppose I can sleep on top of the covers. That might make things less awkward, right?"

So he is nervous about sharing a bed with me. I want to delve deeper into this realization, but it won't do any good. This is just one of those weird situations we didn't foresee but will get through. Friends can share a bed.

"Um, whatever you want. The bathroom is across the hall. There should be toothbrushes and towels under the sink."

"Good idea. I probably should shower and get the grime off me. Do you want to use the bathroom first?"

"No, you go ahead."

While Zach is across the hall, I lecture myself on how to behave. *It's just a friendly sleepover. Nothing is going to happen. We're adults who can handle this.* I've just about got myself convinced when Zach pushes open the bedroom door. He's still toweling off his damp hair, but my eyes are locked onto his bare chest. His very muscular bare chest. I guess making furniture requires a lot of muscle. I try to look away, but instead, my eyes travel down to my gray sweatpants. Since we're about the same height, they fit him *very* well. He looks so good right now, it's all I can do not to leap across the room and drag my fingers across the planes of his torso. Instead, I sit on my hands to keep them from reaching out.

"Shower felt good. Excellent water pressure. Highly recommend."

When he moves to the other side of the bed from where I'm sitting, I leap up, grab my clothes, and dash into the bathroom. Zach's right about the shower. I feel less flustered and more relaxed by the time I'm dry and clothed.

He's propped up against the headboard, leafing through an old teen magazine when I return. He looks up and the smile freezes on his face. His eyes, which start at my face, skim down my body and stop on my bare legs. I run a hand down my shirt and suck in a breath when I realize how short it is. It covers my underwear, but that's about it. Well, I suppose it's only fair that both of us are showing lots of skin.

Trying not to show how much his brazen perusal of my body affects me, I walk as casually as I can over to the bed and slide under the covers. I look over and Zach's face is buried in the pages of the magazine.

"Reading anything good in there?"

He drops it and faces me, one side of his mouth quirking up. "I took the quiz and found out that Chace will make my heart sing this spring with a sporty date. Whoever that is."

I laugh. "He was on a show called *Gossip Girl*."

"Oh."

I turn on my side and prop my head up with my hand. "I think you and he could be friends. He likes hiking and is a nice guy."

He slides down the bed and models my position. It's very challenging trying to keep my eyes on his face.

"You know him?"

"We were in a movie together. He was very respectful."

We stare at each other long enough for me to notice his blue eyes have a greenish ring around the pupil. Suddenly, he winks at me and my body flushes. What is it about his winks? Maybe the fact that they feel like they're just for me. Like he's acknowledging that we have a genuine connection. I yawn, covering my mouth with my hand.

"You're right," he says. "We probably should get some rest before the long drive tomorrow."

He gets up to turn off the light. My eyes follow his path to the switch and back, relishing the view of all his muscles. My fingers really do itch to feel them, but I distract myself by adjusting my pillow. The bed dips when Zach lies down and I have to press my hands into the mattress to keep from rolling into him. At least the sheets are a barrier between us. I need to do something to distract me from the fact that I'm laying shoulder to shoulder next to a half-naked man I find quite sexy.

"Zachary Kyle?" I ask into the dark.

"Nope."

"Elijah."

"Wrong."

"Timothy?"

"Goodnight, Katie."

I sigh dramatically, even though I'm grinning like a fool. "Night, Zach."

I lie there with my eyes open for a long time, acutely aware of the warm body next to me, before I finally drift off to sleep.

CHAPTER NINETEEN
Zach

To say yesterday was surprising would be an understatement. I had so much fun road tripping with Katie to Atlanta. She kept me engaged and entertained the entire time. The visit to a spot she frequented in her youth was fun. And that kiss... I knew we were eventually going to have to, but I honestly wasn't prepared. Even though it was fake, it sure didn't feel like it to me. Even now, I can still remember the feeling of her lips against mine. It was possibly the best kiss of my life. Too bad I'm the only one who seems to be struggling to contain my feelings. Guess that makes sense since I'm not a professional actor.

Having to share a bed with Katie did not make things any easier. She looked so hot in her oversized T-shirt. I couldn't stop staring at her legs. And then to wake up in the middle of the night with her cuddled against me, one of those long legs slung over mine...oh, man. I was dying to wrap my arms around her and squeeze her against my chest. My mind wants to believe her snuggling up to me meant something, but it's just because that bed was tiny. It was almost impossible not to touch.

Of course, I didn't exactly scooch her back over to her side either. Nope. I laid there, indulging myself in the feeling of sharing a bed with someone I care about more than I probably should. The warmth of her body eventually lulled me back to sleep. When I woke again, the other half of the bed was empty and my heart felt like half of it had been scooped out and thrown away.

"Whatcha thinking?"

Katie's question startles me from my thoughts. I look over at her, amazed at how beautiful she looks without the makeup she usually wears. I didn't know she had a few freckles dotting her cheeks. Each new thing I discover about her makes me like her more.

"I really enjoyed meeting your family. Everyone was very nice."

"Except Mason. I apologize for him. Thanks for helping me calm down. It was nice to have someone in my corner."

I look over at her in the passenger seat. Her hands are twisting the bottom of her shirt. Is she worried about what I think of him? Or embarrassed that I interrupted their sibling spat?

"I'm sorry if I overstepped. It's hard to just stand there when someone I care about is being unfairly attacked."

She glances over at me, her eyes brightening. There's that smile I've been missing.

"You were my knight in shining armor. If you hadn't pulled me away, I might have done or said something I'd now regret."

My gaze moves back to the road, more to avoid her penetrating gaze than to check the traffic ahead.

"My dad really likes you."

Mom made sure I had impeccable manners growing, but I really wanted to make a good impression on Katie's parents. It seems pointless since I'll probably never see them again.

"He's a cool guy. I hope he's happy with the new shelves."

I risk a look at the passenger side of my truck and notice Katie's eyes are sparkling.

"You really worked some magic on him. He'll be talking about your project for the next month. If you're not careful, he'll have you back to visit just to tackle another home chore."

It feels good to hear I was a hit with Larry. He was really fun to spend time with. I would have loved to have grown up with an encouraging, kind man like that.

"I'd be more than happy to help him out sometime if he has any other carpentry work. I bet he's a great dad."

She nods. "Oh, yeah. The best. What was your dad like?"

I guess I walked right into that one. She opened her family world up to me; it's only fair I share at least a little of mine.

"My dad left when I was five, so I don't really remember much about him."

I feel a warm hand on my arm. "Oh, Zach. I'm sorry. I didn't mean to pry."

I shrug. "It's fine. From what I've gathered, his absence wasn't much different from his presence. He never came to any of my T-ball games, even though I asked every time."

Katie's hand moves from my forearm up to my shoulder and squeezes. I have to look away from her sympathetic smile. This is why I don't talk about it. No one enjoys being pitied. I shrug my shoulders, effectively breaking our contact. I immediately regret it. Her touch is becoming something I crave.

"Anyway," I say, searching for a new topic. "What road trip game should we play next?"

She's silent for a minute, but I dare not look at her for fear of what expression I might find on her face.

"How about two truths and a lie?"

I'm thankful for her willingness to drop the uncomfortable conversation. "Sure. You go first."

"Okay...give me a minute to think. You be thinking about yours, too."

We ride in silence for a few minutes until I sense her shift her body in my direction.

"Alright. I once got locked out of my house in my underwear and had to hide in the bushes until I saw someone come by and used their phone to call my assistant to give me the code to get back in."

The thought of Katie in her underwear is one I definitely shouldn't linger on, but that's the part that gets stuck in my brain. "No way! Did you have to wait long?"

She shushes me. "You're supposed to hear all of them before you respond."

I curb my smile and nod somberly. "Sorry. Continue."

"Thank you. While making a rom-com, I had a gyro for lunch one day, not thinking about the fact that it was the day we were filming the big kiss scene. When I leaned toward my co-star, he leaned waaaay back and suggested we pause for some mouthwash and mints."

I cringe on her behalf. "Wait, we're only sharing embarrassing stories about ourselves?"

She smacks me lightly on the arm.

"Right," I say. "No talking."

I mime zipping my lips and motion for her to continue.

"At my eighth-grade talent show, I was giving a monologue and right in the middle of this big, dramatic speech, I let out an enormous burp. It pretty much killed the mood. Everyone laughed—because it was a room full of middle schoolers—and I ran off the stage without even finishing."

I sit there, my gut churning with compassion for Katie having to experience all those things. Even if one of them isn't real, I'm mortified on her behalf. She's had a lot of public humiliation and apparently bounced back every time. I know it's a risk to put yourself out there, but she seems to throw herself into things with gusto, regardless of the potentially mortifying outcome. I could stand to be more like her. For as long as I can remember, I just go with the flow, choosing whatever seems easiest even if it isn't what I really want.

"You're awfully quiet over there," Katie says.

I look over with a quick grin. "Am I allowed to talk now?"

She shakes her head, an amused smile on her face. "Yes, silly. You have to guess which one is not real."

"First of all, I'm sorry that any of those are real. You're so amazing to have gotten through those awkward situations and be able to talk about it now. I prefer to keep all my foibles locked up."

Her smile grows, and it pricks something in my chest. Does she not get complimented often? Guess I'll have to keep them coming.

"If I have to pick, I'm going to say the 'locked out of the house' one. With as many scripts as you've had to memorize, there's no way you'd forget a code."

Her mouth forms a pout. "Boo."

"What?"

She sighs. "You're right. I really thought I'd stump you."

I shrug. "Sorry, I guess."

She claps her hands together. "It's fine because now it's *your* turn!"

"Okay, give me a minute."

I think through the parts of my life that make me squirm a little, then try to come up with something equally mortifying that sounds like it could be true but isn't.

"When I was in high school, my friends and I snuck over to the pineapple fountain and put yellow dye in the water so it'd look like pee. Turns out the city has cameras in that area and we not only had to scrub the fountain to get rid of all traces of the dye, but my mom made me volunteer at the historical center for a month."

I look over at her, and her eyes are shining. She's definitely enjoying this game. Her eyebrows raise, encouraging me to continue.

"I used to work at this event in Asheville called Winter Lights. I helped families make s'mores over an open fire. One time, I got a little too close and burned off one of my eyebrows. My boss made me wear a fake eyebrow for the rest of the season so I wouldn't freak out the kids."

I see Katie's shoulders shake and realize she's holding in a laugh. It feels good to know I'm the source of her entertainment. Does she have a close group of friends she gets to be silly with? I bet it's hard staying connected due to her job. If she barely sees her family, maybe she doesn't have good friends either.

"At a friend's wedding, I was coerced into doing a choreographed dance with the rest of the groomsmen. I'd gotten the moves down in tennis shoes, but our dress shoes the day of the wedding were super slick on the dance floor. Halfway through the dance, my feet slipped out from under me. I fell, slid into the cake table, and had four tiers of jam-filled cake fall onto me and the dance floor. The strawberry filling on my linen tux made it look like I was the victim of a crime."

Katie laughs out loud and shakes her head. "No, sir. That did not happen."

I raise an eyebrow. "Are you saying the last story is false?"

She giggles uncontrollably for a long minute, her arms around her waist. She raises a finger, but is gasping for breath. I can't help chuckling at her unrestrained amusement. After a few minutes, she gets herself under control.

"Two of those are real?"

I nod. "As per the rules. What's your guess?"

She wipes tears from her eyes. "Oh man, I wish they all were real. I'm going to have to say the cake one. There's no way you ruined your friend's wedding."

I scowl, but it quickly morphs into amusement at the memory. "I wouldn't say I *ruined* it. Though, every once in a while, Greg or Tara will hand me a strawberry cupcake and then tease me mercilessly."

Katie's eyes round and her mouth drops open. "That's real?! Oof. Then it must be the fountain."

I make a buzzer sound. "Wrong again. It was the eyebrow thing. Though I did work the s'mores station for a number of years."

She purses her lips and glares at me. "That's cheating."

I shake my head. "I don't think so. If anything, you were cheating by putting the image of you in your underwear in my head."

I clamp my mouth shut, horrified at what just came out of it. Sure, I'm a guy and we notice attractive women, but I worry acknowledging I have the hots for her will make her uncomfortable. I can't believe I ever thought not catching feelings would be possible. She's funny and nice. Who wouldn't fall for a woman like her? Quickly, I change subjects, keeping my eyes out the front windshield.

"What are you doing at work tomorrow? Filming a new scene?"

"That's the plan. If we wrap it up quickly, we'll probably start prepping for the next one. Grady is a true professional. We've gotten a lot of filming done in only a couple of takes, which has us ahead of schedule. I may be out of your hair sooner than expected."

Her words have the opposite effect than she probably intended. I don't want to let her go just yet. Yes, I know I'm not really her boyfriend, but I think maybe I'd like to be. Should I tell her I'm developing real feelings for her? I don't want to ruin the friendship developing between us. Perhaps I should wait until our arrangement wraps up. That would probably be the smart thing to do. That way, if she doesn't feel the same, we don't have to keep seeing each other to keep up the ruse. I can do this. I'm no actor, but I'm pretty good at keeping my wants and desires in check.

We stop about an hour outside of Charleston for gas, snacks, and to play the gift game again, at Katie's insistence. Back in the truck, I have Katie close her eyes and hold out her hands. When she opens them, she picks up the T-shirt and opens it up. It says, *We be trippin'* and has a curvy dotted line with a little truck at the end of it. She narrows her eyes at me.

"Is this repayment for the lame shirt I got you?"

I lean back, surprised at the annoyed tone. "What? No. I love the shirt." I lift the front of my sweatshirt. "See, I'm wearing it today. I thought it'd be fun if we both had road trip shirts."

"Oh. Sorry. I thought you were making fun of me."

I shake my head. "No. I'd never." I pause. "Do your other friends do that?"

She deflates in her seat, swivels to look out the side window, and mumbles something.

"What? I didn't hear you."

She sighs, and turns back, not meeting my gaze. "I said I don't really have any friends."

Her words pierce my heart. How can this wonderful woman not have any friends? Surely, there are plenty of other people who see how great she is.

"Why not?"

She shrugs. "I'm too busy, I guess. If I'm not working on a film project, then I'm doing commercials or promotions. I don't have a lot of free time."

"You don't hang out with your co-workers?"

She wrinkles her nose. "Not really. I've been asked to hang out a few times, but I know they're just being nice. They don't really want to spend time with me."

I scowl. "I bet that's not true. You're so fun to be around. If you gave them a chance, you could probably make some genuine connections. Plus, maybe you'd be able to hang out when you're not filming. Everybody lives in L.A., right?"

"Not everybody. My current co-star lives somewhere near Asheville with his wife. I guess he's from that area and moved back a few years ago."

"Relationships are important. My friends have gotten me through some tough times. I can't imagine how I would have survived without my support system."

She leans back against the seat. "I know you're right. Maybe I'll try to make an effort. It's just that I've been burned several times in the past. I'm a little skittish about opening myself up again."

I want to reach across the seat and pull her against me, so I grip the steering wheel instead to keep myself in check. My heart twists with sorrow for how lonely Katie must have been these past few years, how lonely she probably still is. I'm more determined than ever to keep my feelings to myself and show her what true friendship looks like. It's what she needs most right now.

"Alright, your turn," she says suddenly. "Close your eyes and hold out your hands."

I oblige and feel something soft that covers most of my palm. When I open my eyes, I'm staring at a stuffed hamburger. It has beads or something in it to give it a little weight and sports a smiley face and a little RiverDogs hat.

"It reminded me of lunch yesterday," she says.

My heart is in my throat as my mind hurdles back to the kiss. I squeeze the plush in my hand to try to get myself under control.

"Zach?"

I meet her gaze, worried she's going to be able to read the emotions on my face.

"Don't turn your head, but there appears to be someone filming us. What do you say about putting on another show real quick?"

I don't trust myself to speak, so I tip my chin up in response. Her eyes drop to my lips, her lids lowering in a very enticing way, and the last shred of my restraint snaps. I lean over, my hands dropping the toy on my lap so I can reach up and cup her face. Our lips touch and everything feels right in the world. One of her hands slips into my hair, the other wraps around the back of my neck possessively, and she sighs. A growl wrenches from my throat and I wrap an arm around her waist and drag her body flush with mine. I don't know where my assertiveness came from, but Katie's hold on me tightens, so I guess she doesn't mind. We stay locked in the embrace, thoroughly exploring each other's mouths until she breaks off, panting. I have to force my arms to release her and give her some space.

"They're gone."

"Who?" I ask, my brain clouded with desire.

"The girl with the phone."

Oh right. We were kissing for a reason that wasn't simply because we wanted to. I definitely forgot, but Katie obviously didn't. Just like last time. I'm the only one who keeps forgetting these kisses aren't real. I concentrate on buckling my seat belt so I don't have to look at Katie and risk her seeing the disappointment on my face.

I clear my throat. "I guess we'd better get back on the road, too. I'm sure you're ready for some time to yourself."

"I've actually enjoyed this weekend. It was a good idea to get away. I really should visit my parents more."

Her parents. That's why she came on this trip. Not to hang out with me or get to know me better. I'm just a means to an end with her. I'd do well to keep that in mind.

I get us back onto the road and pull a package of Gummy Clusters out of my hoodie pocket.

"Want some?"

Katie smiles, but shakes her head.

"No, thanks. I've got my own snack."

She reaches into a paper sack and pulls out a plastic container. I do a double take, not quite believing my eyes.

"Is that...sushi? Did you really get gas station sushi?"

She shrugs. "It looked good."

"Katie, don't you remember the first rule of road tripping?"

She scoffs. "Yes. No hot food, only prepackaged snacks." She tilts the container. "This is not hot, and it's prepackaged."

I shake my head. "But it's got fish. I don't think it's a good idea."

"Lucky for you, I'm not making you eat it. It'll be fine."

I give her side-eye, but keep my mouth shut. She's an adult, able to make her own choices. I just hope it doesn't come back to bite her.

CHAPTER TWENTY

Kat

I've been casting furtive glances over at Zach for half an hour. He's been pretty quiet since our last stop. Is he annoyed about the sushi thing? It didn't taste as good as it looked. In fact, I sort of regret it now that it's bouncing around in my belly. I can't quite tell if I'm just being paranoid or if it really is making me feel a little squeamish. Or maybe it was that jaw-dropping makeout session before we left.

I was expecting another kiss like in the diner, wondering if I'd feel a little spark again or if it was just an anomaly. I'm not sure how it turned into tightly entwined limbs and bodies so close I could feel his heart pounding in his chest. Or maybe that was mine. All I know is that throaty growl of his made my scalp tingle and goosebumps erupt on my arms. For a minute, I forgot we were kissing in a truck for an audience. I'm sure I made some sounds I'd rather not think too hard about.

When was the last time I experienced a kiss like that? Maybe never. The kisses certainly weren't that hot with my last boyfriend. Of course, he was an immature twenty-something, whereas Zach is decidedly a man. Perhaps that's the difference. Or it could be the fact that I've gotten to know Zach and am attracted to the person he is in addition to his good looks. All I really know for sure is that we have some chemistry, and I like it. Would it be bad for me to allow myself to indulge in this little ride we're on and pretend like it's real? You know, fully immerse myself in the role of Zach's girlfriend.

My body seems into this idea, especially since it latched onto him while I was sleeping last night. I woke up this morning snuggled up against his chest, an arm and a leg tossed over him. The realization was enough to jolt me awake. Zach hasn't said anything about it, so maybe he slept through my clingfest. I must admit there was something nice about waking up next to him. It's something I could get used to very quickly.

My stomach gurgles disconcertingly. I don't think Zach heard it. Another look his way and he's still staring out the window, his knuckles white on the steering wheel.

"Are you okay?"

He turns toward me, and I motion to his fingers. He loosens his grip.

"Yeah, fine. Just ready to be home, you know?"

I don't know. I'm kind of dreading him dropping me off at my hotel. After all this time with him and my family, I can admit how lonely I've been. Most of my time recently has been spent in groups of strangers or with my employees. That's no way to live. Maybe I will go out with the cast if they invite me again.

Is Zach just ready to be away from me? Has he not enjoyed my company like I've relished his? I suppose this is just a job for him. One where he's not getting paid. I scowl at the realization. What is he getting out of this arrangement? Nothing. I need to change that.

My stomach lurches uncomfortably and I drop a hand to it. The rumbling continues until my abdomen spasms with a cramp. Uh oh.

"Zach?" My voice shakes.

"What is it?"

"I think we need to find a bathroom. *Soon.*"

As if to prove my point, I feel bile climb up my throat and clamp a hand over my mouth.

"You look a little pale. And sweaty. We're almost at your hotel. Can you make it?"

I give a tiny, slow nod, keeping my hand where it is. When the truck starts slowing, I grab the handle, ready to jump out, but then I see a group of cameras and people with microphones standing out front. I turn to Zach, panicked.

"Don't stop. Reporters can't see me like this."

I burp, the taste of my ill-considered snack making my stomach heave even more.

Zach presses the gas, casting me concerned looks while steering us somewhere. He turns down a narrow drive, then parks in front of a two-story brick house. He jumps out of the truck and races around to help me out. I stumble, feeling dizzy. He steadies me with his firm grasp, putting a hand to my forehead.

"You're burning up."

Effortlessly, he bends, scoops a hand behind my knees, and picks me up. I tighten in his embrace, worried I'm going to lose my tenuous hold on my bodily functions. He gets the door open without putting me down, then carries me upstairs to a bathroom.

"Trash can is there if you need it. I'll be right back."

I slam the door in his face, then rush over to the toilet, making it onto the seat just in time. The relief is brief as I feel the bile rise again and grab the trash can.

An unknown amount of time later, I'm laying on the bathroom floor curled up in the fetal position, letting the ceramic tile cool my blazing cheek. There's a knock on the door and I moan in response.

"Katie, can I come in?"

I manage another moan. In my rush, I must have failed to lock the door, because Zach pushes it open.

"Oh, Katie," he says, and the tenderness in his voice makes my stomach flip.

He carefully picks me up off the floor, carries me to a bed, then tucks me in. He brings me a plastic bucket and a glass of water, then carries a cleaning caddy into the bathroom. I cringe at the fact that he's in there cleaning up after me, but I'm too weak to do anything about it.

He leaves, presumably to throw away the trash can I desecrated earlier, then comes back with another bucket, which he deposits in the bathroom.

"Can I get you anything right now?"

My stomach cramps suddenly, and I rush from the bed back to the bathroom. A little while later, I drag myself back into bed, mortified when Zach goes back in with the cleaning supplies. All I can do is clutch my stomach and hope I don't need it while he's in there. While he's cleaning, I fall asleep, waking up a while later sweaty and disoriented. Followed by another run to the toilet.

There's a bottle of Gatorade by my bed along with some clean clothes when I emerge again. I'm too drained for a shower, but I change clothes before collapsing back into bed. When I wake again, Zach is sitting in a chair at the end of the bed.

"Hey, there," he says. "How are you doing?"

I groan, then clap a hand over my mouth when I realize how rank my breath is. Zach is immediately out of the chair. He grabs the bucket from the side of my bed and holds it up. I shake my head and wave him back.

"Do you have any mouthwash?"

His shoulders relax when he realizes I'm not going to be sick just yet.

"Yes. Under the sink with the toothbrushes and toothpaste. Do you want me to bring it to you?"

"No, I can do it."

"Do you think you could handle some broth?"

My stomach rumbles uncomfortably, and I shake my head.

"At least a few sips of Gatorade, then? I'm sure you're a bit dehydrated."

I nod, and he unscrews the top of the bottle and hands it to me. I keep my mouth clamped shut until he realizes my hesitation and backs toward the door.

"Is there anything else I can do for you right now?"

I shake my head. He leaves, closing the door behind him. When I'm sure he's gone, I test out a sip of Gatorade. The liquid feels good on my throat, but the sweetness is too much. I drink a few sips of water from the glass on the nightstand, which feels better.

The walk to the bathroom is a little wobbly. Guess I am dehydrated. I clutch the sink while rooting underneath for the mouthwash. I close the toilet lid and sit while swishing. After spitting it into the sink, I look up into the mirror and recoil at my reflection. My skin is deathly pale and my hair looks like I was electrocuted. I'm horrified that someone is seeing me like this. Especially Zach. If he was ever attracted to me before, this is sure to have killed it. No one finds a corpse sexy.

I drag myself back to bed after locating a comb in the cabinet under the sink. Once I crawl back under the covers, my energy is zapped and I let the comb drop onto the duvet, staring at it mournfully. I'm still trying to get myself to pick it up again when Zach returns with tea and an iPad.

The tea smells like Christmas and a small sip tells me there's peppermint in it.

"I brought you some entertainment in case you're feeling well enough to be bored." He hands me the iPad. "I took the password off so you can check out any of my streaming services or play a game. Download whatever you need."

His sweetness is touching. A tear slips out of the corner of my eye and I quickly wipe it away. Zach's hopeful face morphs into concern.

"What's wrong?"

Why does he have to be so caring? I'm full on crying now. Not just at the tenderness, but because of my frustration at being sick and knowing

I look hideous. I want to reassure him I'm okay, but all that comes out is, "My hair."

He blinks a few times, obviously confused, but then seems to understand and picks up the comb. "May I?"

I nod, and he hands me a tissue box. While I wipe my face, he sits down on the bed beside me and begins working on the knots in my hair. He's achingly gentle and I feel only a few tugs. He leans away from me and sets down the comb. I reach up to feel my smooth hair. It's a little greasy, but at least I probably don't look like an electrocuted squirrel. I'm so grateful for Zach's kindness that I burst into tears again.

He hugs me to his chest and I wrap my arms around his waist, appreciating how solid he feels. I can't remember the last time someone took care of me like this. Last year when I had the flu, I shivered and sweated alone for several days until Lila showed up to see why I wasn't responding to her texts and called a doctor out to my house. This is much nicer.

I could stay in his embrace indefinitely, but when I get a whiff of his woodsy cologne, I realize I probably smell like sickness and let go.

"I need a shower."

"Do you have the energy for that?"

Good point. I take another sip of tea. My stomach isn't revolting. "Maybe?"

"There's a bench in there if you need to sit down. Clean clothes are in the dresser."

I glance down at the T-shirt and sweats I'm currently in.

"Where did you get these, anyway?"

"Your assistant brought them over."

At my confused look, he continues.

"She kept calling, and I didn't want her to be worried, so I answered your phone and told her what was going on."

I can always count on Lila. My eyes widen as a thought occurs to me. "What time is it?"

"A little after noon."

"On Sunday?"

He shakes his head. "Monday."

I yank back the covers and jump out of the bed, swaying precariously at the action. Zach steadies me with his hands, gently pushing me to a sitting position on the bed.

"Whoa there, Tiger. Lila told your agent and the director what's going on. The goal right now is for you to heal. Work will pick back up when you're recovered."

I shake my head. "I'm a professional. I don't miss work."

"Even professionals get sick."

I give him a withering look. "Do professionals get themselves sick by making careless decisions?"

He presses his lips together, possibly to hide a smile, but there's still a sparkle in his eyes. "No one knows about the sushi but us. I said you appeared to have a stomach bug. Similar symptoms, right?"

He covered for me? Why does that make me feel swoony? Oh right, I haven't eaten anything in over a day.

"Thank you."

"Anytime. Now, go shower and, if you survive that, maybe we'll try some broth. How does that sound?"

"Sounds nice."

"Good." He gives me a smile that warms me to my toes, then leaves.

Is this what it's like to be in a relationship with someone who actually likes you and isn't just with you for your fame? If so, I could definitely get used to it. Is it possible this might be more real than I thought?

CHAPTER TWENTY-ONE
Zach

Katie's cell phone buzzes on the couch cushion next to her. She silences it without looking, her eyes never leaving the TV screen. It buzzes a second time, and she silences it again. When it starts up a third time, she sighs and picks it up to look at the screen. When she sees who's calling, she bolts up off the couch, her arm brushing mine. She turns to me with an apologetic look.

"I'm sorry, Zach. I have to take this. It's Rick."

It takes me a second to remember he's her agent. I pause the movie and give her a smile. She answers on her way upstairs. A few seconds later, I hear a door closing and assume she's sequestered herself in the guest bedroom where she's been staying the past few days.

Her food poisoning only lasted about a day and a half, but since I told her assistant it was a stomach bug, Katie's been instructed not to return to work until tomorrow. Mom has brought over soup, bananas, and homemade sourdough for toast. I've stayed busy cleaning, food prepping, and worrying. It's been an interesting experience caring for another person while they're sick. It's definitely created an added layer of affection for Katie. Seeing her so vulnerable brought out a protector instinct I didn't realize I had.

Since she's been feeling better, we've spent a lot of time hanging out on the couch watching movies. First, we watched her favorite: *The Princess Bride*. Then we watched mine: *Kill Bill: Vol. 1*. What can I say? I like a determined woman who takes names and kicks butt. We started out on opposite ends of the couch, but somewhere between Wesley's return from the dead and Uma Thurman wiggling her big toe, we ended up shoulder to shoulder in the middle. Until Katie's phone call. We were right in the middle of one of her films, *Love Undercover*, where she plays a singer who falls in love with her bodyguard. I had no idea she could sing, but she confirmed it was her real voice.

When Katie remembered I hadn't seen any of her movies, she decided we needed to remedy that immediately. It's one of her first rom-coms. She looks very young. Probably because she was nineteen when she made the movie. Regardless, the woman can act. If I didn't know it was her, I would have thought the movie cast a real pop star to play the lead.

I raise my head to the ceiling when I hear Katie's raised voice. The conversation does not sound pleasant. She comes back downstairs a few minutes later, a frown on her face, and plops down on the far end of the couch. She put on a hoodie while she was upstairs. A second look tells me it's one of mine. I don't know what it is about seeing a woman in my clothes, but I want nothing more than to lean over and kiss her. Okay, maybe it's not just because she's wearing my sweatshirt.

"Everything okay?"

She crosses her arms and huffs out a breath. "Just my agent being a jerk." She looks straight at me. "Not once did he ask how I was feeling. He was all, 'You missed the endorsement deal we set up with so and so' and 'You're lucky you were so far ahead of schedule that your disappearing act isn't going to cause filming to run long.' Am I just a product to him?"

He does sound like a jerk. Is she expecting a real response from me? What I want to do is breach the space between us and pull her into my arms. She looks so small curled up way over there, her fingers twisting the hem of her shirt.

"I'm sorry, Katie. What can I do?"

She sighs. "I'm just being ungrateful. Forgive me. I have a fabulous life and Rick is responsible for all the money I've made."

I shake my head. "I'm pretty sure it's you and your talent that brought in the money. He just got lucky being the one representing you."

She gives me a small smile. "Thanks, Zach. That's sweet."

Her phone buzzes in her hand. She looks at the screen and scowls.

"Is he calling you again?"

"No."

She puts the phone down, but her hand hovers over it. It buzzes again, and she snatches it back up.

"I'm sorry," she says. "There's this account I follow and there's a new post. I know I shouldn't look, but I just can't help it."

Must be a social media thing. I've never gotten into it. My business has a website, but that's about it. Nora keeps trying to get me to create an Instagram account for it and post finished products, but that seems like a lot of work. Plus, I'd have to learn how it works. Nora said something about reels and my eyes glazed over.

Katie opens her phone and her whole body slumps like she's just been kicked. Before I can think about it, I'm up off the sofa and crouched by her side, trying to figure out if I should rub her back, squeeze her arm, or just pull her into my chest. Indecision freezes me. Maybe she wouldn't like any of those things.

Her phone is open in her lap and when I glance down at it, I do a double take.

"Is that my truck?"

She nods, then picks up her phone and swipes over to a video. Whoever took it zoomed in through the windshield to the two people furiously making out inside. Whoa. How weird is it to watch yourself on video?

And if that video is of you kissing a beautiful woman, well...at least I look like I know what I'm doing. We both seem to be enjoying it. If I didn't know better, I would think it was very real kissing. The video stops, then starts over again. I should tear my eyes away, but I can't. Perhaps I should get an account just to be able to watch this video again. Realizing that's not the point, I shake my head and force my gaze back up to Katie's face. She looks horrified, which makes my gut twist. Definitely not the face you hope for in this kind of situation.

"I can see you're upset, but didn't we do that specifically for this purpose?"

She sighs. I'm clearly missing something.

"Did you read the post?"

There are words? Guess I was focused too much on the media. Below the video it says, "Looks like Katie definitely doesn't care about Talon's broken heart. What a —"

I cough when I read the last word, anger rising inside me. Who in the world would call any woman that name? A creep, that's who. My eye roams the screen, catching on the user's handle. @katsonnettistrash That confirms it. I grab Katie's hand and meet her eyes.

"Katie, none of what it says is true. You're not evil and you're certainly not trash. You are a kind, caring person who doesn't deserve to read such vitriol. Why do you even follow this account?"

She drops her head back against the couch. "I *know*. It's nothing but pure torture for myself, but it's like a scab I can't stop picking."

"Have you thought about deleting the app?"

She's quiet, nibbling on her bottom lip, and I can't stop staring at her mouth. Knowing what her lips feel like against mine makes me want to pull her into my arms and kiss the worry off her face. When I find myself leaning in, I mentally kick myself and plant my back firmly against the ottoman. It slowly slides backward on its wheels, and I feel myself inching closer to the ground every second. When my head is laying on top of the ottoman like a pillow, it stops rolling, but now I'm awkwardly holding myself up by my core and neck.

Katie looks in my direction, and I startle. The ottoman slips out from under my neck and I fall onto my back with a thud.

A laugh escapes her before she can school her features into concern. "Oh Zach. Are you okay?"

I chuckle, my gaze on the ceiling. "Nothing's hurt but my pride."

"That's good. Should we finish the movie?"

I'd nearly forgotten about it. I pull myself up off the floor, push the ottoman back to the couch so we can prop our feet up, and take my seat near the middle. Katie grabs the remote off the back of the couch and scoots closer to me. We're not quite touching, but her proximity settles something deep in my gut. Why does this feel so right and natural? I should focus on enjoying this time with her, but it's hard when I know we've got an expiration date.

CHAPTER TWENTY-TWO
Kat

I'm surprised by how much I've enjoyed staying at Zach's house these past few days. I haven't had a roommate since my days on the teen drama and I must admit it's really nice knowing there's another person nearby. It feels cozy. Maybe I should see if Lila wants to share my suite at the hotel. It has two bedrooms and I only need one. I could even pretend we're two friends on a trip together. She's the closest thing I have to a friend at the moment. Well, and Zach.

Spending so much uninterrupted time with another person has gotten me thinking about a number of things. First, it's made it glaringly obvious how lonely I've been. All I've been doing is working. Any social interactions have been work-related obligations, and that's just not healthy. Second, it's up to me to change my schedule to make room for friends and family. No one else is going to do it for me. Third, maybe I've been too hasty in completely cutting off dating. If this thing with Zach has shown me anything, it's that there are nice guys out there who can see beyond my celebrity and are trustworthy. Maybe my problem was dating other people in the industry or industry-adjacent.

Too bad this thing with Zach is only temporary. Once the filming wraps up, I'll be gone and he'll still be here. I couldn't ask him to come to L.A. with me, could I? It sure would make my big house feel more homey with a second person living there. There's plenty of space in the garage where he could set up a workshop to make furniture. It'd also be nice to have someone to go to events with. Maybe I should broach the idea of making our situation more permanent.

Assuming, I can get up the courage to actually do it. I couldn't stand it if he declined and then there was all this awkwardness between us. Maybe I'll feel him out a little more, make sure the vibes I've been getting from him are more than him just being nice.

While I wouldn't wish food poisoning on anyone, it has sort of been a blessing in disguise for me. It gave me a break from my normal, famous life. Well, except when we were watching one of my movies. It felt a little surreal watching my work with another person. I was so nervous about what Zach would think. We probably should have watched *For Love or Money* since it was the one that got me my little statue, but I've always been proud of how well I pulled off the singer role.

He seemed to like it, though he commented several times about how young I looked. I was nineteen when I made that one, so he's not wrong. It probably would be weird to watch someone almost half your age in a romantic role. But I'm not nineteen anymore. I've had a full twenty-seven years, learning a lot more than most people.

The more I get to know Zach, the more I'm drawn to him. Of course, how could I not be after he tenderly took care of me while I was sick? I've never seen a man clean as much as Zach has. Sure, it's been out of necessity, but he didn't complain once about anything. I mean, he combed my hair, for goodness' sake. Who does that? And not once did I see a look of disgust on his face. If there were any doubts about him being a keeper, they've all been obliterated.

There's a knock at the front door. Zach's upstairs in the shower, something I've been trying not to think about. After spending the night in my childhood bedroom with his torso on full display, the memory has popped into my mind more than I care to admit. Forcefully casting that thought to the side, I get up from the couch and answer the door.

"Hi, I'm Elaine, Zach's mom. You must be Katie."

It sends a pleasant sensation through my chest to hear her use my real name. Is that what Zach calls me when he talks to his mom about me? Wait. *Does* he talk to his mom about me? That thought only increases the warmth I feel.

"Yes, hi. Nice to meet you."

She's got a book in her arms. I step back from the door, and she comes in, heading for the kitchen table.

"I'm sorry you were sick. I heard you were feeling better and thought you might like to see a few photos of Zach when he was a kid."

My eyes brighten. Would I love a look into who Zach used to be? Yes, please! I need to know if his handsomeness was noticeable from an early age. I follow her over to the table and she pats the chair next to hers. She slides the album between us and opens the cover.

The first page shows a young, pregnant woman with a very attractive man next to her. I point at the photo.

"Is this Zach's dad?"

"Yes. Isn't he gorgeous?" She sighs. "Those dimples should have been a dead giveaway he was trouble. That and the fact that his nickname was Fox."

Zach doesn't have any dimples. Maybe he looks more like his mom. I'm not sure what to say to her comment, so I turn the page instead. There's a red squishy face that looks like it's gearing up for an epic scream. Elaine chuckles.

"Zachy sure was a crier. A little colicky, but he turned into a very mellow child."

My eyes roam the page, a glimpse at the first year of Zach's life. When I flip the page, I slap a hand over my mouth to keep from laughing. Toddler Zach is standing with his back to the camera, stark naked.

"This is one of my favorites," she says, tapping the photo with her fingernail. "Once he learned to walk, he was always on the go. He was also a master at undressing himself. I could hardly keep clothes on him, so eventually I gave up and just potty trained him early. Other than the untimely death of a few potted plants, it went fairly well."

Oh. My. Gosh. I would be mortified if this were my parents sharing this info. I'm very grateful my parents didn't think to pull out the baby books when we were visiting them. The water shuts off above us and I realize my time with these books is limited. I flip a little faster, catching pictures of Zach in baseball pants and ball caps, different team names for different seasons.

"He was so good at baseball," Elaine says. "Played third base and had a few colleges scout him, but was never interested. Just loved the game, I guess."

"Most parents would have made their kids go if they had a free ride."

Her smile dims. "He didn't have a lot of control over things that happened when he was younger. He's a good boy and likes making other people happy, but I've always wanted him to choose his own path. To make his own way and discover his own passions."

"He seems to have found it with woodworking."

She nods. "Yes, he's quite skilled. It just feels lately that something's off with him, like his life isn't quite what he wants it to be. I don't want to pry, but it's hard not to worry. I'm his mother, after all." She pauses, lips pursed together and forehead wrinkled in thought. "Though, these last few weeks, I've seen him more alive than he's been in a while, and I think that's because of you." She reaches up to my hand resting on the photo album and squeezes it. "You've been so good for him."

I swallow down the lump in my throat. If only she knew the truth. No wonder Zach was concerned about lying to his family. There's no way I want to hurt this kind, sincere woman. But maybe I wouldn't have to.

"He's been good for me, too."

She smiles. Feet clomp down the stairs and we both turn to see Zach pulling a shirt down over his damp hair. My breath catches at the sight of his washboard stomach. There's a chuckle next to me, and I realize I've been caught.

"What's going on here?" Zach asks, approaching the table.

His eyes dart past my head, and he groans.

"Mom, no. You talk about wanting me to find a nice woman and then you try to scare her away with photos of my bum."

He's definitely wrong there. I didn't mind seeing his baby backside at all. In fact, I wouldn't mind seeing the updated version as well. Almost like he's reading my mind, he turns and walks over to a cabinet for a glass. My eyes follow him, noticing just how well his jeans fit him.

"He's still got a cute one, huh?" Elaine whispers and my eyes widen in horror.

I've just been ogling Zach with his mom right here. Heat rises to my face and I swivel back to the album, closing the cover.

"It's okay, dear," Elaine says, trying to temper her amused smile. "You're dating, after all. It's a good thing to be attracted to one another."

My eyes dart over to Zach, hoping against hope he didn't just hear her. The glass of water is halfway to his mouth, but he's frozen like a statue, his eyes darting between me and his mom. Oh, no. I need a distraction. Fast. Unfortunately, my brain is still partially occupied by the possibility he's attracted to me like I am him. Does his mom know something I don't?

"Well," Elaine says, standing. "I'll leave you lovebirds alone. It was nice to put a face to a name, Katie. Don't be a stranger."

She heads to the door, patting Zach on the shoulder as she passes him. And then it's just the two of us. Alone. With her words still floating between us. Zach takes a long drink of water.

"So..." he says, breaking the awkward silence. "That was my mom. She likes to stir up trouble."

I smile. "She's sweet."

There's a knock at the door, and then it swings open.

"Sorry to interrupt again," Elaine says, "but I completely forgot the reason I came over."

"Oh, I think you embarrassed me enough, thanks," Zach says with a teasing smile.

She swats away his complaint. "You love it." She turns to me. "Katie, I know you're heading back to your hotel soon, but I wanted to invite you to come to supper tonight."

"Mom," Zach says, "Katie's very busy. I'm sure she has a lot to catch up on."

He's not wrong, but I'm not quite ready to leave this little cocoon of warmth and kindness. I've really missed genuine connection with others. "I'd love to, Mrs. Worthy, thanks."

Zach coughs. "It's Fontaine, actually. She kept her maiden name."

Elaine tsks him. "Zach, don't be rude. Call me Elaine, honey. I'll see you for supper."

She shuts the door behind her, and Zach rubs his forehead.

"Do you not want me to go?" I try and fail to keep the hurt from my voice.

It takes three strides for him to reach my side and he stops just at the edge of my bubble, his hands fisting and releasing, like he wants to reach out and touch me but is holding back.

"No, that's not it. Mom just failed to mention that dinner at her house means you'll also be eating with her three very nosy tenants. I'm not sure you want the kind of scrutiny they'll give you."

"I can handle it. Why don't you tell me who I'm going to meet so I can be prepared?"

He gently takes my hand and leads me over to the couch. The contact makes my heart spike and part of me hopes he doesn't let go once we sit down.

"There's Jonah, the marine biologist you met at the aquarium. As you know, he's a big fan, so he might ask you a lot of questions about your work. Or Hollywood in general. He's into all that."

I remember him. A little eager, but no worse than any other fan. "Okay, who else?"

"Nora." His brow furrows in thought. "You may have seen her, actually. She works the front desk at your hotel."

"My assistant checked us in when we arrived, so there's a good chance we haven't met."

"The last person is Will. I believe you've already met him as well. He works at Bliss, so he's used to hanging around fancy people."

I quirk an eyebrow, amused at his phrasing. "*Fancy* people, huh? Do I look fancy to you?"

I'm wearing a pair of baggy sweatpants along with one of Zach's hoodies. It's so soft on the inside. I'm not planning to give it back unless he asks for it. Especially because it smells like him.

His eyes roam my body, and I warm at his appreciative perusal.

He shrugs. "For all I know, those sweatpants could have cost five hundred dollars."

I scoff. "Who would pay that much for lounge wear?"

"Not me, but that's mainly because I can't afford to."

Is he jealous of my money? If he's short on funds, why didn't he accept my offer to pay him to be my boyfriend? Oh right, the whole *Pretty Woman* thing. Does that mean I need to ride up in a white limo to prove my love is real? Whoa, now. No one said anything about love.

"Okay, truthfully I *can* afford to," he says, distracting me from my thoughts. "I just prefer to spend my money on other things like really good food."

My stomach grumbles from the memory of the shrimp and grits I had last week. Zach smirks.

"Do you need a snack? You definitely want to go hungry to Mom's, but a little something won't hurt."

"I could eat something. Do you have an apple?"

He releases my hand and stands. I immediately miss the feel of our fingers intertwined. "Give me a couple of minutes. I'll bring something to you."

While he's occupied in the kitchen, I sneak over to the table and grab the photo album his mom left behind. I flip through his elementary days, noting that he was a cute kid. Not a stunner like he is now, though. Even in high school, he was still growing into his body. And boy, was he right about the acne. I probably would have overlooked him if we were in school together.

"Did you go to your ten-year high school reunion, Zachary...Fontaine?"

He turns away from the cabinet, his eyes dropping to the album in my lap. He shakes his head, but he's smiling.

"Not my middle name, but good guess. Yes, I did."

"I bet your female classmates were beside themselves that they let you get away."

He grins. "Are you saying I'm a catch?"

I give him a wink. "Maybe."

His smile grows. "There may have been one or two who gave me their number."

A flush of outrage rises inside my chest. There were people hitting on my man? *Relax, Kat. This was years ago. Plus, he's not your man.*

I drop my gaze back to the pictures, not wanting Zach to see the emotions on my face. I flip a few more pages until I see him in a green graduation cap and gown.

"What was the name of your high school?"

"Bishop England. What was yours?"

"I had a tutor because I was working full-time by then."

He turns. "Does that mean you didn't go to college?"

I shake my head. "Not all careers need formal education."

He nods, then turns back to the counter, picks up a tray and brings it over to the couch, setting it on the ottoman. There's an assortment of crackers, cheeses, and apple slices. My stomach growls in response, and I'm not sure if it's because of the food or the delicious man presenting it.

"This should hold us over, don't you think?"

He grins down at me, his eyes sparkling, and my heart feels like it's perched on a ledge. I smile back, but internally I'm panicking as I feel myself beginning to tip over the edge.

CHAPTER TWENTY-THREE
Zach

Even though Katie seems fine about having dinner with my mom and her tenants, I'm freaking out a little. Are they going to spend the whole evening teasing me and telling Katie all my embarrassing stories? Though Mom's already showed her the scrapbook she's made of my life. What could be worse than that?

I don't even know why I'm worried about this. Most likely they're going to ask Katie all kinds of questions about acting and people she knows. It's what normal people do. Next to her, who cares about me?

We step into the house and my stomach gurgles when I smell the scent of Old Bay seasoning in the air. I lead her to the dining room, noticing her head swiveling to take in the interior. It can really be a shock to see how updated the interiors are on historic homes. There are tons of rules and regulations about the exterior of historic homes, but the interiors can be as modern as the owner desires. Our family kept most of the architectural integrity with its floor-to-ceiling windows, ornamental framing, detailed fireplace mantels, and heirloom furnishings to make you feel like you've traveled back in time. It barely even registers to me now, but always makes guests stop and stare. Which is exactly what Katie has done.

"What do you think?"

She turns to meet my gaze.

"I feel like I'm walking through some historical figure's house."

"It's really just this front room and the dining room that seem museum-like. The rest of the house has more modern touches."

I grab her hand and pull her into the kitchen, where Mom has several large bowls overflowing with Low Country Boil. She hands one to each of us, which we carry into the dining room. Mom follows behind with cornbread. There are already empty bowls and condiments on the table. I pull out the chair next to Mom for Katie to sit in, and then take the place next to her. Mom rings the bell and soon there are people clomping down the stairs.

"Do I smell Low Country Boil?" Will asks, before entering the room and freezing when he sees Katie. Nora, who's right behind him, slams into the back of him.

"Hey, man. Uncoo—" Her mouth drops open. "No way."

"What's the holdup?" Jonah asks from behind, blocked from entering the room.

Will and Nora step to the side to let Jonah in. He walks to the table and sits down at the end next to me. He smiles at Mom and only pauses momentarily on Katie's face before grabbing his napkin and tucking it into his lap.

"Hey Kat. Good to see you again."

Now it's my jaw that hits the floor. Why is Jonah not as fazed as the rest of them? Whatever. It's probably better this way. The other two sit down at the table across from me, trying and failing not to stare at Katie.

"Hi, Jonah," she says, then points across at Will. "You're the bartender at Bliss, right?"

He straightens up, nodding emphatically. "I was in your apple cider mimosa photos."

She nods. "You were a great sport. Thanks for your help."

He preens like a proud peacock. "You know, I'm serious about wanting to be in the movie. If there are any crowd scenes or bit parts, please put in a good word for me."

"Everything has already been cast," she says. Will deflates in his seat. "But if something comes open, I'll definitely keep you in mind."

"Yeah, I get it," he says.

Okay, so I thought things might get awkward, but I hadn't imagined it would be because Will asked for a job before we've even taken a bite.

"Alright everyone," Mom says. "We should dig in before everything gets cold, but first I need someone to bless the food. Whose turn is it?"

Jonah raises his hand. "Mine."

He prays, and then we pass the food. I pile my plate up with the corn, red potatoes, sausage, and shrimp. Katie observes me before taking an ear of corn, two potatoes, and a few pieces of kielbasa. I lean over and whisper in her ear. "Are you not very hungry?"

"Starving," she whispers back, "but after the sushi incident, I'm a little wary of seafood."

I press my lips together in order to keep a straight face. "Understandable, but I can promise you all of this is well cooked and fresh out of the pot, so you should be fine."

I peel a shrimp and offer it to her. She hesitates, then shakes her head. I shrug, dip it in cocktail sauce, and pop it in my mouth.

Jonah passes me the cornbread. I take a piece and hand the dish off to Katie, who takes one as well. I slather mine in butter and honey, eating half of it in one bite. I sure missed Mom's cooking when I lived in Asheville.

Defying my expectations, conversation flows smoothly as everyone shares bits of their day. Jonah spent the day preparing one of their sea turtles to be released back into the ocean. Often the turtles are so injured they spend the remainder of their lives at the aquarium, but some are able to return to the wild. Will slept most of the day in preparation for his shift at the club tonight. Nora has a new big wig client staying at the Marion Fox.

"In fact, they're staying in the suite next to yours," she tells Katie.

"Who is it?" Katie asks.

I can tell she's dying to share, but her professionalism wins out.

"Unfortunately, I can't say. We try to keep our clients' privacy. I'm sorry the reporters found you at our place. We have a back entrance you could use if you don't want to be bothered."

She looks at me briefly. "That would have been good to know when I was sick, but I'll keep that in mind for the rest of my stay, thanks."

Did she not like staying with me these past few days? Maybe she prefers to be left alone when she's not feeling well. I thought I'd given her plenty of privacy, but maybe she's just been a good sport and watched movies with me so I'll continue to go along with this whole charade. The idea that she's humoring me causes my gut to clench. The food on my plate doesn't look quite so appetizing now, but I force it down. Can't waste good food just because I'm an idiot for thinking there might actually have been something real going on between us.

I'm quiet for the rest of dinner, seeing the past week's activities in a whole new light. Just because it feels like we have a connection doesn't mean it's true. Katie's an actor, for goodness' sake. And a good one, too. This is just an arrangement. That's all it will ever be. Even if I'd really like it to be more.

I help clear the table with Mom while Katie stays at the table with everyone else.

"She seems like a genuinely nice person," Mom says when we're alone in the kitchen. "I have to admit, I was a little worried about my son dating a movie star. Not only is your relationship considered public consumption when I know how private you are, but if you two don't work out, it'll be national news."

I smile wryly. "I doubt David Muir would report on our breakup."

She clucks her tongue. "You know what I mean."

"You don't have to worry about me, Mom. I'll be just fine, no matter what happens."

She squeezes my arm. "I know, honey. It's just been so long since I've seen you look at a woman the way you look at her, and I can tell you're in this pretty deep already. But I'm not too worried because she looks at you the same way."

I want to believe her words. My heart leaps at the thought that it could be true. But Mom doesn't know what I know, and Katie is very believable in the roles she plays. Sure, it's seemed like she's genuinely warmed up to me, but I'm scared that if I tell her how I feel, she'll laugh in my face. Who am I that someone like her would truly want to be in a relationship with me? A nobody, that's who.

I head back to the dining room, where Katie and the others are chatting. "You ready to go?"

She smiles at me. "Yes. I'm sure you're ready to get me out of your hair."

If only she knew.

The drive back to the hotel is quiet. I'm not sure what's got Katie lost in thought, but I doubt she's thinking about how lonely my house is going to feel without her in it. I offer to park around back, but she wants to make an entrance.

After finding a spot out front, I grab her bag from the bed of my truck and pull up the handle. I motion for her to lead the way, but she grabs my free hand instead, cuddling up against my arm and planting a kiss on my cheek. A flash goes off somewhere nearby. We're being watched. I smile down at her, allowing my real feelings for her to show through.

She tugs my hand gently and we walk into the hotel, through the lobby, and to the elevator. The doors shut, and she releases my hand. We disembark on the top floor and I follow her down the hall to her room. She removes a room key from her pocket and swipes it at the door. It flashes green, and she pushes it open, stopping just inside with a loud gasp.

I push through the door behind her, my heart rate spiking when I see clothes strewn around the room, drawers pulled onto the floor, and papers scattered every which way. Wrapping my arm around her waist, I tug her back through the door.

"Stay here," I say, then step back inside and shut the door, leaving her alone in the hallway. I walk cautiously through the entire area, making sure no one is here. When I'm confident it's empty, I open the door again. Katie has slid down the wall and has her arms wrapped around her legs, shaking.

I drop to my knees and pull her to me, kissing the top of her head.

"I'm going to call Nora right quick."

My arms loosen around her, but she reaches out and pulls me hard against her. "Don't leave me."

My heart is in my throat, worry constricting my stomach. "I won't."

Keeping one arm around Katie, I fumble for my phone, then call Nora on speaker.

"It looks like someone broke into Katie's room. No one's here now, but could you call the police or someone at the hotel?"

"I'm on it. I'll be there shortly."

Now that the wheels are in motion, I sit down on the floor, put my back to the wall, and pull Katie onto my lap. She curls into me, obviously shaken. Not sure of what else to do, I run a hand over her hair and down her back, whispering reassuring things while my mind spirals, wondering what might have happened if she had been here during the break-in. My hold tightens on her and I whisper a quick prayer of thanks for food poisoning.

CHAPTER TWENTY-FOUR

Kat

The police have done a thorough sweep of the room, asking me to point out things that are out of place so they can capture some fingerprints. They took mine, Zach's, and Lila's so they can zero in on foreign prints. They asked me if anything had been taken. All my stuff is accounted for, which makes me wonder what they wanted. Were they just after me? My veins turn to ice at the thought.

I'm trying really hard not to be freaked out that some crazed person—or persons, the thought stealing my breath—broke into my room and rifled through my things. How did they even get in? The door shows no sign of forced entry, and my room is on the twelfth floor, so they didn't come in the windows. How am I going to stay here without worrying about being attacked while I sleep? Maybe if Lila moved in? No, I can't risk her being in danger, too.

The officer who took my statement lets me know I can clean up and tells me to let her know if I find something missing later on. Lila, who's been hovering nearby with Zach, tells her she'll be in touch as needed.

I give her a grateful smile. When all this is over, I'm giving her a raise and a vacation. It's reassuring how calm and confident she is in a crisis.

"You can't stay here," Zach says. "Let's gather up your things and I'll take you back to my place."

A wave of relief washes over me. I never would have asked to impose on him any more than I already have, but I also couldn't think of any other options. "Are you sure?"

He looks at me like I'm not quite right in the head. "I won't take 'no' for an answer. I'm sorry to be bossy, Katie, but your safety is the most important thing right now. I wouldn't be able to sleep if you were still here after this."

"Again, Ms. Sonnett," the hotel manager says. He's been hovering just outside the door since the police arrived. "I am so sorry. We've given the security tapes to the police, who I'm sure will catch whoever did this. We are comping your stay and can assure you we will staff security outside your door twenty-four hours a day if you wish to remain here."

I'm sure he's terrified of how this incident might affect the hotel. It's not his fault, and I certainly won't say anything bad about the hotel. At this point, there's no proof they could have prevented it. Crime happens. But given a choice between having strangers posted outside my door and cozying up with Zach on his couch, there's no contest. He makes me feel safe even if logically I'd probably be more protected here.

"I appreciate your offer, but I don't think I could stay in this room after seeing it like this. But maybe Lila would feel better with someone outside her door?"

Zach leans into me, causing me to shiver when I feel his breath puff against my ear. "Would Lila like to come with us?" he asks.

I'm touched by his concern, but selfishly hesitant because I was kind of excited about the prospect of spending more time alone with him. His house only has two bedrooms. I bet he'd sleep on the couch and give her his room. I can't let him inconvenience himself so much for me. "I don't want you to have to sleep on the couch."

He shakes his head. "My mom has a free room right now. Lila could stay in the main house if she wants."

Oh. Well, that would work out quite well. I wouldn't worry about her, plus I'd still get time alone with Zach. A twinge of guilt for my self-absorbed thoughts twists my stomach as I realize how much I want to hang out with him.

"I'll ask."

Lila's putting some of my clothes in a suitcase. I hadn't even realized she'd started packing for me. I walk over to where she is and place a hand over hers to stop her.

"You don't have to do that, but thanks."

She pulls me into a hug. "I'm so sorry about this. I feel better knowing you won't be staying here."

Her tight embrace warms me. I wonder if we'd be real friends if our professional relationship ended. Not that I'm anxious to get rid of her. I pull away after a bit.

"About that. I don't feel comfortable with you staying here, either. Zach's mom has a spare room in her house you could use. What do you think?"

She bites her lip, thinking. "I mean, it would probably be ideal to be close to wherever you are. How far is Zach from his mom?"

I smile. "He lives in the carriage house on her property, so about thirty feet away."

She laughs. "Yeah, I think that'll work. Thanks."

Once we're all packed, Zach pulls his truck around to the back entrance and we load everything up. There's no way I want to see reporters right now. Especially not if they realize the police were here because of me. I just want to try to forget the violation of my privacy and hope the video reveals the culprit so they can be apprehended. That's the only way I'll truly have peace of mind. And maybe an answer for why they broke in.

When we get to Zach's place, he carries Lila's luggage into the main house, promising to be back for mine soon. Not wanting to feel like someone who needs to be rescued, I drag my luggage into the carriage house and up to the guest room. The bed is rumpled from when I threw the duvet cover over the sheets this morning and the sight almost makes me feel like I'm coming home. The side table still contains the bud vase with a magnolia blossom, cut from one of the trees out front. I lean in and smell the fragrant flower.

I've gotten most of my clothes put away when I hear the front door open. My pulse picks up at the sound of footsteps on the stairs. Zach knocks at the half-open door, then pushes it open.

"Guess you wanted to get unpacked," he says. "Sorry I took so long. Mom had to give Lila a tour and then insisted on fixing us some food. She says it'll help us feel better. I've got it set up down in the kitchen."

I'm not really hungry, but I'm still wired from the evening, so maybe a little food will help me settle and get ready for bed. I don't have to be on set tomorrow until ten, but if I can't manage to get any sleep, it won't bode well for my performance. I gasp.

Zach crosses the room to me in an instant, reaching for my hand, his face a mask of concern. "What's wrong?"

I squeeze his fingers, allowing the touch to center me. I chuckle, shaking my head. "Sorry for scaring you. I just remembered I need to run my lines for tomorrow." The gasp may have been a bit dramatic, but I'm still a little on edge from the scene at the hotel.

His alert posture relaxes, and he smiles. "I can help. We can do it while we have a snack."

Most of the time, my running lines involves me recording the other parts and then using them as my cues. It would be nice to have a real person to look at and feed off of. "Sure, that would be great."

It only takes a minute to find my script, and then we head to the kitchen. There's a variety of sliced fruit, almonds and pistachios, and a few squares of dark chocolate. My stomach rumbles at the sight. Zach slides out a chair and helps me get situated, then makes me a cup of tea before joining me at the table.

"This looks great."

He grins. "Mom thinks food can fix anything. She said to tell you she's sorry about what happened and that you and Lila are welcome to stay as long as you want."

The hospitality on display is nearly overwhelming. I can't believe Zach's mom is so willing to help people she barely knows. But then I remember she thinks I'm dating her son. Of course, she'd be kind to his girlfriend and her friends. I hate that I'm lying to such a compassionate woman. I can see where Zach gets his kindness from. My heart wrenches at the thought that I'm going to hurt two amazing people when this ends.

I mentally shake my head. Zach will be fine. He knows the deal and is just playing a part. Any affection I've received from him has just been because of our arrangement, not out of any genuine feelings for me. What a depressing thought. Of course, this is what I asked for. I can't change the terms now even if I am struggling to tell the difference between real and pretend. It wouldn't be fair to Zach. Plus, I'm an actor. If I can pretend to care for someone, I should just as easily be able to pretend I don't. Ugh. Maybe it's actually me who will be hurt when this is over.

Zach and I run lines until my eyes are heavy and I can barely keep my head from hitting the table. He's surprisingly good, even modulating his voice for the different characters. It's a scene where my character shows up to a party and runs into her high school nemesis. I'm supposed to be angry, but it's a bit of a struggle to direct wrath toward Zach. He's just so sweet. There's no way someone would ever be mad at him.

Zach helps me up the stairs because I'm stumbling a bit. The adrenaline that was coursing through my body earlier has left me feeling drained. Once we reach the bedroom, I drop straight onto the bed, my eyes closed before my head even hits the pillow. Zach pulls the covers up around me and there's a whisper of a kiss on my temple before my mind lapses into nothingness.

I scream, feeling the weight of something on my chest. The room is dark and I have no idea where I am. I wrestle with the covers until I'm free, realizing it was just the duvet.

The bedroom door swings open, and then a hand wraps around my wrist. I fill my lungs with air to yell for help.

"Katie, what's wrong?"

I sag at Zach's voice, realizing I must have been having a nightmare. My heart feels like it's going to beat out of my chest. I grab Zach's arm and pull him onto the bed with me. He wraps his arms around me, pulling me to him. I snuggle into his bare chest, his woodsy scent already clearing away some of the terror in my mind.

As my breathing slows, I realize I can feel his heart beating against my cheek. It seems faster than normal. I focus on taking a few more deep breaths, then gently push against his chest to put a little space between us. It's too dark to see his face, but I imagine there's a divot between his eyebrows telegraphing his concern.

"I'm okay. Just had a bad dream."

"Was it about tonight?"

I nod, though he probably can't see it. The nightmare is already fading, though my mind is now on high alert.

"Maybe? It's already fuzzy. But I don't know if I'll be able to go back to sleep."

"You need sleep for tomorrow. Would it help if we talk for a bit?"

I'm touched that he's offering to keep me company. He's been doing that a lot lately. It occurs to me he hasn't been to his store in nearly a week. Am I going to be the reason his business goes under? There's got to be something I can do to repay Zach for all his kindness. Maybe I'll ask Lila tomorrow for her ideas. She's great at that kind of stuff.

"Sure. What should we talk about?"

While I wait for him to respond, I realize his arms are still draped loosely around me. I'm tempted to snuggle in close again, but that would be weird. I just told myself I have to pretend he doesn't affect me so he won't find out I've really fallen for him. I can't now pretend like we're really a couple, no matter how much I may want to. Even if my hand is still on his chest, appreciating its muscular planes.

"What is the movie you're making about?"

"It's a rom-com about two people who hated each other in high school but get teamed up for a race event and have to put aside their issues if they have any hopes of winning."

"And let me guess," Zach says, humor in his tone, "they end up falling in love."

I scoff. "Well, of course. Otherwise it wouldn't be a rom-com."

"What do you like so much about those types of movies that you've made so many of them?"

This is a question I've been asked a lot while doing publicity. Without thinking, I give him my standard reply.

"It's nice knowing that, regardless of whatever challenges the people face or crazy situations they find themselves in, by the end, they will be happy and together. I like the thought of having someone by your side through thick and thin. You could even say I'm a hopeful romantic."

Usually after this, I'm asked about my personal life, but Zach already knows that information.

"Have you thought about trying a different role? Maybe see how you'd fare at a serious part?"

"Are you reading my mind? I've been trying to get my agent to set me up for auditions, but he thinks I'll make more money staying in my lane."

He's quiet for a minute. "Is money the main reason you're an actor?"

I shake my head before realizing he probably can't see me. "No. I like the challenge of embodying different people. It's kind of like trying on different jobs, seeing what life might be like as a small business owner, author, dog-walker, chef, athletic trainer, or whatever the role calls for. I really want to be challenged, even if it ends up being a supporting role that pays less than my rom-com leads."

"Then you should do it. Doesn't your agent work for you?"

His words echo Lila's. Why am I letting Rick dictate my career? His focus is money. Mine is personal fulfillment. Sometimes they overlap, but if they don't, shouldn't my goals be what direct my time and attention?

The conversation veers into other topics including favorite flavor of ice cream (mine is rainbow sherbet which Zach claims is technically not ice cream, his is cookies and cream), first kiss (Zach's was Laura in sixth grade, mine was Todd in seventh and included way too much tongue, yuck), and pets (I've never had one, Zach had a dog named Barkley who died when he was seventeen). I try again to guess his middle name, coming up empty. I make him promise to tell me if I don't guess it before I finish filming. Eventually, there's a lull in our conversation and I stare into Zach's eyes. I've adjusted to the low light in the room, so I catch his gaze flicker down to my mouth. My stomach clenches at the flare of desire in his eyes. I'm so tired of resisting my feelings for him. The night's events have made me vulnerable and aware that life is fleeting, so I give in.

I lean forward, my eyes closing when my lips find his. His arm tightens around my waist, drawing me closer. My hand slides up his chest to cradle his jaw, enjoying the prickle of his beard on my skin. He turns me onto my back, raising himself up with his other arm to keep his full weight off of me, his lips never leaving mine. My hand slides down to his shoulder, enjoying the feel of his muscles. He breaks the kiss, only to press his lips along the curve of my jaw and down my neck. His mouth on my skin elicits a soft moan that makes him growl in response. He blazes a trail of fervent kisses back up to my mouth. I wrap my arms around his neck, needing to be closer. After a few luxurious minutes wrapped up in each other's arms, he pulls back. His forehead drops onto the pillow beside me, his breathing as ragged as mine. He rolls onto his back, but his arm is still curled around my waist and he pulls me with him until I'm laying half on top of him, my head on his chest.

"We should probably try to sleep," he says, voice husky.

As amped up as I am, that seems impossible. It feels like live currents of energy are zinging every which way underneath my skin, traveling the full path of my nervous system. Absently, my finger traces a pattern on his chest. It takes me a minute to realize I'm drawing hearts.

He presses a kiss to the crown of my head. His free hand rests on his stomach, and I reach over to twine our fingers together. He lets me, giving me a gentle squeeze with the arm around my waist. I shut my eyes, but my brain is focused on the fact that we definitely just crossed a line with our late night kissing. None of that was for show and there's no doubt we were both very into it. I want to know what this means for our relationship, but am too emotionally wiped to broach the subject. I finally drift off to sleep.

When I wake the next morning, my cheek is resting against firm, smooth skin. Keeping my eyes closed, I do a body scan, noting the arm wrapped around my waist and my arm casually draped across a bare stomach. Guess that dream I had about snuggling up with a hot lifeguard on a beach towel was a reflection of real life. And that fiery makeout session also definitely happened. My heart picks up speed just thinking about it.

I lift my head off his chest. Zach's eyes are open, staring up at the ceiling.

"Good morning," I say. "Did you sleep?"

He turns his head and meets my gaze, his face blank. My stomach twists. He isn't regretting last night, is he? Because I certainly wouldn't mind a repeat if he's up for it.

"A little. You?"

I nod. "What time is it?"

"A little after eight. If you want to shower, I'll make breakfast."

My chest tightens. What would it be like to wake up next to him every day and have him make me breakfast before I go to work?

"A shower and food does sound great. But I usually just eat a banana or some yogurt before filming. They normally have a spread I pick from while I'm there."

He inches away from me and I realize he's trying to get out from under my weight. I slide over on the bed, freeing him, and he stands up. His hair has more curl than normal and is a little messy, but something about his just awake look is very appealing to me. I can't help but appreciate his body. Oh, my. He's wearing gray sweats again. They're more tapered than the ones he wore at my house. More like joggers. Whatever they are, he is so hot right now. When I realize I'm practically leering at him, I jump out of bed and rush to the bathroom, shutting the door firmly behind me. My cheeks are hot and I place my hands over them, staring at myself in the mirror. We should talk about last night, but what if he was just going along with it because he wanted to comfort me after what happened at the hotel? He may have seemed like an eager participant, but I definitely started it. If I hadn't, would he have initiated?

Doubts are filling my head, crowding out the courage I felt mere minutes before. I know I should just talk to him. It's the only way to know anything for sure. While I prepare for the day, I try to psych myself back up to talk about last night.

When I get downstairs, Lila and Zach are sitting at the table. Lila's got a plate of scrambled eggs and toast in front of her. Jealousy blooms in my chest at the realization that Zach made her breakfast. I guess it wasn't anything special that he offered to make some for me. He was just being thoughtful. I walk over to join them, noticing there's a banana and several small containers of yogurt at an empty seat.

"Hey," Lila says. "The car should be here for us in about fifteen minutes."

"I wasn't sure if you liked plain or flavored yogurt," Zach says, "so I got a few options for you."

I smile to cover my disappointment at Lila's presence and force myself to eat the banana. "I'm not very hungry this morning, but thank you."

I head upstairs to brush my teeth and grab my shoes. The sound of laughter trickles up the stairs and I feel left out. I know there's no reason to feel envious that Zach and Lila are enjoying one another's company, but I'm feeling a little territorial today. There's no way Zach would kiss the daylights out of someone just because he's nice. But I was a damsel in distress and he's been so good at rescuing me. What if that's all it was for him? My confidence that last night meant something to him has evaporated. Is it all in my head? I can't ask him now while Lila's here, but I dread having to sit in uncertainty all day while I wait to find out if he has real feelings for me. Now I remember one of the reasons I don't date. So much emotional turmoil.

CHAPTER TWENTY-FIVE
Kat

The day's filming is in full swing. Grady and I have fun pretending to hate each other at a family picnic. The food created for the scene is amazing. The script had me taking a few bites of several things and I wasn't acting when I raved about the rice dish. A local restaurant made the food and is now on my list of places to try while I'm here. I wonder if Zach has been to it.

As if thinking of him has conjured him into existence, I see someone who looks like him across the set with Lila. When she points at me and they both wave, I realize it actually is Zach. What's he doing here? My heart pounds at his nearness. We really need to have that talk. I can't take much more of this emotional limbo.

The director is ready for the next scene, so I tamp down my emotions and find my mark. After a quick fine-tuning from make-up, I scowl at Grady while talking furtively with the actor who's playing my sister. We're supposed to be identical twins and makeup has done an amazing job of turning the raven haired actress into a believable carbon copy of me with a wig, blue contacts, and a little contouring. If I didn't know any better, I'd think I really do have a sister.

We shoot the scene a couple more times with a few tweaks until the director is satisfied. With my part done, I sit back and watch Grady do his thing. He's very expressive and gets into character in a way that makes me forget who he actually is. I'd love to talk to him about his process and how he prepares for his roles.

A warm hand on my shoulder startles me, but I relax when I see Zach's easy smile.

"What are you doing here?"

He drops his hand. "Lila invited me. She thought I might like to see you at work. And I must say, you're quite impressive. It's like you transformed into a whole different person."

My heart swells from his praise, though I feel a little guilty I didn't think to invite him to set. I'm too used to being single, I guess.

He leans in closer. "I hope you don't mind that I'm here. I can leave if I'm a distraction."

I mean, I suppose he might be a bit of a distraction with his warm smile and addictive woodsy scent, but nothing that will keep me from doing my job. I'm a professional. Besides, I've never had someone besides my parents come see me on set before, and they haven't watched me work since I was a teenager. Probably because they have jobs and can't just drop everything to fly to wherever I am at a moment's notice. Speaking of which...

"Shouldn't you be at the store?"

He frowns. "If you want me to leave, you can just say so."

He takes a step away from me, and I reach out and grab his hand.

"No! It's not that. I'm glad you're here." I smile, hoping to convey my pleasure. "It's just that you've been spending so much time with me lately. I'm worried about your business."

Zach shrugs, his mouth in a straight line. "It's fine." He turns away to face the scene before us. The director is talking to the actors in preparation for another take. "What's happening here? It looks like a party."

He's changing the subject, but I don't want to pry. "It's the scene where my character runs into her nemesis for the first time."

"Shouldn't you have already filmed this scene? You've been filming for several months."

It's hard to believe I've already been here that long. Time sure has passed quickly since I've started hanging out with Zach. And my time in Charleston is going to come to an end far too soon, I fear. "We don't film the movie in order. The director decides what we film when. There are a lot of outdoor scenes, so we're filming them when the weather is projected to be nice. Rainy days mean inside shooting. Though there is a rainy scene in the movie, but we'll use machines to control the timing and rain consistency."

He shakes his head. "You work in a strange industry."

I laugh. "Yeah, it is kind of silly."

The director calls cut. Grady catches my eye, says something to the actor next to him, then walks over.

"Hey, Kat. The director thinks we can get the wedding scene shot today since we're already here and ahead of schedule. You cool with that?"

I'd thought we were done, but I don't mind knocking out as much as we can. Plus, I get to wear the gorgeous dress that's been hanging in my trailer since we started filming. It's already been fitted to me so I know how awesome I look in it. I cast a furtive glance at Zach. What would he think of seeing me in a wedding dress?

"Yeah, that's fine. I'd like you to meet my boyfriend, Zach. Zach, this is Grady, my wonderful co-star."

They shake hands and I realize it's good Zach came by. Him visiting the set makes our relationship look even more believable. And now I'm wishing he was here just because he wanted to see me again even though we were at his house together only a few hours ago.

"You and Kat should come out with us tonight after we wrap," Grady says. "Someone found a restaurant with a back room we can hide out in. It's called Bronze Dahlia. The food's supposed to be amazing."

Zach looks over at me and shrugs, like he's okay with whatever. I have been thinking I should attempt to connect with people in the business. Surely not everyone is a jerk.

"That sounds fun, thanks."

Grady beams like he really wanted me to accept his invitation.

"Excellent. My wife will be there and I know she'll enjoy having someone who's not in the business to talk to." He looks at Zach. "Sometimes we can get a little wrapped up in shop talk."

"I get it," Zach says. "Passion is hard to contain. I know I can get a little overzealous when someone asks me about wood grains."

Grady's forehead creases like Zach's speaking a foreign language he doesn't understand, but then grins. "Passion, exactly." He points at him. "This guy gets it. Looking forward to seeing you both."

"Are you really okay going out with a bunch of actors?" I ask Zach when Grady leaves to get ready for the next scene. "We don't have to go. Or I can go alone." I don't really want to show up by myself, but since Zach isn't really my boyfriend, I don't want to force him into an awkward social event.

He nods. "I haven't been to Bronze Dahlia in a while. They have great pimento cheese."

"I hate to interrupt," Lila says, "but Kat needs to get over to wardrobe to prep for the next scene."

"Oh, yeah. Sorry. You're welcome to stay if you want."

He looks around. "I think I'll go. A new commission came in today and I should get started on it."

I'm glad to hear he's got work coming in, but am disappointed he'll miss me in the gorgeous white dress. We really haven't talked a lot about his business, but he doesn't seem to want to talk about it.

"Okay. I'll see you at the house then, I suppose."

He nods, then leans forward and gives me a quick peck on the lips. "Can't wait."

My eyes follow his exit. When I stand up and turn to Lila, she's smirking at me. "Oooh, you've got it bad, girl."

I frown. "What are you talking about?"

She laughs. "You practically undressed him with your eyes just now. Not that I blame you, of course. If I was dating someone like that, I'd never let him out of my sight."

There's an odd mix of possessiveness and satisfaction swirling inside. It feels good to have Lila's approval, but, since he's not really my guy, I don't like the reminder that he's not likely to be single for long after our arrangement ends. The thought of letting him go tugs at my heart a little, but I can't just hold on to him because I want to. That's not fair to him. Which is why we need to talk. Maybe there will be time before we head to the restaurant this evening.

The wedding scene is a blur. I spend a moment fantasizing about what it'd be like to wear a white dress for real and have the man of my dreams standing down at the other end, eagerly awaiting my arrival. Grady makes an excellent groom, but I keep swapping out his face for Zach's, trying to imagine what that experience would be like. The thought helps me find the emotions needed for the scene. After our tearful vows, we end the scene with a kiss.

Movie kisses are always weird. Everyone is watching you. The director is analyzing how it looks on the screen. We do several takes with varying camera angles before she's satisfied. It is nothing like my kisses with Zach. Even the peck he gave me earlier possessed more emotion than this one.

Back in my dressing room, I've changed back into comfy clothes and am removing the last of my makeup when Rick marches in. I haven't laid eyes on him since my Atlanta trip and I can't say I've missed his face.

I'd have thought he'd come to see me after Lila called to tell him what happened, but he never showed.

"There she is, the woman of the hour!"

I look at him through the mirror. "What are you talking about?"

"You're all over the news. All everyone is talking about right now is the break-in. You'll have to be sure to mention how violated you feel at the premiere this weekend. Everyone will eat it up and I bet your movie will soar to number one in no time."

I scowl. "I do feel violated. This isn't some publicity stunt, Rick. Someone broke into my hotel room. And how did the news find out? I haven't told anyone."

He frowns briefly, like he's trying to convey sympathy, but the light in his eyes reveals he's actually pleased by this turn of events. He probably sees a bunch of tiny flashing dollar signs. Has he always been this insensitive?

"It was bound to come out sometime. Since we can't undo it, we might as well capitalize on it."

Yikes. Maybe I should check out a few agents while I'm in Los Angeles.

"Are you taking your boyfriend with you to the premiere?"

I hadn't really thought about it, but it would be fun to show Zach around the area and play host to him for a change. Would he be willing to go? He's been pretty agreeable thus far, but a premiere is a very intense experience that might scare him away. My chest tightens at the thought.

"I haven't asked him yet."

Rick looks down at his phone, typing something. "If he passes, I'll find someone to escort you down the red carpet. We can't have the star show up alone."

I roll my eyes at his comment, like I'm helpless or something. Have I just ignored his rude comments all this time? "I'll find my own date, thank you."

He shrugs. "By the way, there's a new hard seltzer brand looking for a celebrity endorsement. What do you think? It's just a print ad right now, but it might turn into commercials and public appearances if it's successful."

I wrinkle my nose. At least he's asking me for once. Perhaps I'm getting through to him about wanting to set my own schedule. Which makes me wonder if he's budged on another area.

"What's the latest on dramatic roles? I've heard there's a World War II script with a female lead that's already making a buzz."

He doesn't even look up from his phone. "They want to film in the fall, but we're already in talks for your next rom-com and the two will overlap."

"What if I skip this rom-com and go for the drama instead? I can do a rom-com after."

He scowls, but doesn't look up. "The rom-com is a sure thing. If you don't get the drama role, you won't have a back-up project."

"Would it really be that bad to have a break? Besides, who says I won't get the role?"

Rick sighs and tucks his phone into his pocket. He puts a hand on my shoulder. I have to force myself not to shrug it off, already anticipating disagreeing with whatever he's going to say.

"Look, kid. You're a star in the rom-com world. You could make a movie about a woman who falls for a duck and people would flock to it. But no one's going to watch you in a serious role. You don't have the gravitas."

Now I do shrug his hand off. "Maybe I do and you just don't believe in me. Maybe I should find someone who will help me get the roles I want."

He raises his hands in defense. "Now hold up. I didn't say I don't believe in you. If you really want to try drama, I'll find you something, but not this one, okay?"

I cross my arms, dissatisfied with his answer. The posture feels foreign to me and it occurs to me that in all the years we've worked together, I've never really fought him on anything. Sure, I may have voiced some displeasure, but in the end I went along with what he wanted. Now, however, I'm not content to let someone else steer my ship.

"I want to see three potential serious projects by next week."

He narrows his eyes. "Or what?"

He's got me there. I'm not sure what recourse to take. I don't want to burn a bridge I may need to cross later, but I also want him to know this is important to me.

"I may have to reconsider whether our partnership is still serving my interests or if it has reached its conclusion."

Rick must realize I'm serious because his eyes widen slightly. He tilts his head, possibly to consider if I'm serious. I press my lips together and wait. Finally, he nods.

"Fair enough."

He leaves, and I exhale sharply. That was stressful. It's much easier playing strong, brash people than being one in real life.

When I get back to the house, Zach is there, freshly showered in dark jeans and a black button-down shirt with the sleeves rolled up to his elbows. The view of his muscular forearms is quite appealing.

"You look nice," I say.

"Thanks. What time do we need to leave?"

I glance at the clock. "About twenty minutes. Hey, can we talk?"

There's a tiny divot between his eyebrows, but he nods. I sit down on the couch and pat the cushion next to me. He joins me, but leaves a foot of space between us, his posture rigid. It almost feels like he's bracing for a breakup talk. I reach over and grab his hand, trying to put him at ease.

"I have a movie premiere this weekend in California and wondered if you'd be my date."

He leans back against the couch, his posture still rigid. "What do I have to do?"

I don't want to say because I know it's not his thing, but he probably has a general idea.

"You'll wear a tux and walk me down the red carpet. Take a few photos, watch the movie, and spend a little time at an after party. That's all."

He's quiet for a few moments, then nods. "Sure. I've never been to California before. Will there be time to do a little sightseeing?"

I smile, relieved that he's agreeing to this. I may have told Rick I'd find my own date, but there was no one else to ask if Zach said no.

"Of course. We'll fly out Saturday morning, have the premiere in the evening, and then have some fun on Sunday before we fly back."

The smile he gives me makes my heart flutter. I'm so grateful for his willingness to help me out once again. He really is too good to me.

He chuckles. "Jonah is going to faint when he hears about this."

Zach drives us over to the restaurant. I'm nervous about this evening, but am also anxious because we still haven't talked about last night. I was going to ask him after he agreed to go to the premiere with me, but his mom came over to drop off some cookies and chat until we had to go. I've been thinking all day about what I've wanted to say. Part of me wants to admit that I've grown to care for him and am interested in seeing where this goes. Another part is terrified of his rejection and wants to chicken out and pretend it was a mistake. It was most definitely not a mistake to me, but what if he thinks it was? I'm still drumming up the nerve to broach the subject when we reach the Bronze Dahlia.

Zach parks, then turns to me. "Hey, before we go in, I wanted to talk about what happened last night."

My heart stutters. Is he about to tell me he wants this thing to be real? I sure hope so, but I'm not about to blurt that out without some reassurances. I inhale deeply to keep myself steady, then give him a reassuring smile. "What about last night?"

"I'm sorry for kissing you when you were vulnerable. I wanted to comfort you after what happened at the hotel and got a little carried away. You needed support and I let my own desires get in the way of that. It won't happen again. If you change your mind about me going to L.A. with you, I understand."

I'm stunned. He regrets kissing me? That's definitely not good. But wait. He said he gave in to his own desires, so does that mean he does like me, but is simply remorseful because he thinks he was thinking more about what he wanted than what I wanted? Does he not remember I was the one who initiated the kiss? Can he not tell that I've essentially given up on us only fake dating? If anything, I'm pretending I *don't* like him as more than a friend. Perhaps my acting award really was well deserved. Well, this is something we should straighten out right now.

I gather my wits about me, trying to figure out exactly how to reassure Zach and confess my feelings. Aware that I've been silent for too long, I decide I'd better say something.

"I want you to come to L.A. with me. Very much. And I need to tell you that I really li—"

I'm startled by someone pounding on the window near my head. When I look over, Grady is waving and grinning at me. I sigh. For an actor, his timing is less than stellar at the moment. We'll have to finish this conversation later. I wave back, then turn to say something to Zach, but he's already out of the truck and coming around to open my door.

Grady introduces us to his wife, Bex, and the four of us head inside. A few people are already in the room when we arrive. I introduce Zach to Maddie, the woman who plays my twin sister in the movie, and Derek, the tall actor playing Grady's best friend.

"Great name," Zach says, shaking his hand. "I enjoyed your performance in *High Wire*."

Derek smiles. "Thanks, man. That was a fun movie to make. I worked with a circus performer so I could do some of the stunts myself."

It hadn't occurred to me that Zach might recognize someone from work. Derek's a nice guy, so maybe tonight will be fun for Zach. I'm sure it'd help warm him up to the idea of moving out west. Except would he be willing to leave his mom? They're super close. And why wouldn't they be after what they've been through together? It's no use worrying about any of this until we actually have a talk about our feelings.

A bunch of sharable plates are placed on the long table in our private room and everyone picks off of them while we mingle. Someone comes by for drink orders while plates are added and removed. At some point, the savory food disappears and is replaced with fruit and desserts.

I do regular visual checks on Zach throughout the evening to make sure he's doing okay. When I head over to the corner he's occupying with Derek, Grady, and another actor, they're loudly debating the best action movies ever made. Zach pulls me to him in a side hug and places a quick kiss on my cheek, whispering in my ear, "Are you having fun?"

It does something to my heart that he's concerned about me when I was the one who dragged him here. "I am." And I'm telling the truth. Everyone has been so nice tonight. I'm regretting not joining them earlier in our shooting schedule.

"When you're ready to go, give me the signal."

"What kind of signal?" I like the idea of us having secret communication in a group setting.

"How about you tap your chin three times like you're thinking?"

I giggle. Silly, but not too obvious. "Okay, and if you want to get out of here, slide your finger along your beard from chin to ear."

The low chuckle he emits makes my heart flip. "Deal."

"I'm going to go socialize some more."

I place a hand on the back of his neck, then lean in and kiss him on the lips. It's only when I'm halfway across the room that I realize what I've done. Glancing over my shoulder, Zach has reengaged in the men's conversation. I place a hand to my lips, surprised by how natural that felt. I definitely wasn't acting and hope Zach doesn't think it was just for show. Of course, until I tell him otherwise, what else is he supposed to think?

Needing a minute to compose myself, I stop at the table and pop a grape in my mouth. I feel a presence next to me and turn.

"You sure won the boyfriend lottery, Kat," Maddie says. "Not only is he nice, but he's very easy on the eyes. Plus, the way he looks at you from across the room makes *me* swoon."

Instinctively, I look over at Zach. He raises his hand to his face. I think he's going to give the signal, but then he grins, his eyes twinkling with mischief, and scratches his forehead. My lips quirk up, amused at his playfulness. I draw my hand up, closing my hand into a fist except for my index finger. It angles toward my chin before detouring and scratching just beside my nose. He shakes his head, then turns back to the group.

"What was *that* all about?"

I forgot Maddie had been talking to me. My face warms. "Just a little inside joke. Sorry."

"Don't be. You two are adorable."

I'm not sure how to respond, so I turn the conversation to work and what projects she has lined up after we're finished filming here in Charleston.

The party winds down a little while later and I'm a little disappointed neither of us got to use our secret signals, but that just means we actually enjoyed ourselves. We share stories of our conversations and debate the best food offerings on the ride home. I really liked the blue crab fritters while Zach raved about the braised pork belly. The name kept me from trying it even though it just looked like thick bacon. Maybe if we come back to the restaurant sometime, I'll be brave enough to try it.

Back at the house, I disappear into my room to remove my makeup and get into comfy clothes, humming to myself while I complete my evening skin routine. When I finish, I remember we need to finish our conversation from earlier, but Zach's bedroom door is shut. Perhaps all the socializing wore him out. Maybe it's better not to make a big deal out of things and just let them progress naturally. I know I'm chickening out, but tonight was really nice and I don't want to risk souring the memory by forcing a relationship talk. I've just settled into bed when there's a knock at the door.

"Come in."

Zach enters and takes a seat on the edge of the bed. "You seemed like you had something you wanted to say on our way to the restaurant. Care to talk about it now?"

My heart pounds against my ribs. So much for chickening out. Zach is calling my bluff. I nod, swallowing because my throat feels really dry. He reaches out and takes my hand. I want to look at him, but I think I'll lose my nerve if I do, so I zone in on our entwined fingers. I take a deep, fortifying breath.

"I've really enjoyed spending time with you and getting to know you. You've been so gracious to allow me to stay with you after everything that happened. Going to events with you like the one tonight has made my life much more enjoyable. Knowing I have someone to support me has given me courage I didn't know I was missing."

I pause, realizing I need to see his reaction when I say this next part. When I look up, his expression is guarded. Is he worried about having to shoot me down? Whatever, there's no turning back now.

"I like you, Zach. I've developed more-than-friendly feelings for you. I know it's not what we agreed to, but I have to know if maybe you feel the same way. If not, totally cool." Though my heart would break. "But if so, I was wondering if maybe you'd be interested in dating for real?"

His eyes widen while I'm speaking. One corner of his mouth twitches, but then he draws his lips into a straight line. My forehead crinkles in worry. He lets go of my hand and my heart drops until it comes up to cup my face. He leans in and kisses me with purpose. I wrap my arms around his neck, pulling him closer. When we break apart, Zach draws me against his chest.

"That's a yes, right?"

He chuckles. "Yes, of course. I like you so much, Katie, but I didn't want to mess things up for you. I wanted to honor our agreement."

I pull back to stare into his eyes. "Me too. I hate to ask, but what does this mean for the future?"

He runs a hand through his hair and sighs. "I don't know. Would it be okay if we just focus on being open about our feelings for now? That seems like enough."

I nod, then, because I can, I reach for his jaw, enjoying the feel of his beard against my hand for a second before leaning in and kissing him. We spend a good while trading kisses before Zach decides we should probably get some sleep. I agree only because he promises to wake me up with a kiss in the morning.

CHAPTER TWENTY-SIX
Zach

The bow tie feels tight against my neck, so I slide a finger under my collar and tug, hoping for a little relief. Katie grabs my hand, lacing our fingers together.

"I promise it won't be too bad. When we arrive, we'll take a few pictures and I'll probably have to answer a few questions, but then we'll be in the air-conditioned theater and get to sit for a couple of hours while everyone judges my performance."

When I look over at her, she's giving me a teasing smile. Right. I shouldn't be nervous. I'm just her plus one, not the focus of everyone's attention.

"Is it nerve-wracking for you? I mean, putting your art on display for the first time?"

She tips her head to the side, considering. "Not as much as it used to be. I've learned to mostly ignore all comments, especially the negatives."

At the lift of my brow, she bites her lip and looks away. She's still following that one loser account. I saw her scrolling through it in the airport earlier and caught some comment comparing her feet to water skis. I don't know why that bothered her. They look like normal feet to me.

I'd never flown in first class before, but it wasn't much different from economy. More leg room and a bigger seat mainly. Katie had me sit in the aisle to keep her presence incognito, but it was only moderately successful. Halfway through the flight, Lila, who was sitting across from us, leaned over and showed us a social media post of us in our seats with the caption, *Kat Sonnett and her hot boyfriend are on my flight!* I didn't see anyone take our picture, but it obviously happened.

Thankfully, it's all that's happened thus far, but we're about to enter the lion's den. Of course, publicity is the goal of a movie premiere.

This is my first time riding in a limo and I have to say it's not as exciting as I expected it to be. Sure, I've got plenty of leg room, but there's no sunroof to stick my head out of. I thought all limos had them. A major disappointment for sure.

What wasn't disappointing? Having the talk with Katie the other night. It was a bit of a surprise to find out she has feelings for me, but what a relief that I no longer have to keep my own under wraps. The only thing that's really changed is I don't have to second guess myself when I want to show affection. We agreed to take things one day at a time and not worry about the future just yet. We can figure out what we'll do after her movie's finished. Right now, I'm on top of the world knowing Katie is officially my girlfriend.

"So there are just two photo stops on the red carpet and one person doing interviews," Lila says from her seat on the bench perpendicular to ours. "Zach, make sure to smile the whole time. It's going to feel unnatural, and that's okay. Focus on making sure the smile reaches your eyes and you should be good. Stay behind Katie so everyone can see her dress."

I nod my understanding. Katie is in a gorgeous blue-gray dress that hugs her torso and hips, then flares at the legs. Her hair is down in loose waves flowing over one shoulder and she wears sparkling silver chandelier earrings. I feel like I'm going to prom with the most gorgeous woman alive.

The car stops, and I am stunned at the number of people outside the window. Most of them have cameras and there's a buzz of conversation. Lila gets out first, then motions for me to go next. I reach back to give Katie a hand. It feels like she exits the car in slow motion, looking so dazzling my breath catches. She gives me a wink, then lets go of my hand to slide her arm through mine and waves to the wall of spectators on one side of the red carpet. The loud cheers confirm she's got a lot of fans in the crowd.

Lila catches my eye and mimes a smile. I lift my lips in response, trying to remember what all she said in the car. Something about eyes and behind. My eyes round as I look around at all the people with cameras pointed at us, yelling questions. It's just one big racket to my ears. I turn my focus back to Katie. She looks at ease. We reach a backdrop with what I assume is an image from the movie and stop. Katie shifts her body, so it's angled toward me and puts a hand on my chest. Unsure what to do with my hands, I keep them by my sides until she whispers out of the side of her mouth to put an arm around her waist.

I have no idea where I'm supposed to be looking, so I peek at Katie's face, finding that focusing on her calms me almost immediately. Someone calls my name and I turn, getting a face full of flash. I blink a few times, not enjoying being blinded every few seconds. How do people stand this?

Katie reaches back and grabs the hand around her waist, tugging me along the carpet. After a second stop at a different backdrop and another barrage of camera flashes, we move on to a woman in a sleek black dress with a microphone.

Katie steps up onto the little platform where the other woman is standing and greets her like an old friend. Grateful to be out of the spotlight for a bit, I study Katie as she laughs and chats with the reporter.

Katie says my name and, when I look at her, she's motioning for me to join her on the platform. When I step up, she pulls me to her side, our arms linked.

"Meeting Zach was such a wonderful surprise," she tells the woman. "I had no idea I could be this happy."

My heart soars at her words. It feels good knowing she really means it. I hated all the limbo, wondering if I was the only one with my heart invested. She squeezes my arm affectionately and I brush a light kiss on her temple.

"Awww," the woman says, and I remember anew that we're being filmed. I'd forgotten for a second.

The reporter's smile morphs into an exaggerated frown. A look of concern crosses her face.

"We heard about the break-in at your hotel room. How are you doing?"

"Yes, it was a bit troubling. Thankfully, Zach was with me when I discovered it. I feel safer knowing he's here with me."

The woman smiles again. "You have your own personal bodyguard."

Katie thanks the woman, and we step off the platform. Lila leads us through the doors of the theater and away from so many watchful eyes. Katie pauses, letting go of my arm and taking a deep breath.

"Are you okay?" I ask.

She gives me a small smile. "I hate when they ask invasive questions like it's nothing. Does she really think I want to talk about a recent violation of my privacy?"

I step closer to her, wrapping her loosely in my arms so I don't wrinkle her dress. "I'm so sorry. What can I do?"

She shakes her head and nestles closer to me. "Just be you. I'm so glad you agreed to come."

"I'm here for you. Anything you need, I'll do it." As I say the words, I realize I truly mean them. I would do anything for Katie.

"The hardest part's over," Lila says. "Let me show you to your seats and then I'll find you some popcorn."

"There are snacks?" I figured we'd have to behave like we were at the opera or something.

Katie chuckles. "The usual theater fare. Popcorn, nachos, M&M's, caviar."

I narrow my eyes at her. "Is there really caviar?"

She nods solemnly. "And duck pâté if you're into that."

I wrinkle my nose. "I'll stick with the popcorn, thanks."

"Good choice," Lila says.

The theater begins to fill. I feel silly sitting in a fold down chair and holding a tub of popcorn while wearing a bow tie, but when in Rome, right?

"Well, well, well. If it isn't Kat Sonnett."

I look past Katie to see a guy dressed exactly like me smiling down at her. She pops up out of her seat and gives him a hug. A wave of jealousy washes over me at their obvious affection for one another.

"Hey Colin!" Katie says. "So good to see you. What are you working on right now?"

He gives her a dazzling smile. "I'm doing an action film in South America. Finding a lost treasure while rescuing someone's kidnapped son. It's pretty hot in the jungle, but I'm having fun. What about you?"

She rolls her eyes. "Another rom-com."

He motions toward the screen. "Hey, don't knock rom-coms. You're killing it with those right now."

"Yeah, but I'd like to try something new. Maybe make my own sweaty action film."

His brow furrows. "Really?"

She purses her lips. "Well, maybe not *action*, but I could afford to spice up my acting resume. Maybe take on a serious role."

He nods. "I heard they're still looking for people for that drama Ananda Cortez is directing."

Katie stands taller. "I know. I've been trying to get my agent to hook me up."

"Well, don't wait too long, as I hear they want to get rolling pretty soon."

She sighs, then looks around and startles when she sees me like she forgot I was here. "Oh, Zach. Let me introduce you to Colin Stone. He's my co-star in this movie."

I stand and shake his hand, trying not to squeeze too hard and give away my less-than-kind feelings toward a probably stand-up guy. "Nice to meet you."

"Same," Colin says. "Have you met my wife, Jenna?"

We pass around greetings before everyone sits down. Knowing Colin is married has quelled the green monster prowling around in my gut, but I'm disconcerted at how strong my feelings were. Even though we're official, part of me still worries everything could fall apart at a moment's notice. I mean, what sane person wouldn't want to be with Katie? She's fun, sweet, gorgeous, and brightens my day every time I see her. A man could really get used to that feeling.

Katie and Colin chat while I watch the people come in and sit down. Lila ends up next to me, but she's on her phone until the lights dim. Someone stands up front with a microphone and welcomes everyone. Katie leans over and whispers that it's the director. Then the movie starts.

The audience seems pretty responsive to the movie, laughing at the appropriate parts and sighing at sweet moments. I feel Katie's eyes on me at one point, and when I turn, she's got a nervous smile on her face. Is she worried about what I think? I grab her hand and give it a squeeze I hope feels comforting. She slides her fingers through mine and we hold hands for the last part of the movie.

When she and her co-star have their swoony kiss, I have to look away. It looks so real on the screen, even though intellectually I know it isn't. I mean, I just met his wife and they're obviously very much in love from the way they're snuggled up together. Kissing attractive guys is part of her job, and I have to be okay with that.

When the movie's over, Katie looks over at me expectantly. "So?"

I smile. "You were great. It was a really sweet story. You two were very believable as a couple."

She squeezes my hand. "Thanks!"

We stand and I stretch. Colin leans over toward Katie. "Are you going to the after party?"

She chuckles. "We kind of have to, since it's for our movie."

He laughs. "Yeah, just wanted to make sure there would be someone cool there. See you in a bit."

He and his wife wave and head up the aisle. Lila directs us out the other way and takes us right to the car. I guess it's nice being one of the stars. There's not much waiting around; everything is ready when you need it.

When we get in, it smells like burgers and Katie grabs one of the brown bags and dives in.

"Thanks, Mac!" she says.

The window partition is open, and the driver waves his acknowledgment. Lila hands me a bag before opening the third.

"It's nearly impossible to eat at the after party with everyone wanting to talk to Katie about the movie," Lila says, "so we make sure to have something on the way."

I eat the burger and fries in my bag, glad for more than popcorn in my stomach. When we arrive at our next destination, we make a pit stop at the restrooms before heading up to the party on the top floor. Apparently, in addition to not being able to eat, you don't get any other necessary breaks either. Okay, so maybe being famous has a few drawbacks.

Colin and Jenna are the first to approach us, but Katie and Colin are quickly overwhelmed by people who want to talk with them, leaving me and Jenna alone.

"Do you want to get a drink and hide out in a booth?" she says.

That sounds like a great idea, but I don't want to abandon Katie. I look over to where she's standing, surrounded by a dozen people.

"Don't worry. They'll find us if they need us."

She seems to know what she's doing, so after a stop at the bar for some water, we find a quiet corner.

"How long have you and your husband been together?"

"Married for five years, but together for four years before that."

She must be a pro at all this stuff by now. Yet, she doesn't seem caught up in the glitz and glamor. I mean, she's not trying to rub elbows with everyone.

"You're experienced at handling all this," I say, motioning around. "Any tips?" Might as well find out what I've signed myself up for as a celebrity's significant other.

She smiles. "First, ignore everything you read about her. They just want to cause drama and if you buy into it, your relationship is going to struggle. Second, the kissing they do for work means nothing. It's a weird aspect, but there's no emotion behind it. The music and cinematography are tricks to make the audience believe it's real, but she'll never kiss them the way she kisses you."

It's funny she's bringing it up since it is a real concern of mine. If Katie and I are together long term, I'll figure out how to handle it. It's a weird part of her job, but I trust her.

"Third, find some real friends. A lot of people in Hollywood are just out for themselves, so it can be hard to make true connections. I'm sure you have plenty of friends, but my guess is Kat doesn't." I nod. "Colin was the same way. I think it's why we work so well. My non-celebrity status made me more appealing because he can let down his guard and be his true self with me. I bet Kat feels the same way about you."

Does she? My life feels very boring compared to hers. Of course, it also allows me plenty of privacy, which hers doesn't. Would my life become more public if we stayed together?

"This is helpful. Can I ask you something? Has it been harder for you to keep your privacy being married to an actor?"

She gives me an understanding smile. "Yes, and no. It's Colin who's recognized when we're out together, but we live in a gated community for privacy and vacation in secluded locations. And a lot of people are good about keeping their distance when we're at dinner or in public. Sure, we often end up on someone's feed, but you get used to it."

Her answer isn't surprising, but I still don't like the idea of people feeling entitled to document their encounters with us for public consumption. I've already gotten a taste of it and it makes me uncomfortable. I mean, are there really people who got a thrill watching me kiss my girlfriend? Okay, so maybe I've watched that video a few times myself, but still.

"Have you still been able to work? Actually, I'm sorry. I don't even know what you do."

"I'm a scientist at UCLA. I teach classes and conduct research. The students are a little excited when they find out who I'm married to, but Colin doesn't visit me at work, so it's fine."

Her answer is reassuring that a normalish life is still possible, but would I have to move to L.A. where celebrities are ubiquitous in order to be afforded privacy? Bill Murray lives in Charleston and I've only seen him once at a RiverDogs game. A few people approached him for autographs, but most people left him alone, so it's not impossible. And Katie's current co-star lives in Asheville, which means maybe it's becoming more common, but would she even want to relocate to Charleston?

I don't know why I'm even thinking these thoughts. We promised not to think about the future yet, but I really don't know if I could move to Los Angeles. I'm not leaving my mom knowing there's a chance her cancer could come back. I don't know how Katie feels about living on the east coast. The logistics seem impossible, which is probably why we're avoiding talking about them right now. However, it feels like we're being reckless and ignoring the inevitable collision course with reality.

Jenna and I continue chatting while Colin and Katie make the rounds. I'm exhausted just watching her. This life is fun to visit, but I don't know if I want it to be permanent. Eventually, the actors find their way back to us.

"We're finally done," Colin says, bending down to kiss his wife, then shake my hand. "Thanks for entertaining Jenna while I worked. I know these events aren't the most fun."

"I think she kept me company, actually," I say.

"And what fine company it was," Jenna says, smiling at me. "I told Zach they should come over for dinner the next time he's in town."

"Oh, yes, that would be fun," Colin says, smiling at Katie. "I can show off our new wood-fired pizza oven."

"It's a date," says Katie.

"You have my number."

Back in the limo, Katie slumps against the seat, exhausted. She kicks off her heels and props her feet on my lap. Instinctively, I take one of them between my hands and massage the sole. She groans when I run my thumb down the arch of her foot. I continue pressing and rubbing, moving to her other foot after a few minutes. When we reach her house, she's so relaxed she's nearly asleep.

"We're here," I say, nudging her gently. "Should I carry you so you don't have to put your shoes back on?"

She shakes her head, then reaches into a side pocket and removes a pair of rubber flip-flops.

"Lila always leaves these in the car."

When we left the party, Lila declined Katie's offer to drop her off at her place, saying she was meeting some friends later. "You've got a great assistant."

"I sure do."

I grab her heels, then help her out of the car. We walk hand-in-hand up to the front door of Katie's massive house. When we arrived this afternoon, I was surprised at how empty and impersonal her home felt. There aren't any knickknacks on shelves or disheveled blankets on chairs or couches. She doesn't even have a table in her dining room, just a small round table in an alcove off the kitchen. Has she never hosted people at her place? Maybe she doesn't spend a lot of time in it if she's filming in various locations like Charleston. I think I'd feel lonely being the only person in a place this big and sparsely furnished. It makes me grateful for my full life back home.

As soon as the door's closed, Katie pushes me back against it, her mouth finding mine while her hands burrow into my hair. My arms go around her waist, hugging her to me, but letting her set the pace. Her hands roam down over my shoulders to my chest. She breaks the kiss, her eyes dancing with desire.

"You look so good in a tux. It was a struggle not to attack you before we left the house earlier."

I run my hands up and down her arms, appreciating how good she looks in her dress. "I know exactly what you mean."

She buries her face in my neck, but I hear her yawn. I chuckle. "You've had a long night. Let's get ready for bed."

She gives me a hopeful look. "Can we cuddle in bed for a bit?"

Who could say no to that? I playfully tap her on the nose. "Sure thing, Tiger."

She turns her back to me, looking over her shoulder. "Would you mind unzipping me?"

I swallow thickly as I pull down the zipper, revealing a lot of skin and making my mind go haywire.

"Thanks, Zachary Isaac."

I shake my head. She shrugs a shoulder, then heads down the hall to her room. I watch her until the door closes, then run a hand through my hair. I am a goner. No wonder I'm ignoring the giant red flags waving in our future. I'm willing to take whatever attention and affection she'll give me for as long as I can. Which means, when she opens the door dressed for bed and invites me to cuddle with her, I don't hesitate.

CHAPTER TWENTY-SEVEN
Zach

I've been awake for several hours when Katie's bedroom door opens and she breezes into the living room wearing a cute ruffly tank top and short jean shorts, her hair loose around her shoulders, looking like a true California girl. She smiles at me on her way to the kitchen for a cup of coffee. She brings it over to where I'm sitting on the couch and takes a seat on the cushion next to mine, giving me a quick kiss. This room is the only one that really feels homey. There are two big white couches with light blue accent pillows, a high pile rug under a glass coffee table, and two chairs the same color as the pillows. The pops of color in this room make me think this is where she spends most of her time.

"Sleep well?"

"Eh," I say with a shrug. "I don't always sleep well in a new place. What about you?"

She nods. "Like a baby. Though I was a little sad when I woke up alone."

It makes me feel good to know she enjoys the cuddling as much as I do. "I woke up with the sun but wanted to make sure you got all the rest you needed, so I came out here."

"You're so thoughtful." She gives me a lingering kiss. "So, listen…"

My heart skips a beat. Did I do something wrong last night? Is she breaking up with me already? The fear must be written across my face because she reaches over and pats my hand.

"Lila set up a few appointments for me this morning and a lunch this afternoon with someone I used to work with on *Sun City*. I know we planned to do some sightseeing together, but it looks like that's not going to happen. I'm so sorry."

Is that all? As long as we're still dating, I don't care about much else. My body relaxes. "That's fine. I'm fine to do some solo exploring."

"Are you sure? You're welcome to come with me, though it'll probably be pretty boring."

"No, that's okay. Take care of what you need to and I'll play tourist for the day. We'll meet back here and head to the airport together."

She gives me a hug and I inhale her floral scent. "Thanks for being so understanding."

The doorbell sounds. Katie's head swings toward the front door. "That must be Lila." Her gaze turns back to me, conflict written on her face. "I feel bad leaving you after I promised we'd be together today."

"Don't be. It's fine." I stand up, pulling her with me into another hug. Even though I'm fine spending some time alone, I can't say I won't miss having Katie near me. I kiss her, hoping to convey my affection for her.

"You're awesome, Zachary Griffin."

I shake my head, smiling widely. She snaps her fingers like "aw shucks," then grabs her coffee and is out the door with Lila. My stomach growls, reminding me it's still following eastern time and wants some breakfast. Katie's fridge is empty. Unsurprising, since she's not currently living here. I check Yelp reviews and settle on a local cafe not too far from here with outdoor seating.

I people watch while I eat, wondering if anyone around me is famous. Jonah would know. At least one of these attractive people must be in the business. Maybe they all are, but work behind the camera. Or maybe it's filled with tourists like me. While considering my next venture, I think of where Katie might have taken me if we were sightseeing together. Julia Roberts and Rodeo Drive pop into my head and I decide I have to get a photo of me on the iconic street if only to mess with her.

The half hour drive reminds me just how big Los Angeles is. There are so many people and cars. I don't think this is the place for me. Though, maybe if I get my eyes on the ocean, it might feel more like home. That'll be my next stop.

I get out and wander the streets, finally searching for the building on the internet. It turns out the iconic store from the movie was technically on Santa Monica Boulevard and is currently a very expensive shoe store. I take a selfie, making sure the address is in the picture, then send it to Katie with the caption, *Feeling a little Pretty today*. She quickly responds with a gif of Julia Roberts holding shopping bags saying, "Big mistake. Big. Huge." I chuckle.

I wander down the street, enjoying the palm trees lining the sidewalks and peeking into the windows. When I see an Hermès store, I remember Mom's birthday is coming up and step inside. The products are beautiful, but nothing calls out to me, so I leave and continue down the block, now on the hunt for a birthday gift.

A loop through Burberry yields nothing either. I don't think clothing is what I'm looking for. Nearing the end of the street, I'm just about to give up, but then I spot Tiffany & Co. on the corner and know I can find something for her in there.

The first counter I come to has bangles and bracelets. They are pretty, but nothing sticks out to me. A woman approaches and asks if she can help. When I tell her who I'm shopping for, she suggests earrings, but after looking through them all, I shake my head. A case of colorful stones draws my eye. Inside are several rows of rings. Mom usually has at least three rings on at all times, so I'm sure she wouldn't mind adding one more to her collection. I study each of them, trying to decide which might be best when a deep blue square cut stone nestled inside two rows of diamonds makes my heart squeeze. I point to it and the clerk picks it up and hands it to me. I study it, trying to figure out why it's calling to me.

"You know," she says, "that color is a perfect match for Kat Sonnett's eyes."

I look up, startled at her words. She has a knowing expression on her face. Does she recognize me? Yikes. I didn't realize it would happen this quickly. What the clerk said is true. The stone is as captivatingly blue as Katie's gaze. Is that why I like it so much? *No*, I remind myself, *it's Mom's favorite color. That's who I'm purchasing it for.*

"This is perfect. I'll take it."

"Would you like me to wrap it?"

"Just the little blue box is all I need, thanks."

She nods, takes my credit card, then hands it back along with a small blue bag.

"I hope she loves it," she says with a wink.

I thank her and head back out front. I'm ready for some fresh air, so I order a car to take me to Santa Monica Pier and people watch from my spot on the sidewalk until it arrives. More than one tan woman eyes my shopping bag and gives me a big smile. What is it about this store that women like so much? I've never understood it, but then I'm a guy. I'd much rather be given free rein in Rockler, my favorite woodworking tool purveyor. It takes twenty minutes to get to the pier. I decide to give myself an hour and then head back, so I'll be at the house when Katie's finished with lunch.

The pier is crowded with people and noise, so I bypass it until I find an entrance onto the sand. There are still plenty of people on this gorgeous, sunny day, but they're spaced out. I sit down, take off my shoes and socks, roll up my pant legs, and stuff my wallet and phone into the bottom of my shoes, putting the socks on top to camouflage them. I then eye the blue bag on the sand next to them. It's too conspicuous. I stand up, brush the sand from the seat of my jeans, remove the ring box from the bag and put it in my pocket, then throw the bag into a nearby trash can before wading into the water up to my calves. I'm shocked by how cool it is. After a few seconds, I retreat up the beach to my shoes. I stretch out on the warm sand, using my shoes as a pillow, and close my eyes.

A buzzing wakes me out of my nap. I dig in my shoe for my phone, surprised I've been out here for three hours. I answer, my voice froggy from sleep.

"There you are!" Katie practically shouts.

I sit up quickly, my heart pounding. "Everything okay?"

"Yes, fine. I was just worried when you weren't here at the house."

"Sorry, I fell asleep on the beach."

I squeeze my eyes shut, trying to fully wake up. The movement feels tight on my face. I lift a hand to my cheek and wince at how hot my skin feels. Definitely sunburned.

"Where are you?" she asks, concern lacing her voice.

My heart squeezes at the thought that I've upset her by my lack of awareness. I should have set an alarm, but how was I to know I'd fall asleep? "Santa Monica." I've shoved my feet back into my shoes and am heading away from the water. "I'll get a car and head back."

"No, don't. We have to be at the airport in a couple of hours. By the time you get here, we'll just have to head back across town again."

"What about my suitcase?"

"Lila and I will pack your things. Why don't you pick a place for us to eat dinner near the airport?"

"I'm sorry. I'll find something and text you the address."

After a quick search, I send the address to a Mexican place. Katie responds with a thumbs up, so I order a ride. When I get it, the driver commends me on my destination, saying it's his favorite taco truck in the city. He takes me by an ATM after informing me the truck only takes cash, then hands me a scribbled note of what to order before I get out of the car. I stand under the pop-up canopy because I don't need any more sun. I'd sit, but there aren't any empty chairs. If there wasn't a crowd of diners plus my driver's recommendation, I'd be very skeptical about this place. The truck's parked on a side street next to a building with bars over the windows. Not exactly a welcoming ambiance.

Half an hour later, a sleek black SUV pulls over in front of the food truck. I approach the back passenger door, relieved when the window rolls down and I see Katie's face. She's turned toward the truck, frowning.

"Um, this is a food truck."

I grimace. "I know, but my driver said the food is good. If you want to go somewhere else, I understand."

"This is fine. Some of my favorite meals have been from food trucks."

She slides out, then does a double take when she sees me. "Zach, your face is very red."

"Yeah, that's what happens when you fall asleep on the beach."

Everyone orders and then Lila holds out a credit card. The guy shakes his head and points to the "Cash Only" sign. I pull out my wallet and pay.

Katie looks at me in surprise. "You still carry cash?"

"My driver took me by an ATM on the way here. Otherwise, this really would have been a disaster."

After our food comes through the window, we sit down at a table, taking the only empty spots. It looks and smells amazing, making my stomach growl. The first bite is a heavenly mix of spices that tantalizes my tongue. I close my eyes to savor the flavors, but they fly open when I hear a satisfied moan across from me. Katie's hand slaps over her mouth. Lila looks at her strangely and I try hard not to chuckle.

"Sorry about that," Katie says. "I've missed good Mexican food. I'm sorry, Zach, but they have nothing like this in Charleston."

"No offense taken. This is amazing."

After we finish, the three of us pile into the SUV that's been waiting at the curb to take us to the airport. Katie puts on a baggy sweatshirt and hat before we get out of the car.

"You sure you don't want a hat too?" she asks, pulling a blue Dodgers cap from her bag.

"You think I'll need it?"

Lila holds her phone out to me. On the screen is a picture from the premiere last night. I have to admit Katie and I look fantastic all dressed up together.

"This picture is all over the websites and has been circulating on social media. People are debating whether you two are head over heels for each other. They've been dissecting all the shots from last night, including some unauthorized ones fans took."

That must be why the clerk recognized me earlier. I reach out and take the hat, adjusting it to fit on my head, then slide it on. "Am I incognito now?"

Katie scrutinizes me. "That color really brings out your eyes. I like it. But no, not really. I think people are going to notice a hunky muscular man with a sunburn in or out of a hat."

Whoa. There's so much about that sentence to dissect.

"You think I'm hunky? Is that sexy-adjacent?"

Her mouth drops open, and she blinks a few times before pressing her lips together, her cheeks tinged pink. "I mean...look at you. You have to know you're very attractive."

I give a casual shrug. It's rare I see Katie frazzled. "But the real question is, do you find me attractive?"

Even though we're dating, I still need reassurance that she's attracted to me. Our fiery kisses are definitely a strong indicator, but what can I say? I'd like to hear that I have an effect on her from her own lips. Her two very kissable lips.

Katie's saved from answering by Lila, who clears her throat.

"We'd better get moving. LAX is always a zoo and I don't want us to miss our flight. We have a tight window in Atlanta, and if we miss it, we won't get home until tomorrow."

When we're in the air headed east, Katie turns to me. "To answer your earlier question, you are the sexiest man I've ever seen. It's very hard not to just stare at you all day."

Okay, now that felt good to hear. It's encouraging to know the attraction is mutual. I'm grinning like a madman, but I can't help it.

She chuckles. "By the way, was that a Tiffany box I saw you take out of your pocket at security?"

What is it about those blue boxes? "Yes. My mom's birthday is next month, and I found something while I was on Rodeo Drive."

She frowns. "I hope you're not still bothered by me offering to pay you. I promise I really wasn't trying to *Pretty Woman* you."

I shake my head. "No, I just like teasing you. If it bothers you, I'll stop. It's just fun having an inside joke with you."

Her lips quirk up slightly. "It's fine. Can I see what you got your mom?"

I lean over and rifle through my backpack under the seat in front of me until I find it. Straightening up, I hand the box to Katie. She opens the lid and gasps.

"Zach, this is beautiful."

"Thanks. I hope she likes it."

Katie looks between the ring and me several times, a strange expression on her face. Finally, she fixes her gaze on me, looking sheepish.

"Would it be okay if I tried it on? Is that weird? It's just that I don't have anything from Tiffany's and I'd like to pretend. Just for a bit."

I grin, happy to be able to do this tiny thing for her. I take the box back and remove the ring.

"It's size five and a half. Which finger do you want it on?"

She grins and wiggles her left ring finger. "This one."

My heart flips. I know we're just having fun, but my mind imagines what it might be like to actually propose and hear her say yes. I slide the ring on, surprised by the perfect fit.

Katie sucks in a breath, holding it up in the air in front of her. Her eyes are wide as she stares at her hand. She seems frozen for a few seconds, but then she releases a breath and drops her hands to her lap, squeezing her eyes shut. She seems to be debating with herself about something. She removes the ring and hands it back to me. I return it to the box and slide it back into my backpack. When I straighten up again, Katie's eyes are closed and her head is against the window.

My mind is flying all over the place, now with images of me sliding a ring onto Katie's finger, front and center. Oh boy, things are getting muddled. I could have sworn it was longing I saw on her face while she was wearing the ring. But for what? To be so totally in love with someone that they ask her to spend the rest of her life with them? To get married? Because I'm definitely starting to think about it now. I know I should pull back on this kind of thinking until we figure out what's going to happen when her work wraps up in Charleston, but the inevitable has already happened. If she leaves, my heart is going with her.

CHAPTER TWENTY-EIGHT

Kat

My time in L.A. flew by. It was only a day and a half, but so much was crammed into those thirty hours. I had a successful movie premiere and a fun after party where I reconnected with one of my former co-stars at lunch the next day. I met with a couple of agents to chat about what working with them might look like. I'm worried word will get back to Rick, but maybe it'll freak him out enough to finally get me that audition I've been after. Both of the other agents were eager to work with me and were willing to set me up with whichever auditions I'm interested in. It was a refreshing feeling knowing I wouldn't have to fight as hard for what I want.

Unfortunately, most of those good things prevented me from show-ing Zach around town. How can I reasonably present the idea of him moving out here with me if I can't show him all the great things L.A. has to offer? I'm not surprised he ended up at the beach. The city can be a lot. I'd kind of forgotten how crazy the traffic is. Charleston is practically a small country town by comparison. Which definitely has its perks, one of which is that I don't feel like I'm on display all the time when I'm out in public. I know it's part of the life, but I don't want to have to hide away in a gated house just to be able to let my guard down.

Plus, my life in L.A. has been pretty lonely as of late. I've made more connections in my current temporary town in the past couple of months than I have in the five years since I bought my house in the Hollywood Hills.

"You're all set," says Melissa, stepping back and appraising my face. "You know, you look just as natural as a brunette."

I gently pat the wig I'm wearing for the movie. Normally I'd dye my hair for a part, but I was also scheduled to shoot some ads for a couple of products and they requested my natural blonde hair. Plus, the wig looks fabulous. If someone didn't know what I normally look like, they'd be fooled. I actually bet I could wander around the city like this and no one would recognize me. Well, unless they've been visiting our outdoor shooting locations. Then they'd have already seen me with this new hairstyle.

I head over to the stage where we're filming today's scene. It's an inside shoot of a scene near the end when the competitors finish the race and find out who won. I'm supposed to be injured, so I limp as I approach Grady and the director who are already in place.

"It's your other ankle," Grady says.

I look down and realize I've been walking on the bandaged foot. Oops. "My bad."

"We're going to film the finish line scene first," the director says, "and then after that, we'll set up for the award ceremony."

I nod in understanding, and she heads over toward the camera. Looking around the room, I spot a familiar face among the crowd of people who will cheer for the competitors as they cross the finish line. Will must feel my stare because he turns toward me. I smile and give him a wave. His face lights up and he makes heart hands while mouthing 'thank you.' I nod, pleased I could help him out after all. He doesn't have any lines, but hopefully his face will show up for a second here and there throughout the scene. His good looks definitely make him stand out from the crowd, so I wouldn't be surprised if this turns into something bigger for him.

Grady hands me the backpack I've worn most of the movie. I put it on, then he bends down and I hop up onto his back.

He grunts like the weight surprised him.

"Sorry."

He laughs. "I'm just teasing you. You're fine. Hey, Bex is in town for a couple of days. Would you and Zach want to go to dinner with us tonight or tomorrow?"

I had fun hanging out with them before the L.A. trip. I'd been nervous about socializing outside of work just because it's been so long, but it was a lot of fun. I didn't spend much time with Grady's wife so it would be nice to learn more about her and their life together. Zach seemed to feel better about dating an actor after hanging with Jenna in L.A. Maybe Bex could fully convert him to the idea of marrying an actor. My eyes widen at the realization that I was just thinking about the two of us married. That's so much more permanent than dating, which we've only been doing for about two months, and only officially for a few weeks. However, marriage conjures up images of safety, comfort, and love. Those are three things I wouldn't mind having more of in my life. And after trying on that gorgeous ring, I've had more and more thoughts about a life with Zach as my partner.

"That sounds great. Let me check with Zach to make sure he doesn't have anything going on."

When we take a break for lunch, I grab my phone and call Zach.

I smile when I hear his voice. "How's the store?"

"Like a ghost town, per usual, but I've managed to whittle out a squirrel and two ducks, so I'm keeping myself occupied. How's filming?"

"It's going well. Grady asked me about us having dinner with him and his wife tonight or tomorrow. Would one of those work for you?"

"Tonight would be preferred, as I have plans tomorrow."

I really want to know what these plans are, especially since I'm feeling a hint of jealousy that he's doing something without me, but Lila is motioning to me we're ready to get started again, so I wrap things up. "Great. I'll see you later."

Grady is thrilled about meeting up and picks a place and time for dinner. When I get back to the house, it's empty. I hop in the shower then pick out a cute floral dress for the evening. I'm just slipping my shoes on when I hear the front door open and close. Zach is home! My heart pirouettes in my chest and I hustle down the stairs, stopping myself just before I crash into him. He hands me a bouquet of light pink peonies that smell divine.

I grab a handful of his shirt, pull him to me, and kiss him soundly. "Thanks, Zachary Rupert. These are beautiful."

He chuckles, not even acknowledging my guess. "You're welcome. You look beautiful."

He fills a vase with water, then takes the flowers from me. While he's arranging the flowers in the vase, I take a minute to appreciate the view. He's wearing khaki pants and a blue dress shirt with the sleeves rolled up. The man is *hot*. When he turns, I notice his beard is a little shorter and his hair has some sort of product in it that makes him look even better than usual.

"You look great. Did you get a haircut or something?"

He runs a hand over his hair, then rubs the side of his beard. "Yeah. I thought you'd appreciate it if I cleaned myself up a bit. I should have done it before we went to Los Angeles. Sorry about that."

I shake my head. "Don't be sorry. You look good all the time."

He chuckles. "Thanks. So do you. Especially when you show off those fantastic legs."

My cheeks warm under his appreciative gaze.

"We should go," I say, even though I'd be content just to stay in and stare at each other.

Grady and Bex are already seated in a private circular booth when we arrive. I slide in next to Bex and Zach sits next to me, placing him across from Grady. After the server takes our order, Grady leans forward. "So, is it true?"

"Is what true?"

He motions between me and Zach. "That you two are engaged?"

Zach's perplexed look tells me this is the first he's heard of this. I turn back to Grady. "Where did you hear that?"

He pulls out his phone, types for a bit, then turns it around. There's a photo of Zach standing in front of Tiffany's with a small blue bag next to a grainy shot of my hand wearing his mom's ring. I click on the photo and it takes me to a social media post where someone claims they saw Zach propose on the plane. Oh no. I click on the hashtag "katsengaged" and see post after post with these same photos plus a few from our public kisses. The public seems excited about the news. My fingers itch to grab my own phone to see what my least favorite fan is saying, but Zach's right; I don't need to torture myself. I really should delete my private profile.

Zach, who has been reading over my shoulder, lets out a deep sigh. "Whoa."

I shake my head and hand back the phone. "As believable as that looks, it's not true. We're just dating."

Grady smiles. "Don't let them force you into anything you're not ready for. Bex and I were pronounced married once or twice before I ever proposed. Fans can be a little hardcore sometimes."

"How did you adjust to everyone peeking into your personal life?" Zach says, looking at Bex.

She smiles. "I pretty much just ignore it. I'm not on social media, so I don't see all the gossip. Plus, I've never been interested in being famous. Grady has his work and I have mine. He keeps me mostly shielded from celebrity life, which I appreciate."

"It's one reason we live in Asheville rather than L.A.," Grady says. "We have a more normal life there."

Zach and Grady discuss their favorite hikes in Western North Carolina while I listen to Bex talk about her jewelry-making process. She offers to design me some custom earrings and we exchange contact info.

I'm enjoying this dinner so much it almost makes me forget why I closed myself off from trying to connect with other people in the industry. I'm a people person by nature and I can feel part of myself reawakening from a deep slumber. There's no way I'm going back to my old habits of all work and no play. I just have to keep a firmer hand on my schedule.

As the evening winds down, I feel a tug of disappointment that it's almost over. If we didn't have an early start tomorrow, I might suggest finding some live music and doing a little dancing. I'm feeling so energized it might be hard to sleep tonight.

"This has been fun," Grady says. "We should get together again soon."

I smile and nod. "Yes, definitely."

Zach gives me a look, his raised eyebrows trying to convey a message I'm not receiving. I shrug to let him know I don't understand, but I think it gets lost in translation.

"I don't want to be too forward," he says, turning to Grady, "but I'm hosting a game night tomorrow. You're both welcome to come if you want."

Zach hosts a game night? He hasn't had one since I've been staying with him. I assume this means I'm invited too. Is it a charades, poker, or board games kind of game night?

"What kind of games?" Bex asks, looking interested. Is she a competitive person? That glint in her eye makes me think so.

"Various card games. Mostly ones my family made up, but occasionally we'll play normal games like Rummy or Phase 10. We take turns choosing. But I'm going to warn you now that Uno is off the table. The last time we played, I had to buy a new chair."

Bex knocks Grady's shoulder with her own, rubbing her hands together. "Ooh, sounds like my kind of people. Can we go, Hawksy?"

Hawksy? I press my lips together to hide my smile.

He puts his arm around her shoulders and pulls her against him, placing a kiss on her cheek. "Sure thing, Bextra."

Okay, now that's cute. I've never had a nickname with a significant other. Zach has called me "Tiger" a few times, which I really like. Does that count? What could I call him? "Sexy" seems too on the nose. Maybe I'll just play it by ear.

"I'm a little bummed we're just now getting to know each other," Grady says, looking at me. "You're both pretty cool. We'll have to stay in touch after our shoot wraps next week."

His words hit me in the gut. My remaining time with Zach is running out. I glance at him to see what he thinks of this news. I hadn't had time to tell him yet, but his face gives nothing away. I smile at Grady.

"Yeah, that'd be great. I mean, we'll definitely see each other to do publicity, but I agree."

Zach tries to pay the check to everyone's protests, but his card is rebuffed. Turns out the chef heard we were here and comped our meal. When we get up, Zach drops some cash on the table for our server.

We're both quiet on the short ride home. I don't know what Zach is pondering, but I'm thinking about how we can make our relationship work. Would he possibly consider coming back to Los Angeles with me to see if this could become something real? His mom is here. So is his business and a lot of friends. I don't know that I can compete with weekly dinners, game nights, and a lush social life. Heck, if I had all of those things, I'd certainly stay put.

I sneak glances at him all the way home, wishing I could read his mind. I thought things would get easier when we decided to make our relationship official, but all I can think about is what will happen when filming is over. Will we try long distance? Will one of us move? Are we serious enough that moving is even reasonable?

We're both quiet while we get ready for bed. We've fallen into the habit of cuddling before falling asleep and I wonder how I'll be able to sleep in the future without his arms around me. These thoughts are still swirling in my head when I hear Zach's breathing deepen, letting me know he's asleep. I stare at the ceiling trying to figure out a way for us both to be happy and together. All I know for certain is I've got it bad for the bearded man lying next to me.

CHAPTER TWENTY-NINE
Zach

I thought about prepping the group for our game night guests, but I'm interested to see how Greg and Dane react when they meet two well-known actors. Will and Jonah both had conflicts. I know they'll be bummed when they find out they missed meeting Grady Hawkins.

The kitchen counter is covered with food and drinks. Katie spent most of the afternoon in her room, prepping for tomorrow. It's the last day of filming and then she'll be heading back to L.A., I suppose. We've been avoiding talking about what's going to happen when her work wraps up and I'm not looking forward to that conversation.

Truthfully, I don't feel like I've earned the right to ask her to stay. Nor do I feel like I can just leave my mom and my job for someone I've only known a couple of months. I guess that leaves long-distance dating, which sounds terrible. How am I going to survive days and weeks without seeing her gorgeous smile or holding her in my arms? I'm completely smitten with this woman.

A knock on the door interrupts my thoughts. Greg and Dane each have a six-pack and Nora's carrying a foil-covered plate. She hands it to me and I uncover it to reveal my mom's famous lemon-glazed cake. She usually only makes it for special occasions like my birthday, but that's not for another month.

"What's this for?"

Nora shrugs. "Dunno. Elaine just handed it to me."

Maybe this is a sign things are going to work out between me and Katie. Not that I believe in that sort of thing.

"Just us tonight?" Greg says.

I shake my head. "I invited some new friends to join us. They should be here soon."

The doorbell rings. "Right on time."

"I'll get it," Nora says, pushing past me to get to the door first.

I try to hide my smirk when I hear Nora's loud "Oh!" She comes back to the kitchen looking a little dazed.

"Zach, your friends are here."

I shake Grady's hand and hug Bex. "So glad you could make it. You've met Nora. This is Greg and Dane. Guys, this is Grady and Bex."

They both have stunned looks on their faces. When they look at me for an explanation, I just shrug. Footsteps on the stairs let me know the last person is about to join us. Katie comes into the kitchen beaming.

"I thought I heard familiar voices down here. Hey guys!"

She hugs Grady and Bex, then looks at me for introductions. "Katie, this is Greg and Dane. We went to high school together."

She smiles, ignoring their shocked looks. "I hope you have some stories about Zach to share with me."

Dane is the first to regain his composure. "Yeah, sure."

It's not often I can catch my friends off guard. Now I have something to tease them about, which I'll need after they humiliate me tonight with stories from our youth.

After everyone's gotten food and drinks, we sit down at the table. I grab the bowl with everyone's names in it and invite Katie, who took a seat next to me, to pull out a name.

"I got my name," she says.

"That means you get to choose the first game." I hand her a paper. "You can choose any of these or teach us something new."

"Oh, um. I don't know many card games. What is Tic Tac Toe?"

"It's fun. Greg, why don't you explain the rules to our guests?"

He shuffles two decks together while talking through the rules of the game, demonstrating with a practice hand. Once everyone has the basics, he deals nine cards to each person. Bex is on his left, so she goes first. When the round is over, I tally up everyone's scores and we play until everyone has dealt once.

"And the winner of Tic Tac Toe is...Katie! Congrats."

"Beginner's luck," mumbles Greg, who usually triumphs at this game.

"Since you won," I tell her, "you get to pull the next name."

She picks Dane.

"Flipper," he says. "I need redemption after Nora's sneaky win."

He explains the rules while I play host and make sure everyone has a fresh drink and more snacks. Grady ends up in last place while his wife wins the game. I was worried about how the newcomers would do with all the trash talk that goes on around the table, but they jump right in with teasing and gentle name calling. At one point, Katie ribs Dane about his sixty-point hand and I feel my heart swell. I can imagine her sitting at this table on the regular, her eyes sparkling with humor. My life is going to feel so desolate when she leaves.

We take a break for bathrooms and cake. I watch Katie take her first bite, smiling when she closes her eyes and makes a pleased moan.

"So good, right?"

She opens her eyes to look at me and nods.

"Think your mom will give me the recipe?"

"Sorry. It only gets passed down to family."

One side of her mouth quirks up. "So you're saying I have to marry you to be able to eat this cake whenever I want?"

My heart beats faster at the thought. "Think being stuck with me would be worth it?"

She gives me a coy look. "Nothing about being with you has been difficult, Zach."

"Hey, Zach," Grady says. "Bex and I are going to head out. I need some sleep before tomorrow. I have a feeling it's going to be a long day."

"Oh, sure. Thanks for coming."

He smiles. "It was great. The new games were fun. Let's do it again sometime. And you're always welcome to come see us in Asheville."

I didn't expect Grady to be so cool and down to earth, but he and Bex fit right in with the guys tonight. And I genuinely think he means his invitation. Katie and I see them out.

"I really like them," I tell Katie.

"Me too. Hey, is it okay if I turn in? I need to rest up as well."

"Of course. Do you want me to have everyone go home so we don't keep you awake?"

She shakes her head. "No, you're fine. Thanks though."

"Okay. Should I sleep in my own bed tonight so I don't risk waking you?"

She twists her lips into a pout. "I suppose so. Good night, Zach Brown."

I smirk. "You're not even trying anymore are you?"

She shrugs. I slide a hand around her waist and plant a soft kiss on her lips. "Good night, Katie."

When she heads upstairs, I return to the table where three pairs of eyes are looking at me expectantly.

"What?"

"I can't believe you didn't tell us Kat Sonnett and Grady Hawkins were coming tonight," Greg says, indignant.

I laugh. "Just wanted to see your faces."

Dane chuckles. "That was crazy. I hope we didn't embarrass you too much."

I dismiss his words with a wave. "I already told Katie the worst stories, so you're fine."

"Oh, so you two are sharing secrets, huh?" Nora says. "How serious are you?"

I sit down, grab the deck of cards from the middle of the table, and start shuffling.

"We're just having fun and taking things slow. You know, easy breezy."

Nora narrows her eyes. "Those looks you were giving her tonight didn't look so easy breezy. I could have sworn you were giving her heart eyes." She cups her chin in her hands, tips her head, and sighs dramatically, batting her eyelashes at me for effect.

Greg barks out a laugh. "Ha! Heart eyes, so true. Zach, I've never seen you look at another woman the way you look at Kat."

Dane grins. "You're in loooove."

I shake my head and sigh, but inside my heart is beating a mile a minute. If they can see through my façade to the truth, can Katie? "Why are you all acting like middle schoolers?"

Time to point the spotlight on someone else. I grab a name out of the bowl. "Nora, choose the next game."

She rolls her eyes at my weak attempt to change the subject. "Fine. Let's play Blackout."

When we're finished, everyone helps me clean up. Nora tries to steal the rest of the cake, but I send her across the driveway with one large slice instead. I want Katie to have more if she wants it. I wrap it up and stick it in a storage container, taping a note with Katie's name to the lid.

"Kat's really cool," Dane says on his way out. "She fits right in with the group, and it's obvious she likes you back. I'm happy for you, man."

I shut the door after him and Greg, my mind spinning out with questions. Where does she see this going? Does she like me enough to consider sticking around Charleston? I guess tomorrow after she's wrapped up her movie, we'll have to hash things out. Am I willing to confess my love for her or will that scare her away? I know she's been hurt by past relationships so I probably need to be patient and let her take the lead on things. It won't be easy, but she's worth it.

CHAPTER THIRTY

Kat

There's been a gray cloud hanging over my head all day. I'm conflicted about what I want to happen with Zach after today. I told him I'd make us dinner tonight after work so we can have a conversation about what's happening next. I don't have to be anywhere else soon, so I've thought about staying in Charleston and spending more time with Zach. It'd give us more time to figure things out.

As long as he's open to that. I had a great time with his friends last night. They teased me like I was just a regular person and even Grady seemed like he belonged there. It was a night of normalcy I haven't felt in a long time. As nervous as I am about admitting I'm head-over-heels for him, I know I need to take that chance. He's shown me nothing but respect and kindness, and I feel safe with him. There's not a deceitful bone in his body and it feels like a breath of fresh air after a long time underwater. He'd be careful with my heart if I allow myself to give it to him.

I step out of the small trailer that's been parked near our filming location for costume and makeup. Lila meets me and walks me over to where everyone is set up. I suck in a surprised breath when I realize where we are. In front of me is the stone pineapple fountain Zach brought me to after our first dinner date. My chest squeezes at the memory of our almost kiss.

"Okay," the director says, coming up to where I'm standing. "In this scene, you're uncertain how you feel about Carlos. All the anger you've harbored against him has evaporated in light of his confession. You can't deny there's an attraction between you two, but you're not sure if you're willing to take the leap and tell him you like him."

Talk about art imitating life. My feelings for Zach are all twisted. I feel like we're on a precipice and I have to be the one to decide if we jump. At least I can channel all this into work. "No problem."

Grady comes over and gives me a friendly smile. "I can't believe this is the last scene. It has truly been a pleasure to work with you."

I nod. "Same here. I've really enjoyed getting to know you and Bex outside of work."

"Places everyone," the director calls.

Grady and I take our marks. When someone yells action, we take off toward the fountain. I pull out the phone to take a picture and Grady grabs it from me before wrapping his arm around me and angling the phone up so the fountain is behind us. I pretend it's Zach by my side and allow my face to show the conflict between wanting to be closer to him and being afraid of getting hurt. The phone dings, Grady whoops when he reads the next clue, grabs my hand, and pulls me out of frame.

"Cut!" The director approaches us. "That was great. Kat, I need a bit more exaggeration of your uncertainty. Other than that, it was perfect."

We shoot the scene two more times before the director is satisfied.

"That's a wrap, people. Great job!"

Everyone claps and congratulates one another on a job well done. It's only mid-afternoon, so I should have time to get to the store and grab ingredients for tonight's big dinner.

While I'm getting out of costume and removing my makeup, Lila pops into the trailer.

"The police finally sent over a still photo from the hotel's video. Whoever it was wore a nondescript hoodie. He must have known there was a camera because he backed out of the room, which means no face shot. The weird thing was he used a key card to get in."

My forehead scrunches. "That's odd. Maybe he was a guest who got the wrong room?"

"But then why would he throw your clothes everywhere?"

She's got me there. That's a disappointing development.

"Can I see the photo?"

She hands me her phone. Sure enough, the person is in black pants and a hoodie. Light glints off his shoes. I zoom in. Why is he wearing dress shoes with sweats? And really nice ones at that. I move the photo around, my eyes catching on a yellow line at the right sleeve. I enlarge the area, and even with the graininess, I'm pretty sure I know what I'm seeing. I pass the phone back to Lila.

"What would you say that yellow thing is on their wrist?"

She studies the photo, then looks up in surprise. "A gold watch?"

I nod, my eyes narrowing as unease prickles my spine. Most people wear watches on their left wrist unless they're left-handed. And I know someone who's a southpaw. "Where's Rick?"

Lila's eyes widen in understanding, and she searches on her phone. "Uh, I believe he said he had a meeting at the hotel."

"I need to see him. Now."

"Your car is ready whenever you are."

I yank my wig off, tossing it onto the counter in front of me, then pull off the cap and use my fingers to comb out my hair. I stand up and grab my bag. "Let's go."

I spend the short ride trying to figure out what to say to him. I cannot believe he would do something like that, but the more I think about it, the more it makes sense. He's been doing a lot of questionable things lately.

When we get to the hotel, Lila leads me to a door just past the lobby. "Rick commandeered this room for business."

I press my ear against it, hearing muffled voices. I knock, then open the door. Rick stands, a surprised look on his face. "Kat. Done filming already? Always the professional getting it done in just a few takes."

I ignore his words. "Why did you pretend there was a break-in at my hotel room?"

He pauses, like he's assessing the situation. "What do you mean? Someone really did mess up your room."

My cheeks pink with indignation. "Yeah, and it was *you*. Rick, I was really scared after it happened."

He puffs up like he's going to deny my claim, and I silence him with a hand.

"I saw the intruder's dress shoes and *gold watch* from the camera footage."

He presses his lips together, obviously scrambling to put a spin on things.

"All press is good press, remember? It helped the public get back in your corner after the whole Talon thing."

"Which you also orchestrated. You don't listen to me. I said I didn't want to be set up. I said I had a boyfriend. I asked for a serious role. I don't think this is working out for me anymore."

He takes a step toward me. "Now, wait a second, Kat. I'm sure we can get everything sorted to your liking. I'm sorry for the miscommunication, but think of all I've helped you achieve. Do you think you'd be a household name if someone else was your agent? Do you think someone else would have seen the talent I saw in you when you were a teen? Are you really just going to throw all that away?"

His appeal to our history weakens my resolve a little. Am I being too hasty? Sure, his methods were a bit unorthodox, but he wasn't wrong about a fake relationship improving my status. Didn't I essentially take his advice even if it was with someone of my choosing?

Movement to my right startles me, and I turn, coming face-to-face with Talon's trademark smirk. "What are you doing here?" I ask.

"Meeting with my agent. Rick doesn't only work for you, you know."

I slowly turn toward Rick, who's suddenly shuffling some papers in front of him on the desk. "You're Talon's agent now? When did this happen?"

"About two months ago," Talon says.

Betrayal rocks through my body. Rick is a snake. He was pushing Talon on me for his benefit, not mine. How have I been blind for so long? My stomach turns, realizing how naïve I've been. Am I just that dumb and trusting?

"How *could* you?" I glare at Rick, but there's no heat in it, just hurt. "I ought to press charges against you for breaking into my room."

His eyes widen briefly, surprised by my words, but then he scoffs, his face taking on a predatory look. "I know you're upset, but you don't want to do anything too hasty."

The steel in his tone makes my heart beat faster. "What do you mean?"

He leans back in his chair, a smug grin on his face. "Your career is in my hands. It sure would be a shame if the gossip rags found out something unwholesome about rom-com queen Kat Sonnett."

I narrow my eyes at him. "I haven't done anything bad."

He shrugs. "We all know juicy gossip travels fast. Even if there was a retraction later, what would people remember?"

I can't believe he's threatening me. This is not how I saw the conversation going. At a loss to how I ended up on defense, I decide it's best to quit for now and regroup later. I spin around on my heels and exit the room, speed walking back out front to where the car is waiting. I'm silent most of the ride to Zach's place, working things out in my mind.

"Did you know about this?" I finally spit out.

Lila looks up at me like I just shot her. "No, of course not."

I slump in my seat. "I'm sorry. It's just...am I really that gullible? I thought I could trust him, but obviously I was wrong."

She presses her lips together, giving me a sad nod. "I'm not his biggest fan, but I didn't think he was that slimy. I'm sorry, Kat."

"Not your fault."

My phone pings with a new notification from my secret social media account. I stifle a groan. You know that phrase, "when it rains, it pours?" I have a feeling I'm about to get soaked. What lovely thing does @katsonnettistrash have to say about me today? My day can't get much worse, so why not find out?

There's a photo of my hand wearing the gorgeous blue ring. The caption makes my stomach sink.

Can't believe her family had to find out she was engaged from a gossip site. Guess she's too high falutin' for the people who loved her before she was famous. Maybe Talon dodged a bullet. And those Titanic-sized feet.

I feel like I've been sucker punched. There's only ever been one person who has consistently tormented me about my feet. How did I not notice it before? I scroll back through the posts and there are more clues pointing to the identity of my number one hater.

#ifoundbigfoot

Look who doesn't need to put on water skis. I bet she could walk on water with those pontoons.

#theyetiisreal

Maybe I really can't trust anyone.

"Lila, how fast can we be on a plane to California?"

"I thought you wanted to stay a few more days."

I shake my head, worried if I stay here I'll discover something terrible about Zach I've somehow managed to overlook. It feels like that kind of day and I can't handle any more heartache. I'm too distraught to have a coherent discussion about our future, even if I know deep down Zach wouldn't hurt me on purpose. "I've changed my mind."

She types away on her phone for a bit. "We can catch a flight out around four. Is an hour enough time to pack?"

"I'll be ready."

When we return to Zach's house, I toss all my stuff into my bags, not even bothering to fold anything. I pull on leggings, a T-shirt, and my favorite sneakers. Zach's hoodie is hanging on the doorknob. After a moment's deliberation, I put it on, pausing for an appreciative sniff. There's only a trace of his woodsy cologne, but enough to make my heart twist. This isn't how I wanted today to go, but I'm at my breaking point. I feel stupid and seeing pity on his face would be too much.

After carting my bags out to the town car, I head back in and notice the container on the counter with my name on it. I unfold the paper.

Even though you can't have the recipe, the rest of the cake is yours. Looking forward to dinner tonight! Zach

Ugh. I'd completely forgotten about dinner. My heart twists with guilt that I'm leaving him in the lurch, but I feel like I'm about to implode and I don't want him to be collateral damage. I pull out drawers until I find a notepad and pen. After scribbling a quick note, I press it to my lips, regretting that this is how things are ending. With one last longing look around the house that has felt more like home than my L.A. mansion, I grab the cake and meet Lila in the car. My eyes scan the front of the house, committing it to memory before slumping against the seat. The historic buildings don't even register as we're shuttled out of the city to the airport.

CHAPTER THIRTY-ONE

Zach

Whistling as I approach my front door, my skin tingles with nervousness as I prepare myself for what's about to come. I've spent most of the day waffling between dread and excitement, unsure of what's going to happen between me and Katie. If she's willing to talk through the options, I'm sure we can find something that works for both of us. I run a hand through my hair, take a deep breath, and push the door open.

I pause, the quiet inside seeming out of place. Shouldn't there be the clang of spoons against pots? And what about the tantalizing aroma of cooking food floating through the house? I sniff. Nothing. I beeline for the kitchen, not bothering to take off my shoes, and find it as pristine as I left it this morning. I open the fridge. No new ingredients. Did Katie change her mind about cooking? Maybe work ran long and we're going out instead. I pull out my phone but have no new messages. Even if she was busy, she'd still text me. Or ask Lila to contact me.

My neck prickles with worry. Something doesn't feel right. I hurry upstairs to the guest bedroom. The closet and dresser drawers are empty. The rumpled bed is the only sign someone was staying here. I pull out my phone and call Katie, but it goes straight to voice mail. Her phone must be off. Dread pools in my stomach.

I head back down to the kitchen, looking around for clues until I spot a notepad on the kitchen table. Picking it up, my heart sinks as I read.

Zach, Thanks for everything. Something came up and I had to return to L.A. I really wanted things to work between us, but I just can't do this right now. I'm very sorry. Katie

She left me a note? Why not call or text? It's not like I was slammed at work and couldn't talk. And why so cryptic? "Something came up?" Surely I deserve more than a clichéd excuse. Unless she lied about wanting to date for real. Maybe she was just playing along because she didn't want to hurt my feelings. I knew she was a good actor, but surely even she couldn't have been faking the whole time, could she?

Not quite ready to give up hope, I call her again, but hang up when I get the recorded message. Is she ignoring me on purpose? If so, leaving a message would be pathetic.

How could I have been so stupid as to think there was something real between us? She pretends for a living, so of course I believed she actually liked me. I'm amazed she's only won one award for her skills.

I drop into the kitchen chair, letting the notepad fall onto the table. I always knew in the back of my mind things seemed too good to be true, and yet I let myself get caught up, anyway. This sucks. Crossing my arms on the table, I drop my head onto them, mentally berating myself for letting my guard down even though part of me knew better.

After giving myself a few minutes to wallow in my feelings, I straighten up, rip the note from the pad, and toss it in the trash. Then I go upstairs, strip the bed, and grab the towels from the guest bathroom. When I stuff everything into the washer, something falls onto the floor.

I pick up the RiverDogs baseball cap and sigh. I adjust the hat and put it on, feeling like a loser for not being able to let go as easily as Katie. After cleaning the bathroom and remaking the bed, I settle onto the couch, turning on the TV for a distraction.

And there she is on the screen, looking lovingly at some other guy. I've seen that look directed at me before, which feels like the final nail in the coffin proving I was duped. I was just another temporary leading man to her. I shouldn't really be mad because it's what I signed up for. It's my fault for ever thinking I had a real chance with her.

I change the channel in search of an action film where lots of stuff blows up, but pause when I see Katie's face again. It's one of those celebrity news shows. They're showing a picture of her at some event in a beautiful blue dress. It switches to one of me and Katie at her premiere. The two photos are now side-by-side and the hosts are dissecting her posture and expression, saying how much happier she looks next to me and pointing out the fact that she's leaning into me like she wants to be closer. It's like the whole universe wants to rub in how amazing she is at acting and how gullible I was.

My finger's on the button to change channels, but then they show a photo of a hand wearing a ring I recognize. One that's sitting on top of my dresser as we speak. After seeing it on Katie's hand, I couldn't give it to my mom. She received a pair of custom earrings from Bex for her birthday instead, while I foolishly hoped for an opportunity to give Katie the ring for real. How deluded am I? Despite the sting in my chest, I can't help but wonder what they're saying about her. I turn up the volume.

"...her team has neither confirmed nor denied the engagement. I don't know about you, Mario, but I'm thrilled for her. Kat deserves to be happy, and it looks like she's found someone who truly appreciates her. And he's easy on the eyes, too."

"Hey, now, Courtney. Should I be jealous?"

She smiles at him. "Of course not, babe. You're my one and only. And I can tell from the way those two look at each other that they've found their special person as well. I wish them all the best."

Oh, how I wish that was true. It's a small consolation I wasn't the only one who fell for our ruse. Thankfully, my mom doesn't keep up with celebrity news, so I don't have to worry about her thinking I'm getting married. I did text Jonah when I first heard the rumor since he follows that world and told him to set everyone straight if they asked. Which I'm glad about now because it's going to be hard enough telling everyone we broke up. My friends were excited to see me dating again. At least I don't have to hide my disappointment about it ending. It'd probably look weird if I wasn't bummed. It's my only solace in this whole terrible situation.

The hosts move on to some other celebrity I don't recognize and I click channels until I'm back around to the celebrity news show. Of course there's nothing on. It's Thursday. My stomach rumbles, reminding me I haven't eaten. I shut off the TV then head into the kitchen to scrounge something up, newly disappointed I didn't get to experience Katie's cooking. I have no idea if she is much of a cook, but I was enjoying the idea of seeing her in my kitchen like she lived here.

I sigh, make myself a sandwich, and then head out to the converted garage I use as a workshop. When I raise the door, the sight of a partially built table soothes me. I know just what needs to be done and lose myself in the process, only stopping when I realize how late it is.

Unfortunately, despite the late hour, I stare at the ceiling for a long time wondering why I agreed to such a ridiculous plan, knowing full well I was probably going to become emotionally involved. At some point I fall asleep, because all too soon I'm jolted awake by my alarm.

I lay there listening for signs of Katie moving around in her room, before remembering she's gone. A wave of melancholy washes over me. It's been a long time since I was dumped. I forgot how much it sucks. I heave myself out of bed, determined to keep myself busy enough so thoughts of Katie don't keep creeping into my mind. I fail miserably.

CHAPTER THIRTY-TWO

Kat

It's only been two days since I was in Charleston, but I already miss it. Okay, maybe not all of it. Certainly not the humidity. Not sleeping in beds with less cushion than my luxury mattress here at home. And definitely not the hours spent in hair and makeup on the days when filming took only thirty minutes. But I do miss some things. *Fine.* I miss one thing. One *person.*

I sigh, perplexed by my own feelings. How can someone I've only known for a couple of months take up so much space in my head and heart? Surely people only fall this quickly in movies. But I know that's not true because I searched the internet for stories of people who got married after knowing one another for only a few weeks. Plenty of successful marriages came from quick starts. Of course, none of them started out as a scheme to get someone's agent off their back.

I groan, flipping from laying on my back to my side. It affords me a better view through my living room window, giving me a glimpse of downtown in the distance.

My doorbell rings. I know who it is, but can't find the motivation to get up off the couch. There's knocking for a minute, and then I hear the faint beeps of the code being entered. A few seconds later, Lila comes into view with two coffee cups in her hand.

"Just as I thought," she says, setting one cup on the table in front of me. She pulls a white paper bag out of her tote and sets it next to the cup. "Sit up and eat something so you'll have some brain power while we formulate a plan."

I heave myself up, making room for her to sit. She hands me the coffee and I sip, appreciating the input of caffeine. Maybe it'll help counteract the lethargy I'm feeling. Curious about what else she brought, I open the bag and pull out a wrapped breakfast sandwich. The bacon, egg, and cheese sandwich tastes heavenly, making me realize I haven't eaten anything in almost two days. Is it just despair at feeling betrayed or is it also the heartsickness I feel over how I ended things with Zach? He deserved more than a hastily scribbled note, but that's all I could manage at the time. I should call him, but what if he doesn't answer? What if he answers and I hear the hurt in his voice? Or worst of all, what if there's no emotion? What if I'm the only one devastated by our separation? He called me twice while I was on the plane, but I'm afraid if I call him back, my greatest fear will be confirmed.

Of course, with everything else going on in my life, Zach is the least of my worries right now. Though I do wish he was here to help me navigate my current predicament. Perhaps I should have thought things through a little more before I just ghosted him. It's a little late to wish for a do over.

Lila leans over and sniffs the air near me. Her lips twist. "Have you showered?"

I shake my head.

"First breakfast," Lila commands. "Second shower. Then we'll talk about world domination."

I chuckle, appreciating her presence and forcefulness. I need someone to help get me out of this funk.

When I'm in clean clothes with my teeth brushed, I return to the living room and look around. The blanket is missing from the couch and the pillows have been fluffed and put back in their corners. Lila is perched in a chair, typing away on her phone.

"Where's my sweatshirt?"

She wrinkles her nose. "I put it in the washer along with the blanket."

"You washed it? But now it'll smell like fabric softener."

"I know. I don't know how you could wear something that smelled so bad," Lila says.

My lip trembles and my vision blurs with tears. Oh, no. It's finally happening. I crumple onto the couch, the last of my defenses gone. I bury my face in a pillow, embarrassed at how much I already miss Zach. The couch beside me shifts and arms come around me.

"Oh, Kat. What's wrong?"

I sob, unable to get enough breath to speak. Everything washes over me. Rick. Talon. Mason. Zach. I'm angry and sad at the same time. Lila is quiet, letting me feel my emotions. Eventually, the crying wanes and becomes heaving breaths.

Lila finds a box of tissues and hands them to me. I focus on some box breathing to get myself back under control.

"Talk to me," Lila says.

I blow my nose, then position myself on the couch so we're facing each other. Her concerned face pricks my heart. At least I have one person who has never let me down. *Two*, my conscience counters, making tears spring to my eyes again. I hastily wipe them away.

"Sorry," I say, taking a few deep breaths to resettle myself. "I've been feeling a lot these past few days."

"Understandable," she says. "You've had the rug pulled out from under you. A person should be able to trust their agent. Maybe it's a good thing you've already put out feelers. I didn't like the look on Rick's face when you confronted him."

I'd forgotten she had been with me at the hotel. "Do you really think he's going to spread malicious gossip about me?"

She shakes her head. "He'd be hurting himself since you're still his client. I just think you scared him with your threat and he wanted to even the playing field."

Her words give me a tiny shred of comfort.

"You're right. I need to end that relationship immediately, as it's no longer serving me. Can you set up a meeting with Lindsay Adams? I felt most confident about her ability to push my career forward. And don't set up any more side gigs. I need a break from commercials and promoting new brands."

She nods. "No problem. You have been working pretty hard. I asked Rick if we should slow down on all the extras, but he assured me it was what you wanted. I should have asked you instead. Sorry about that."

I pat her arm. "Don't worry about it. I haven't been good at pushing back against Rick. It's probably why he thought he could get away with these last stunts. But I'm no longer a naïve teenager. I have a lot of experience in this business and now I know what I want."

"What *do* you want?"

Zach's face flashes in my mind, but I shake it away. Things are so complicated for me right now that I can't even begin to consider how that might even be possible.

"First, I need a new agent. Second, I have to deal with something personal."

Lila gives me a sympathetic look. "Is it Zach? Are you going to ask him to move here?"

"Uh, no. Why do you think that?"

"Isn't that why you've been moping around? Because you miss him?"

Has it really been that bad? I guess if I needed to be told to shower, probably so. "Well, yeah, partially, but I might have burned that bridge."

I scrunch up my nose in anticipation of Lila's reaction to my next statement. "You know my hater account on social media?"

She sighs. "Are you still following it? That's not healthy for you."

"I know, but I figured out who's behind it. My brother."

Lila's eyes widen. "No! How do you know?"

"Some things he's written are phrases Mason used to use when I lived at home. I should have figured it out before, but it didn't click until the other day."

"Oh, Kat, that's awful. What are you going to do?"

"I'm not sure. I mean, what did I do to him that he hates me so much?"

She shrugs. "You're so nice to everyone. I doubt you deserve it. Maybe he's just jealous?"

I suppose she could be right, but I don't feel like a very nice person right now. There's plenty of evidence against me. I threatened my agent. Even if he possibly deserves it, I don't want to be that person. I left Zach with a note when he warranted so much more. And, if I'm honest, I have neglected my family these past few years.

"You're sweet, Lila, but I have to shoulder at least some fault in my current predicament."

Lila's phone dings and she grins. "That was Lindsay. You've got a meeting with her this afternoon. I guess she's eager to work with you."

Well, that's one step forward. "Thanks, Lila."

A buzzer goes off down the hall and she stands up. "I'll switch your laundry before I go. Unless you need anything else."

"Uh, no, I think I'm good."

She disappears and I stare out the window, contemplating what I'm going to say to Lindsay. Our first meeting was very promising. She was excited about helping me find more diverse character roles to play. I really hope it's not too late for the historical role I've had my eye on.

What to do about Mason is more complicated. I don't know why he hates me so much. It has to be more than jealousy. Maybe he's more angry about the baseball thing than he let on. Whatever his reasons, I need to deal with him so we can both move forward.

"I almost forgot," Lila says, coming back to the living room with a small padded envelope. "I found this on your front porch."

I take it from her, my brows scrunching up in confusion when I read the return address.

"How does Zach know where I live?"

"He asked me for your address. Should I not have given it to him?"

I wave away her concerned look. "No, it's fine."

I palpate the envelope, feeling something small and lumpy inside. Did I leave a lipstick at his place and he's returning it? Seems like something he'd do. Some people would just throw it away, but Zach is more considerate than most. I tear open the envelope and shake out a note and a small ball of tissue paper. Opening the paper, my pulse picks up as my eyes scan the page.

Katie, I'm sorry we didn't get a proper goodbye.

That's my fault, I think ruefully.

I really enjoyed our time together.

Me too. Too bad I ruined it.

I hope you get that role you have your heart set on. Zach

Even now he's still showing me kindness. How could I have just left someone this amazing?

P.S.-You left your RiverDogs hat at my place and I'm keeping it. Consider it a fair exchange for my hoodie (yes, I know you stole it).

Still with a sense of humor. He's way too good for me.

P.P.S.-My middle name is Derik.

Tears pool in the corners of my eyes. He isn't mad at me? I'd have been furious if he'd just disappeared on me. Of course, that's because I'm half in love with him. Maybe he wasn't as into me as I thought he was. Though he had to have felt something if he's holding onto my hat. Unless he's planning to burn it. But even that would show he cared about our relationship. This is too confusing. Am I just reading into things because part of me hopes he's sad too? I have no right to feel this way because it was my decisions and actions that led us to where we are. Honestly, it twists my heart to think I might have hurt such a kind, generous, amazing guy. If I'd stayed and shared my feelings, perhaps I wouldn't be so sad and alone right now.

His second P.S. practically rips my heart in two. He must think we're never going to see each other again if he ended our little game. Of course, I didn't exactly leave a door open between us with my note. *What were you thinking, Katie?* I wasn't.

I pick up the tiny package, tearing through it to see what he sent. It's obviously not lipstick. When I reach the small piece of wood, I gasp.

"What is it?" Lila's voice startles me. I didn't realize she was still here.

I place it in her hand. It's an otter laying on its back, its hands folded on its chest like it's floating in the water.

"Aww," Lila says. "So cute!"

My throat is tight with emotion. It's so detailed. Did he make it while we were together? This has to be proof he cares for me. The thought makes my heart soar and then sink. How could I have just left like he meant nothing to me? Tears trickle down my cheeks, pain welling up inside at the damage I've unleashed on a man who's been nothing but supportive toward me. Sure, I was distraught, but I know right from wrong. I was being a coward. I've just been letting life happen to me lately rather than taking charge, and look where that's gotten me. Nowhere good, for sure. It's time to retake the reins of my life, go after what I want, and not let fear or doubt intimidate me any longer.

CHAPTER THIRTY-THREE
Zach

"Earth to Zach. Are you with us?"

I blink out of my stupor and glance across the table at Nora. Her face is etched with concern.

"Sorry, did I miss something?"

"Is everything okay? You look like someone stole your favorite blankie."

My forehead scrunches. "What blankie?"

She shakes her head. "You haven't said a word throughout dinner. What's going on? Are you just sad that Kat went back to Hollywood, or is it something more?"

I look around the table, seeing the same worried expression on each face. I sigh. "Katie and I broke up."

"Oh, no!" Nora says. "What happened?"

Jonah glares at me. "What did you do?"

I glare back. "Nothing. We didn't think long-distance would work. It was mutual."

Only I know this is a lie. It's better than saying I wasn't enough for her. The truth still stings. I tried to wish her well by sending her the otter. Of course, my motivation wasn't completely selfless. I wanted her to know

I really did care for her, but also it hurt me to look at it and remember how hopeful I was that we had a future together.

Jonah shakes his head. "I don't believe you."

I shrug. "Then I don't know what to tell you."

"You seem awfully sad for something that ended mutually," Will chimes in.

He's pretty astute. Technically, Katie and I agreed that this was how things were going to end, and I seem less pathetic this way. Yes, I'm still wounded she didn't even say goodbye, but I'm trying to get over it. I can at least be somewhat honest about my feelings.

"I really liked her. If she wasn't on the other side of the country, maybe things would have worked out, but it's not like I could ask her to move here."

"Why can't you move there?" Nora asks.

I shoot her a look, my eyes flitting briefly to Mom. "My business is here, among other things." Other things like Katie not wanting me enough to talk things out in person.

That seems to satisfy everyone's curiosity, thankfully, and the conversation moves on. I feel a hand on my arm. Mom is giving me a questioning look, so I smile to reassure her.

"Zach and I will clean up," Mom says when dinner is over. "You all go do something fun."

"It's trivia night over at The Laboratory," Nora says, glancing at her phone. "We can just make it if we leave now."

Everyone carries their plates to the kitchen, thanking Mom for another wonderful meal before rushing out the front door. I hear a car start up and then it's quiet again. Mom and I clear the table in silence. She puts me on drying duty and fills the sink with water.

"Alright," she says, "talk to me."

I shrug, not meeting her eye. "What do you want me to say?"

"Do you love her?"

She really cuts to the quick, huh? Surely it's too soon to love Katie. I definitely like her, though. A whole lot, by the way my heart is throbbing at her absence.

I shrug, rather than give her a straight answer. "You think I'd have learned my lesson and not allowed myself to get so attached, but here we are."

"What do you mean by that?"

I don't want to lie to my mom. "Katie did break up with me." I sigh. "Honestly, I should have known this would happen. It's not the first time I've been rejected by someone I love. I come on too strong. I'm too needy and smother them until they leave."

Mom takes off her dish gloves and pulls me into a hug. "You're not too needy. Wherever did you get that idea?"

My eyes sting and I squeeze them shut, embarrassed by how emotional I am. I clear my throat, but my voice still wobbles when I speak. "I'm sorry Dad left us. I just wanted to spend more time with him, to do something that would make him proud of me, but I drove him away."

Mom grabs my shoulders, looking into my face. "What are you talking about?"

"I pestered Dad too much about coming to my baseball games. I thought if he came to just one, he'd see something good in me. But instead, he left us. I was too much trouble and too needy, so he left."

"Oh, honey, no. That's not true. Your father's leaving had nothing to do with you. Come, sit down at the table and let's talk."

She leads me over to the kitchen table and I drop down into a chair. I know she's going to try to convince me it wasn't my fault, but I know what happened.

"If it's not my fault, then why was he gone after we got back from one of my baseball games? The last time I saw him, I begged him to come. He told me I was being whiny and to knock it off. Obviously, he got tired of my cajoling."

Mom rubs soothing circles on my back. "Oh, Zachy. Your father was drunk when he said those things. He didn't really mean them. He struggled with alcohol. I'd told him he needed to deal with his issues because I saw how hurt you were when he dismissed or ignored you. That day I told him if he didn't want to change, then he needed to leave because I wouldn't let him cause you more pain."

Her chin wobbles, her voice breaking on the last word. Her eyes fill with tears. I had no idea this was going on. Of course, I was just a kid. I didn't know anything about substance abuse.

"I'm sorry you've thought it was your fault all these years," she says, wiping the tears streaming down her cheeks. "I should have done better at helping you understand. Please forgive me."

I wrap my arms around her and pull her in tight, my own tears falling. How could I have been so wrong? And now that I know the truth, can I accept it?

"There's nothing to forgive, Mom. You loved me enough for two parents."

She squeezes my shoulders, then pulls back. "I see how much you like Katie, and she didn't seem to think you were too much for her. Why don't you go after her?"

"Because she doesn't want me." The truth hurts, but maybe if I say it enough, the sting will lessen. "Besides, my business is here. *You're* here. I have roots."

She gives me a no nonsense look. "Your roots didn't keep you from going to Asheville and you seemed to find plenty of customers there, if I recall." She gives me an appraising look. "If you're worried about me, don't be. I feel great and the doctors have given me a very positive prognosis. Don't put your life on hold just because I *might* get sick again. I promise I'll be fine."

I open my mouth to respond, but she holds up a hand to stop me.

"I'm not saying I don't appreciate what you did coming here to help when I got sick. You truly were a lifesaver, but I would have managed even if you hadn't been able to come. Go live your life."

I frown. Mom's lived here her whole life. She knows everyone in a ten-block radius and went to school with many of the folks who are in local government and run successful businesses. There were plenty of people who offered their help while she was undergoing treatment. If I'd stayed in Asheville, she still would have been surrounded by people who love her. I think I came back mostly because I didn't want to abandon her like my dad did. And I have enjoyed my time here, but maybe I should venture out again. She must see the realization on my face, because she grins and pats my arm.

"Now tell me why you think Katie doesn't want you. Did she actually say that?"

I grimace. "Not exactly."

"What did she say, honey?"

I release a long breath, then recite her note from memory. I read it so many times it's imprinted on my brain.

She's quiet for a few moments. "Well, baby, it sounds like she had an emergency. It doesn't sound like goodbye. Just see you later. You can still work with that."

"She didn't answer my calls and I haven't heard a peep from her since she left."

I wince, realizing that's not completely true. Mom simply raises an eyebrow, waiting for me to come clean. Sometimes it's a real pain when someone knows all your tells. "She sent a thank you text for a package I sent."

Mom tilts her head to the side, her classic thinking action. "Maybe whatever it was that came up is being dealt with. Perhaps when she's worked through whatever has rocked her world, she'll reach back out."

It's not like I haven't considered this. I've pondered so many scenarios about what happened, one of them is probably true. But I keep landing back on the one where she just didn't see a future for us. Still, maybe it'll feel better to talk through one of the alternatives. "But why couldn't she have talked to me about her issue? I'd have done whatever I could to help."

She hugs me against her side. "I don't know. Maybe she was so overwhelmed she couldn't think straight. Or maybe she isn't used to having people she can count on."

That is a very real possibility from all I know about Katie. It's not like we've been together long enough for her to know she can depend on me, no matter what. The thought of her dealing with hard things alone pierces my gut. As much as I'd like to rush to her aid, I should respect her wish to handle things her way. I just have to hope she'll come back to me.

CHAPTER THIRTY-FOUR
Kat

This week has been full of activity. I met with Lindsay Adams and decided we'd be a perfect fit. I set up a meeting with Rick and told him it was time to part ways. I had been worried about him retaliating, but Lila has been my guardian angel during this tumultuous time. She found clauses in my contract about character defamation and morality. I handed Rick a copy with the important parts highlighted, and the threat of litigation seemed to shut him up. He didn't apologize for his underhanded behavior, but he's never been one to acknowledge mistakes. The meeting was surprisingly anticlimactic after all the worrying I'd done.

Lindsay got me an audition for the World War II script I've been drooling over. I've spent the last few days working on my monologue and figuring out how I want to portray the character. This role would be a stretch for me, but I'm ready to shake things up and see what happens. My meeting to show the director what I can do is in a few days, but I've got real-life drama to take care of in the meantime.

I sent a message to @katsonnettistrash saying I know who they are and want to talk. They responded skeptically, but when I told them I could meet them at Trexler Financial where they work, they realized I was serious. We're meeting at a cafe around the corner from his office.

I showed up early, coming directly from the airport. When the flight touched down, the familiar scenery out the window made me momentarily nostalgic. Atlanta used to be my home base while I was making the teen drama. But once that show ended, the movie roles took me all over the world and I thought I needed to be in Los Angeles, where everyone else was. I probably could have done just fine staying in Georgia, but spreading my wings helped me learn to stand on my own two feet. Of course, I also found out how lonely success can be and only recently discovered that it doesn't have to be that way for me.

My fingers pick at the cardboard sleeve around my cup while my eyes search the face of every person who comes into the cafe. Finally, a guy in a very nice suit and expensive leather shoes crosses the threshold and looks around. When we connect gazes, he freezes. I wave, motioning him over. He hesitates, making me wonder if he's going to turn around and leave, but he shakes his head and makes his way over, sitting on the stool across from mine.

"Katie, what brings you to town?"

I spin my empty cup around.

"Oh, you know, just coming to find out why my brother hates me."

Mason tugs at the collar of his shirt and chuckles nervously. "How did you figure out it was me?"

I lean back, disappointed. I thought an apology would be the first thing out of his mouth, but I guess if he despises me, he's probably happy to know he's hurt me.

"I should have figured it out the first time you commented on my feet. No one else has ever compared them to boats."

He looks away, running a hand through his hair.

"Seriously," I say, leaning forward and resting my elbows on the table. "What happened? We used to be thick as thieves. Was it only about baseball? Because I can't do anything other than apologize. I didn't even know about that until you told me, but I'm still sorry."

He blows out a breath, still not meeting my eye. "It wasn't just that. I was also jealous. Do you know what it's like having a little sister everyone knows and loves? You're all anyone wants to talk to me about when they find out we're related. I was actually glad when you took a stage name because new people had no idea."

That would be hard. I'm not sure how I'd act if the situation were reversed. Still, something tells me that's not the whole picture.

"Some of your posts are pretty vicious, like that engagement one. I told you, Mom, and Dad to ignore any gossip, and that I'd tell you first if something was true. Did you really think I'd keep news like that from you?"

"I don't know what you'd do. It's not like we talk much. And we rarely see you."

Okay, now it feels like we're getting somewhere. I sense some hurt feelings.

"I know, and I'm sorry. I've allowed work to take over my life these past few years and neglected my family. If it's any consolation, I've missed you too and am cutting back on work so I can visit more often. And, of course, you're always welcome to come see me in California."

He gives me a skeptical look. "Really? This is the first I'm hearing about your open door policy."

I sigh. "Like I said, work overwhelmed me for a bit, but I've realized how important it is to cultivate my relationships."

He rolls his eyes.

"Is this because of your new boyfriend?"

My face crumples at the mention of Zach. I've been trying so hard to not think about him, but he seems to keep coming up.

"We broke up."

I bury my face in my hands, embarrassed to be tearing up in public. An arm wraps around my shoulders.

"I'm sorry," Mason says. "What happened?"

I shake his arm off, suspicious. "Why do you want to know? So you can post about it?"

He has the decency to look chastened. "Look, I'm sorry. I never thought you'd see my posts. It was a way for me to vent my frustration. And then when the account started gaining popularity, it kind of felt nice to have my hurt validated by others. I must admit I felt special having something I wrote go viral. I didn't really think about how it would make you feel. I know it wasn't kind or right. I'll delete the account."

I wave a hand. "Do whatever you want. Wouldn't want to stifle you."

"What I did to you was mean. You didn't deserve that."

His admission makes me feel like all is not lost between us. "I appreciate that. Do you think we can start over? I really have missed my big brother."

"Yeah, okay. I kind of missed you, too. And, for what it's worth, I'm sorry about you and Zach. He seemed like a genuinely nice guy."

I nod. "He is."

He raises an eyebrow. "So…?"

He's giving me the first opportunity to rebuild our relationship. There's a risk he's playing me, but I don't want to shut him out if he's really trying. And I can't be suspicious of people forever. Still, I'm too afraid to admit I chickened out, so I say something that could be a real reason.

"Neither of us wanted to date long distance. He's got his job, family, and friends in Charleston. I couldn't ask him to give all that up for me."

"Why can't you move there? It seems to me like you're always off filming somewhere else. What does it matter where your home base is?"

He has a point. Do I really need to be based in Los Angeles? This is something Zach and I could have discussed if I'd stuck around instead of running away.

"I suppose I could, but we've only been dating a couple of months. It seems like a lot of pressure to put on a new relationship. What if it doesn't work out? I'd just move back to California with my tail between my legs?"

"Maybe. But what if it turns into forever?"

My heart skips a beat at that thought. What if my relationship with Zach could be fixed? Am I willing to give up that chance because I'm scared if I reach out, he'll reject me? I'm heartsick now. How much worse could it get?

"You're right. Thanks, Mase."

He smiles and pats my shoulder. "Anytime."

"So, are we good?"

My heart is beating quickly as I wait for his response. I didn't realize how much I've missed connecting with people who have known me my whole life and can call me out when needed.

"Only if you forgive me for being a jerk."

"Only if you promise to tell me when I hurt or annoy you. No more passive-aggressive social media accounts."

He chuckles and holds out his hand. "Deal."

I slap his hand away and pull him into a hug. He squeezes me back, and I feel a wave of relief.

Mason tries to convince me to stay for dinner with the parents, but I'm not ready to see their sad faces when they hear Zach and I are no longer together. He promises not to say anything, so I can be the one to tell them. I know Dad will be disappointed. He's been texting me project ideas to do with Zach the next time we visit.

I'm sitting in the airport lounge when my phone rings. I smile when I see who's calling.

"Hey Grady. To what do I owe the pleasure?"

He laughs. "Hey Kat. I was wondering if you'd be willing to do me a favor. I agreed to be on a panel here in Asheville that talks about the city's representation in entertainment. Since you and I just wrapped a movie based on a book written by an Asheville author, I thought perhaps you'd be willing to join me. If you show up, it's sure to be a sold out event."

I smile. "I'm pretty sure they only need your name for that."

"Nah. Everyone knows me here. I'm old hat. You, on the other hand, would be a novelty."

"When is it?"

"This weekend. I know it's short notice, but it'd be great to see you."

It would be nice to spend more time with Grady outside of our work commitments. This offer feels like his attempt to turn us into real friends. I certainly could use a few more of those. I click over to my calendar.

"You're in luck; I'm available. Text me the details."

He whoops into the phone so loud I have to pull it away from my ear.

"Thanks, Kat. And, hey, bring Zach. We can do some hiking while you're here."

My stomach twists. Yet another person I have to break the news to. I'm afraid if I say it right now, I'll end up crying in the airport and no one wants that. I ignore his comment and wrap up the call. All this angst I'm feeling should help me with my audition tomorrow. And it's something I can use to distract this tornado of emotions swirling in my chest.

After talking with Mason, I need to talk to Zach in person. He may not forgive me, but it's the right thing to do. I'll hop over to Charleston after the Asheville trip and get it over with. The decision does nothing to ease the discomfort in my gut.

I sent Zach a thank you text for the otter carving and received 'you're welcome' back. It's more than I deserve with the way I just disappeared on him, but the curt message still stung. I've been wracked with guilt over how I handled everything with him. I owe him at least a face-to-face apology and explanation.

An idea pops into my head of something I can do for Zach in the meantime, making me feel hopeful. I don't know why I hadn't thought of it before. I shoot off a quick text to Lila before boarding my plane.

CHAPTER THIRTY-FIVE

Zach

"Sorry I'm late," I say, coming into the kitchen. Everyone is standing around the island, plates already full of food. "Oh, good. You didn't start cards without me."

Nora gives me a side hug. "What took you so long? Traffic?"

The counter full of food makes my stomach growl. I snag a pinwheel off the tray and stuff it in my mouth, then pile a paper plate high with food.

"No. The store was unbelievably crowded today. There were even a few people waiting outside when I showed up to open this morning. I sold all my little wooden animals and most of my bookends. The phone has not stopped ringing with people wanting me to either ship something I already have on hand or custom make tables and chairs. I know people say selling is feast or famine, but I've never had so much attention."

"It's probably because of the post," Jonah says, taking a bite of pizza.

"What post?" I say around a mouthful of food.

Jonah shakes his head like I'm a lost cause.

"I forget you don't do social media. Kat posted about your store last night."

Suddenly, everyone has their phones out.

"No way!" Nora says. "Whoa, dude. Her photos make me want to buy one of your tables, and I don't have anywhere to put it."

I make a "gimme" motion, and she hands me her phone. The first photo is of the interior of the store with me sitting at the desk in the background. There are closeups of a chair and one of my river tables. The last one is a selfie of her holding up a tiny wooden elephant with a swooping trunk. My heart squeezes. She's so beautiful. That smile could make me buy a little wooden animal I don't need in a heartbeat.

My brow furrows as I try to figure out why she's doing this. Is this her way of paying me back for dating her? An attempt to make things even between us? My stomach lurches at the thought and I pass the phone back to Nora. "Why would she do this?"

Will shrugs. "Maybe she misses you and this is a roundabout way of showing she cares."

"Oooh," Nora says, nodding. "Yes, you're constantly on her mind and she wonders if you're thinking about her."

I scoff. "Of course I can't stop thinking about her, but I haven't heard from her since she left."

"Because she wants to honor your break up but secretly hopes you'll decide you can't live without her and move to California to be with her," Will says with a wide grin, clearly getting into this speculation game.

"Or she's just helping a friend," I counter.

"I don't think so," Nora says, messing with her screen. "She called you her favorite artisan and told her followers meeting you was the best thing about her time in Charleston."

"No way." How I wish that was true, but I know Nora's just messing with me.

She gives me a disappointed look. "Did you even read the caption?"

"What caption? All I saw were pictures."

"You're hopeless," Jonah says.

I look over Nora's shoulder, reading the words she's pointing to. When what Katie said about me and my store washes over me, it momentarily buoys my previously dead hope that maybe Mom was right about Katie just needing some time. Is this her way of saying she's ready? But then why not reach out to me directly?

"I don't know guys. We haven't known each other very long. Isn't it a little impulsive to consider moving across the country for someone I'm not currently dating?"

"What do you have to lose?" Greg says.

"Besides my business, friends, and family?"

"We'll all still be here," Dane says. "You could at least visit her and see what she thinks."

Duh. I'm glad there's at least one cool head in the group. A visit is doable. And a lot less permanent than moving my whole life across the country if it turns out I'm reading more into things and she just wants to be friends. The thought of seeing her again makes my heart race.

"When should I go? What should I say? Do I tell her I'm coming?"

Nora must notice my wild eyes because she clamps a hand on my shoulder and leads me to a chair.

"Sit. Eat. We'll help you figure out a plan."

My skin feels jittery with nerves. Am I really going to fly to California and give Katie another opportunity to reject me? It's gotta be better than living with the constant ache of missing her and wondering if she's missing me.

"First," Will says, taking the chair across from me. "What do you want to say?"

Do I tell her it feels like I'm missing a limb without her? That she's the first thing I think about in the morning and the last thing on my mind before I fall asleep? That I can't stop carving otters out of wood blocks because I just want an excuse to feel like she's still here with me? That sounds too intense. Maybe start with the basics.

"I want to tell her I really like her, miss her like crazy, and would like to find a way to make this work. I'll tell her I'm willing to move to Los Angeles, if that's what it takes."

Approving nods meets my statements. Jonah's phone beeps. He looks down at it and gasps.

"Guys! Kat is going to be in Asheville this weekend." He looks at me. "Maybe you don't have to go all the way to California just yet."

Nora's eyes widen. "Ooh, I've got a great idea." She grabs my arm firmly. "Zach, you should grand gesture her!"

My forehead wrinkles. "Do what now?"

"Take a page out of her movies and do something special to show her how much you care. Oh! I bet that's why she posted about your business. She grand gestured you. I bet she loves you!"

My heart pounds against my ribs. Could that be true? Obviously, that's what I hope, but how can I know for sure? There's really only one way to find out, and it's going to take all my courage.

CHAPTER THIRTY-SIX

Kat

Although it was awkward telling Grady and Bex that Zach and I broke up, overall it's been a pleasant visit to Asheville. We went for a hike in Dupont Forest and saw a few waterfalls. Bex gave me the earrings I ordered from her, plus a necklace she made that has a little pineapple pendant on it. She said it was a memento to remind me of filming the movie with Grady, but it immediately made me think of Zach instead. I put it on because it's pretty and I didn't want to hurt her feelings. It kind of feels like a way to carry Zach with me. Of course, I was already doing that with the small wooden otter in my purse.

After dinner at Blue Goose Taco Shop, we walk to the Wortham Center for the Performing Arts for the panel. The five-hundred seat theater is sold out, just as Grady predicted, though I doubt it's because I'm here. My name isn't even on the website. I'm a pleasant surprise unless you follow me on social media and saw Lila's not-so-subtle post suggesting people check out the panel if they live nearby. There were more than a few people commenting that they'd gotten a ticket.

We're ushered behind the curtain onto the stage and shown which chair to sit in. I'm seated between Grady and an author. There's also a director who made a movie at Biltmore Estate and someone from the Chamber of Commerce. While we wait, I make small talk with the woman on my left.

"Wait," I say, things finally clicking into place. "Did you write *Stuck With You?*"

"That's me."

I sit up in my chair. "I really enjoyed the fast-paced action and the funny situations. I'm sorry it wasn't filmed here to utilize the locations in the book."

She shrugs. "I heard the film backers had ties to South Carolina and wanted to do something for their community. Can't blame them, I suppose. But that's part of what this panel's about. Figuring out how to bring more publicity to Asheville."

"You've got a great advocate in Grady. I know he's looking for ways to utilize the local landscape in his films. He managed to get his next one made here."

Grady leans in, obviously eavesdropping. "That's because I'm one of the major investors in the film. I don't have much sway as an actor, but executive producers get a little more input."

"I didn't know that."

He smiles and lowers his voice. "Just between us, while I'm glad the city benefits from it, my main motivation is being able to sleep in my own bed at night."

I laugh, wondering how much truth is in his statement. It certainly was nice being able to go to Zach's place after filming and relax. My heart clenches remembering how good it felt not being alone every night. Well, after tonight, I'm headed to Charleston to find out if I can eliminate my loneliness for good. I haven't quite worked out what I want to say, but I know I have to apologize and tell him I'm falling in love with him. Just the thought makes my stomach swoop with fear that he won't feel the same way. I can't stand this limbo of not knowing if I screwed things up permanently.

It's not like we didn't suit each other. We had plenty of chemistry—more than I've ever had with anyone else. And I don't think I'd ever get tired of curling up on the couch with him or having dinner with his mom and friends. Regular game nights are also appealing to me. I could let my competitive nature out and not feel judged by anyone.

My house in L.A. feels cold and empty because it's missing my new favorite person. The only thing I think I'd miss about California is Lila, but we could still work long distance. She fully supports whatever happens tomorrow, which I appreciate. As does my new agent. She believes in work-life balance and wants me to direct my career path. I haven't heard anything back about my audition, but I'm hopeful. My agent said the director was deciding between me and two other actors. Every time I think about it, I cross my fingers and toss up a prayer. I really want the part, but I know Lindsay will help me find another one if it doesn't work out.

The buzz of the crowd behind the curtain grows louder the closer we get to the start time. Finally, someone hands us each a microphone and moves offstage. The curtain parts and cheers erupt from the crowd. There are audience members holding up cutouts of Grady's face. There's one of me too. Other people are waving books in the air. Someone else has a movie poster featuring a couple at Christmastime with a mansion in the background.

The moderator steps out on stage and welcomes the crowd, sharing the format of the event and introducing each of us. I wave when she calls my name, startled by a piercing whistle from somewhere in the audience. It sounds like I have a couple fans in attendance.

We spend an hour discussing prepared questions from the moderator about the entertainment industry. The Chamber representative talks about what they're doing to attract more high-profile events to the area. Then the floor is opened to questions from the audience. There are microphones on stands in the aisles and a young man is the first one in line.

"Hi," he says, waving. "Kat, I'm a big fan. Does your presence on this panel indicate that you're moving to the area like Grady?"

I hadn't thought much about how things might look. I smile, deciding to have some fun, maybe start a rumor. "Great question. I don't have any plans to move to Asheville right now, however, I enjoyed filming in Charleston and have considered spending more time there soon."

The moderator points to the woman at the other microphone, who asks the director a question. I relax, enjoying hearing the questions and answers for the other panelists. Someone asks if the author would sign their books. Same question from someone with a cardboard cutout of Grady's head.

I start to zone out until I hear my name. My skin tingles, recognizing the voice. My breath hitches and my heart leaps when my gaze snags on my favorite pair of blue eyes. What is Zach doing here? There's no way it's a coincidence. It's a four-hour drive between the cities, which I know because I was planning to rent a car tonight. Does this mean he's not upset about how I left? I'm still going to apologize, but I am tempering my hope that he may be willing to give me a second shot at a relationship. The right side of his mouth tips up and he winks. I'm grateful to be sitting in a chair because my knees go weak in response. I lean forward, wondering what he's going to say.

"You mentioned earlier that you were considering a visit to Charleston. Do you have any specific plans?"

Even from this distance, I can feel myself being pulled toward him. How in the world did I think I could just walk away from what's been developing between us? My heart is pounding. I clear my throat, hoping to steady my voice.

"Well, I'm in need of some new bookends, so I thought I might look in one of the local shops." The serious face I'm trying to maintain breaks and I feel my lips tip up on both sides. "Also, I've been jonesing for a road trip and some Nerds Gummy Clusters."

His smile makes me feel giddy. "That sounds like an excellent itinerary. What are you doing after this? I've got a bag of Nerds in my truck."

A few people chuckle at his bold offer. The increased chatter between audience members makes me think some people have figured out what's going on. But I don't care because I can't stop grinning at Zach.

"Sounds like a date," I say.

Zach nods, then tosses something to me. I just catch it, surprised to be holding a little wooden heart. My actual heart nearly stops. Does this mean what I think it means? I look back at the mic stand, but he's no longer there. Glancing around, I don't see him. Of course, I don't remember what he was wearing. I was too busy staring at that handsome face. I just have to trust we'll find each other afterwards.

Questions continue and I'm so ready to be done. I need to see Zach again! My arms are aching to hold him, to tell him I'm sorry and want to figure out how to make things work between us.

Grady motions me closer and whispers in my ear. "Does this mean you're getting back together?"

"I hope so."

He smiles. "Good, because I want another invite to game night. I need to redeem myself after last time."

I laugh, slapping my hand over my mouth when I realize I've interrupted the conversation. I mouth "sorry" to the audience.

Finally, the moderator wraps things up, thanking everyone for coming. The audience is on their feet clapping. I shade my eyes, trying to find Zach in the crowd, but it's futile. Maybe I'll just stay put and let him find me. My leg jiggles up and down in anticipation. Nope, can't do it. I hop up, then head offstage to grab my phone so I can call him.

I've just reached my purse in the little staging room when I hear the door shut behind me. Goosebumps rise on my arms. Slowly, I straighten up and turn, my senses on high alert. When I see who it is, I dart across the room and slam into Zach, wrapping my arms around his neck. He chuckles, pulling me tight against him. He kisses my cheek softly, and I sigh, relishing the scent of his cologne.

"I missed you," I say.

He pulls back and looks into my eyes. "I've missed you, too. I came here to tell y—"

My hand clamps over his mouth. "Me first."

He shrugs and I move my hand, softly tracing his lips with my finger. I've missed those as well. I shake my head, refusing to get distracted despite how desperately my mouth wants to taste his. My gaze snags on his chest and my heart squeezes at the sight of the road trip shirt I bought him. I can't believe he wore it. Actually, I'm still in shock that he's here. It definitely makes me feel more confident about what I'm about to say.

"I'm sorry for how I left. I'd had some devastating news. I should have stayed and talked about it with you, but I was scared and I ran. I've thought about you every day we've been apart. I miss your cologne, your warm hugs, and the way your eyes twinkle when you're amused by me. Zach, I'm in love with you. If you'll forgive me, I'd like to move to Charleston and see where this goes."

He's silent, his eyes wide. Did I scare him? Oh no, I came on too strong with the love thing. Maybe there's a way I can backtrack a little?

I open my mouth, but Zach puts a finger over my lips.

"My turn."

He takes a deep breath that I can feel because we're still pressed against each other. I'm also aware of his heart hammering against his sternum. It's going almost beat for beat with my own.

"First, I forgive you. Second, I'm sorry I let you go without a fight. I was hurt that you didn't talk to me before you left, but I should have trusted that you'd reach out when you could. You're beautiful, fun, and funny. Your presence in my house made me excited to come home each day, and I love the way you wiggle in your chair when you eat something you like. I thought Charleston was my home, but it's actually you. I will move to Los Angeles and support your career however I can. I love you, Katie."

I chuckle, amazed at this wonderful man who would obviously do anything for me. "Well, we can't both move."

He shrugs. "We can talk about it later. Right now, I need to know if you were serious about coming home with me."

I give him a coy look. "Yes, but only if you really have Nerds."

He shakes his head, but is smiling ear to ear. "You think I'd lie about something like that?"

I playfully push his shoulder, my body zinging with happiness. "Za—"

Whatever else I was planning to say leaves my brain when his lips find mine. I sigh against his mouth, feeling like I'm home again. Each kiss feels better than the one before, and it's only the sound of a door opening that breaks the trance.

"Sorry," Grady says, grinning like he's anything but. "Came for my phone." He nods at Zach. "Nice to see you, man."

"Same," Zach says. "Sorry I can't stay to hike. Maybe next visit."

"I'll hold you to it," he says, patting Zach's shoulder on his way back out the door.

Zach clears his throat and releases me, lacing our fingers together. "Need anything before we go?"

My bag with a change of clothes is at Grady's house, but I'll just borrow some of Zach's. I lean forward and press a quick kiss to his lips. "Everything I need is right here."

Epilogue

Kat

One Year Later

If someone had approached me this time last year and told me in twelve months' time I'd be living on the east coast, dating a gorgeous man who loves me like I'm the most precious thing in the world, and be the star of the number one movie in the world with lots of Oscar buzz, I'd have laughed in their face. But, sometimes real life is better than anything you can ever imagine.

I got the role in the World War II drama I so desperately wanted. It feels validating that *Hidden Madness* has been at the top of the box office chart since its release. All the reviews have raved about my performance. Some mentioned how shocked they were that a comedic actor had this kind of range. I'm not sure if that's supposed to be a compliment or a dig. Regardless, I've received offers to play a variety of parts in future movies. I've signed up for a comedy and another historical drama, but the rest of my year is currently free, which is good because right now I'm preparing for the role of a lifetime: Zach's bride.

In a few minutes, I'll be walking up an aisle and repeating lines I've already memorized because I just can't help it. We're getting married in the courtyard of Zach's mom's house. It's a small group—our families and a few friends. Initially, I wanted to have the ceremony at the pineapple fountain where we almost had our first kiss and also got engaged, but Lila reminded me we couldn't block off the area like we do in movie shoots and I'd rather not have uninvited guests angling for selfies or autographs on the most important day of my life.

Zach proposed a month after we got back together, giving me the gorgeous blue sapphire and diamond ring he'd bought in California. He said once he saw it on my finger, he knew it was meant for me. He ended up giving his mom some earrings designed by Bex for her birthday, which she loved. We both would have gotten married within the month, but I got the call for the movie role and shooting started right away. Plus, Zach had a lot of new orders for dining sets to fill, thanks to my social media post. Oops. Sorry not sorry.

Thankfully, the movie was filmed in Atlanta, so we were within driving distance of one another. Plus, I got to make up for lost time with my brother and parents. Mason and I are on much better terms now. He deleted the social media account and seems to appreciate that I'm making more of an effort to keep in touch with my family. I certainly enjoy having them back in my life again.

There's a knock on the bathroom door where I'm putting the finishing touches on my makeup. I pull it open and my dad does a double take. I slide my hands down the dress, a gorgeous V-neck tulle dress with three-dimensional floral appliques and a swishy skirt. My hair is styled in a loose chignon that shows off the low cut back of the dress. I feel like a princess.

"Sweetie, you are so beautiful."

"Thanks, Dad." I motion to his tux. "You look very dapper."

"Are you ready?"

I grin. "I thought this day would never come. Let's get this show on the road."

We head downstairs to the foyer of Zach's former home. With all the furniture orders, he needed a bigger workshop. He found a home a couple of streets over from his mom's and turned the garage into his workspace. The house needs some work, but he's excited to help restore the house to its former glory, and my dad has offered to be a second set of hands whenever he needs them. They've really bonded over house projects. My parents have a fancy laundry room now with custom cabinets, an extendable drying rack, and a folding table thanks to Zach's ingenuity and ability to utilize small spaces.

I peek out the front window. White chairs are set up in two sections for our guests. The end of the aisle is blocked from my view by the side of the house, but I can picture the flower-covered arch at the front where we'll stand to say our vows. I wonder if Zach is out there somewhere mingling with our guests. A bell rings, indicating it's time for people to take a seat.

Zach's mom opens the door and steps inside. She sees me and smiles. "You make a beautiful bride." She turns toward the kitchen. "Alright, ladies. You're on."

My bridesmaids—Lila, Nora, and Bex—grab their bouquets and give me a hug on their way out the door. Music plays. Elaine takes Will's arm, and he walks her down the aisle. Next are Mom and Mason. My bridesmaids follow, which is my cue to head outside with my dad to the little screen set up just behind the last row of chairs. He hands me my bouquet. I guess in my excitement I left it on the kitchen table. I give him a grateful smile, then slide my arm through his as the music changes.

I push my shoulders back and take a deep breath, wondering if I'm going to tear up when I finally lay eyes on my almost husband. We step out from behind the screen and turn to face the center of the aisle. Thirty feet away stands my future. Dane, Greg, and Mason are lined up behind Zach. I lock eyes with my groom as I proceed up the aisle. His mouth is pressed into a line, his chin trembling slightly. Oh my gosh, is he trying not to cry? This thought only causes tears to fill my eyes. I must sniffle because Dad discreetly passes me a tissue. I dab my eyes and shake my head slightly at how ridiculous I must look. Stuffing the tissue in the pocket of my dress, I look up in time to see Zach wipe his eyes with the back of his hand, then give me a sheepish look. I smile, my heart soaring that I get to spend the rest of my life with this sweet man who loves me so completely.

When we finally reach the front, Dad kisses my cheek, then takes his seat next to Mom. I hand my bouquet off to Lila and then take Zach's hands. He gives mine a reassuring press and we turn toward the officiant.

It feels like the ceremony is but a blink before we're both wearing new rings and grinning at each other while our officiant invites us to seal our vows with a kiss.

Zach's eyes glint with mischief. He wraps his arms around my waist and shoulders, then dips me before pressing his lips to mine. My hands cling to his shoulders while I kiss him back with all the love in my heart. After probably too much time for our audience but not enough for me, he breaks the kiss and returns me to an upright position. Slightly dazed but completely head over heels, I grab the lapels of his jacket and pull him back to me for another inappropriately long kiss. When I let go, he chuckles and gives me a long, heat-infused look.

"What do you think about skipping the reception and going straight to the honeymoon?"

I bite my lower lip, liking where his head is at. Unfortunately, I know that won't fly with any of our guests. "As enticing as that sounds, I'm really looking forward to dancing with my new husband on the deck of a yacht at sunset."

"Yeah," he says. "And I suppose we shouldn't let all that food go to waste. I know how much you enjoy your shrimp and grits. But perhaps we could sneak a few more kisses behind the house before we greet our guests?"

I nod eagerly. Kissing Zach is one of my favorite things. Lila hands me my bouquet and I take Zach's hand, loving the way we fit together. We take off down the aisle in a sprint, laughing as we round the end of the aisle and disappear behind the house. Zach cups my face and draws my lips to his. I melt into his touch, my free hand pressed lightly against his chest. It feels like time stops when we're together and I hope it really does, because I want to stay right here in his arms forever.

Zach

One Year and Two Days Later

It's been quite an ordeal keeping our honeymoon destination a secret from Katie, and I'm about to find out if it was worth it. Lila helped me arrange everything, including the private jet, and even packed her bags. I convinced Katie to keep the shades down on the windows when we landed, but didn't think about the fact that the customs agents who come aboard to check our passports and forms would ask her why she was in Greece. Oh well, the look on her face is priceless. Her wide eyes turn to me before throwing herself into my arms.

"Zach!" she shrieks directly into my ear. "How in the world?!"

I laugh, enjoying having her snuggled up against me. "Lila, obviously."

She squeezes me harder before letting go and stepping back. The adoring look in my eyes makes me want to gather her back in my arms, but the agents staring at us help me keep my arms at my sides.

"Do you realize what you've gotten yourself into?" she asks.

"You mean, am I aware that we're going to spend the next week outside in the hot sun following tour guides around to various ruins listening to them explain the history and significance of each piece of rubble instead of canoodling in bed or on a lounge chair by the pool?"

She gives me a sheepish look. "Yes, that."

"Wherever you are is where I want to be, even when that means we are both drenched with sweat and stinking to high heaven. You know why?"

"Because you love me."

"You got that right."

"Thank you so much!" she says, squeezing me tight. "I'm blown away. And I promise to make sure we still do plenty of canoodling while we're here."

"I'll hold you to it, Tiger," I say, pressing a quick kiss to her lips.

Ever since Katie mentioned Athens being the place she wanted to visit most, I've been scheming to make it happen. I can't wait to see this city through her eyes.

My life has been so much more vibrant since Katie entered the picture. I hadn't realized how stagnant I'd been, just sort of going through the motions, not really thinking about what I wanted. But this last year has shown me how much I'd been missing. Sure, I'd had my mom, plenty of friends, and satisfying work, but I now also have a woman who challenges me all the time while also supporting and championing me. She makes me feel like I can do anything. And I'm willing to do anything I can to make her happy.

After our papers are approved, a car takes us to our hotel where we crash onto our bed for a quick afternoon nap since we didn't get a lot of sleep on the plane despite having an actual bedroom and a somewhat comfortable bed. Our room has a balcony and Katie gasps when we open the doors, giving us a stunning view of the Acropolis. The hill and its buildings are visible through the encroaching darkness because of lights illuminating their surfaces. It's our first stop tomorrow and, if I know my wife and her interest in its history, will probably take all day. I've been told we must get up Lycabettus Hill for sunset one day, but this trip is for Katie, so I'll let her make the final decision on our itinerary.

We find a restaurant near our hotel and indulge ourselves in a variety of local cuisine. I grin when Katie wiggles in her chair after popping a piece of hummus-smeared bread in her mouth. Her little quirks are so charming. She dips another piece, then feeds it to me. I hum my appreciation for the delicious flavors.

"See? So good." Her eyes are shining.

Yep, it's official. I'd do literally anything if it means seeing her this happy.

"I love you, Katie."

She sighs. "I love you, too, Zachary Derik."

I hope you enjoyed Kat and Zach's story. Find additional content (like card game instructions) and a special bonus epilogue on my website: MeganByrd.net/my_books

Want to stay up to date on book news? Sign up for my e-newsletter at MeganByrd.net/newsletter

Acknowledgments

Writing and publishing a book is not a solitary event. There were many people who helped and supported me with this project. I will never remember to thank everyone, but I appreciate all the love and help I get from the amazing people in my life.

First, thank you to my family (A, K, & J) who listened to me talk about various parts of the process, shared thoughts on cover designs, and tolerated me when I was worn out from reading and editing the story again. Thanks for encouraging and supporting my creativity!

Many thanks to my writer friends who help me keep going on this journey. Anna, I love our monthly meetups for exercise, good food, and even better conversation. Sherri, our Marco Polos are a highlight of my week. You make me laugh and inspire me to keep going. Lisa, I am amazed by how many words flow from your fingers and the way you write your characters and stories.

Thank you to all of my early readers: Jane, Pattie, Heather, Anna, Hilary, Susie, Maureen, and Tara. Your feedback and comments were immensely helpful in shaping this story. Thank you also to those who voted in my cover surveys: Katelin, Heather, Amy, Lalita, Karen, Tara, Mary Beth, Hilary, Emily, Brittany, Dan, Amanda, Lorie, Olive and Leah, Kim, Jennifer, Cindy, Brooke, Christine, Genie, Megan, Nancy, Helen, and Lisa.

A special thank you to Derik VanVleet who generously answered my questions about woodworking. I didn't end up getting technical in the book, but I appreciate the knowledge.

I wouldn't have any of my marketing materials or book covers without the generosity of my friends, Kristina and Eric, who have graciously shared their resources with me. I appreciate you!

Big thanks to all my ARC readers and Bookstagrammers who shared about the book. It takes a village to celebrate and champion books.

Thanks, Julia Roberts, for starring in movies that inspire me to write fun love stories (especially *Pretty Woman* and *Notting Hill*).

About the Author

Megan Byrd lives in Asheville, North Carolina with her husband and two kids. She hates running, but loves hiking in the mountains toward a waterfall or scenic view and taking kickboxing, HIIT, yoga, and Zumba classes. When she's not reading, writing, or chasing waterfalls, she enjoys visiting local bookstores, wandering through thrift shops in search of special gems, listening to live music, and catching up with friends.

Want to be first to know when the next book is available? Visit her website and sign up to receive e-newsletters which contain behind-the-scenes sneak peeks of her current work-in-progress, life updates, book recommendations, and other fun things. You'll also receive a free story (or two) for signing up! Follow her on social media for all the latest about current and upcoming novels.

Website: MeganByrd.net
Instagram: @megan.e.byrd
Facebook: AuthorMeganByrd